TESSA MIYATA
IS <u>NO</u> HERO

By Julie Abe

Eva Evergreen

Eva Evergreen, Semi-Magical Witch

Eva Evergreen and the Cursed Witch

Alliana of Rivelle

Alliana, Girl of Dragons

Young Adult

The Charmed List

TESSA MIYATA
IS <u>NO</u> HERO

JULIE ABE

LITTLE, BROWN AND COMPANY
New York Boston

Little, Brown and Company
Hachette Book Group
1290 Avenue of the Americas, New York, NY 10104
Visit us at LBYR.com

First Edition: August 2023

Little, Brown and Company is a division of Hachette Book Group, Inc. The
Little, Brown name and logo are trademarks of Hachette Book Group, Inc.

The publisher is not responsible for websites (or their content) that are not
owned by the publisher.

Little, Brown and Company books may be purchased in bulk for business,
educational, or promotional use. For information, please contact your
local bookseller or the Hachette Book Group Special Markets Department
at special.markets@hbgusa.com.

Library of Congress Cataloging-in-Publication Data
Names: Abe, Julie, author.
Title: Tessa Miyata is no hero / Julie Abe.
Description: First edition. | New York : Little, Brown and Company, 2023. |
Series: Tessa Miyata | Audience: Ages 8–12. | Summary: On a trip to visit her
grandparents in Japan, Tessa Miyata inadvertently releases the spirit of an
evil samurai god who wants to destroy Tokyo, and stumbles upon a hidden
part of the city where gods and mythological creatures walk among humans.
Identifiers: LCCN 2022028375 | ISBN 9780316448529 (hardcover) |
ISBN 9780316448727 (ebook)
Subjects: CYAC: Gods—Fiction. | Mythology, Japanese—Fiction. |
Japanese Americans—Fiction. | Grandparents—Fiction. | Tokyo (Japan)—
Fiction. | Japan—Fiction. | Fantasy. | LCGFT: Fantasy fiction. | Novels.
Classification: LCC PZ7.1.A162 Te 2023 | DDC [Fic]—dc23
LC record available at https://lccn.loc.gov/2022028375

ISBNs: 978-0-316-44852-9 (hardcover), 978-0-316-44872-7 (ebook)

Printed in the United States of America

LSC-C

Printing 1, 2023

For Eugene, Emily, and May,
with all my love

After the rain,
the earth hardens.

Ame futte, ji katamaru.

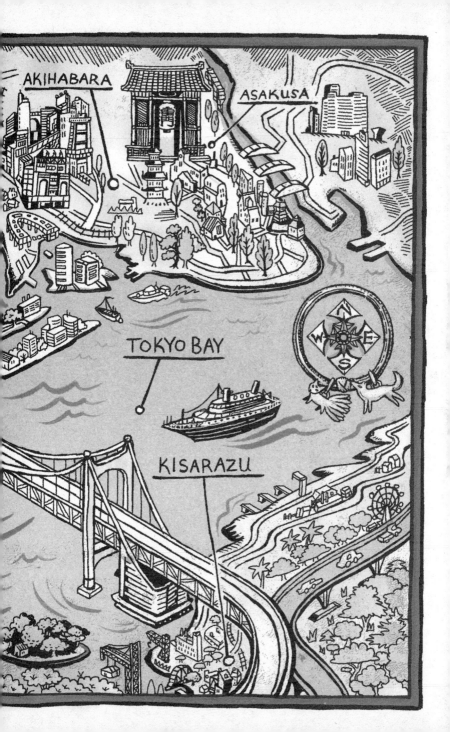

TESSA'S STUDY GUIDE FOR LIFE IN JAPAN

"-chan"/"-kun"/"-sama"—You stick "-chan"/"-kun" at the end of names for friends, like Tessa-chan, Jin-kun (like, if he was actually my friend). "-sama" is an honorific for important people.

bō—A wood staff, definitely not used for playing with at home.

daruma—A round doll, usually red, that has just one eye painted in. The owner makes a wish, and only fills in the other eye when it's completed.

Daruma

Jagabee—Basically potato chips in the shape of french fries, but extra tasty.

katana—Super sharp sword; don't play with these at home.

kitsune—A troublemaking fox with supposedly legendary powers. Seriously, if you see a kitsune, DO NOT

APPROACH IT. They're trouble, I tell you, trouble.

Kitsune

maneki neko—A cat figurine that beckons in good fortune. I need another twenty million of these.

manju—A Japanese confection that is absolutely *divine*. Think of those mochi ice creams, but more like a cake, and usually with traditional fillings like sweet red bean.

Meiji Jingu—A super-majestic shrine built in the 1920s, dedicated to Emperor Meiji and Empress Shōken, located in Tokyo.

Obaachan—Grandma, aka gives the best hugs.

Ojiichan—Grandpa, aka the sweetest old guy ever.

ōkami—A mythical wolf.

omamori—A protection charm, usually with a specific focus, like driver safety or good grades.

omikuji—Fortunes that are usually written out on strips of paper, sorted into levels of luck.

shimenawa—A purification rope made of woven rice straw or hemp. It often has lightning-shaped paper streamers attached for enhanced strength.

shuriken—Also known as a throwing star. Again, definitely don't play with these at home.

Taira Masakado—A formidable samurai from the 900s (seriously, he did exist!) with a really intense history.

He tried to rise up against the government, then got assassinated...but that's not where the stories end. There's tons of tales of him wreaking havoc, even after his death, as a vengeful spirit....

tatami—Traditional Japanese straw flooring, smells *amazing.*

temple vs. shrine—Japanese temples are Buddhist; Japanese shrines are Shinto.

Tokyo—The capital city of Japan.

torii—A gate that's often at the entrance to Japanese shrines; it marks the start of a sacred place.

Torii

tsuba—The nifty guard piece that keeps your hand from sliding onto the sharp blades of katanas and other pointy weapons. Often created in intricate designs.

Yakult—One of the most refreshing snacks in the universe, a drinkable yogurt in the smallest, cutest container ever. There are healthy probiotic-things inside, so I always tell Cecilia and Peyton (my sisters) that Yakult is totally essential for my health. And, um, okay, it tastes amazing, too.

I

The City of Legends
Awaits You

PROLOGUE

Location: San Francisco Museum of Modern Art, California, USA

TESSA MIYATA KNEW SHE WAS CURSED. WHAT ELSE could she call seeing a masked woman in white, gliding toward her in the middle of the modern art museum with an enormous wolf trotting at her side?

And this was only day one of summer art camp. Back in sixth grade, at least she'd lasted a month before Allison Heinrich, her "best friend," told her she was a freak and never talked to her again. She'd spent the past year alone and friendless, fitting for the weirdo that she was.

Right now, things weren't any better. Especially not with that creepy woman heading straight toward her— and this wasn't the first time this ghostly visitor had found her. Long, black hair swirled along the sleeves of her pure white kimono; the woman's face was hidden with a white mask of a wolf. Not to mention the *actual*

gigantic shimmering wolf, its smoky-yellow eyes looking at Tessa like it could easily polish her off as a midday
snack.

The kitsune charm on Tessa's scarlet bracelet clinked
warningly. That wasn't good. She'd had it as long as she
could remember, and whenever she tried to cut the bracelet off, it always reappeared—yet no one could see it but
her. The weirdest part? Without fail, when trouble was
brewing, the fox charm always signaled that something
ominous was to come.

Ding! Her heart pounded in her ears as she tried
to keep listening to the group of four friends she'd met
during the introductions a few hours earlier, as they all
eagerly talked about some sort of watercolor technique.

"That's so neat," Tessa said, fidgeting with the charm,
trying to make it stop—not that anyone else could hear

its sounds. "I never knew
art like this was made
with dog scratching."

"Dry scratching," one
of the girls laughed, her
dark eyes crinkling into a
smile. "Ooh, and look at
this piece!"

Ding, ding! The other
four had been really fun
so far. They'd pointed out

things Tessa would've never noticed about the pastel water-colors hung in silver frames, like all the secret designs hidden in the shapes of the clouds or the way the artist's signature also looked like a cloud. The real reason Tessa was here was because this art camp was a last resort. Unbelievably, though, these four artsy girls seemed to like being around her. But their friendship wouldn't last long if—

Ding.

"Tessa Miyata, this is our last chance to communicate." The woman's voice thundered, ominous as an incoming storm, as her shadowy body walked straight through the closest boy. Tessa's new friends drifted toward the next art piece, still chatting, but dread froze Tessa's feet. *Last chance?* Did that mean she was *finally* going to be left alone? When the woman had first appeared—at the beginning of sixth grade, no less—she'd been silent, her mouth moving but no words coming out. But, over time, she'd begun talking. And saying "Tessa Miyata" in that super intensely serious way seemed to be her favorite phrase.

Not here, not here. My sisters are never going to forgive me. Gram can't afford another summer camp. She tugged her too-long bangs over her eyes, like that would stop the ghostly visitor from seeing her. "Hey, I'm going to run to the bathroom!"

One of the girls piped up, "I'll go with you—"

"No!" Tessa tried to suppress the anxiety in her voice.

"Um, it's okay. I'll go by myself." She couldn't stomach seeing another once-friend stare in dismay, comprehending Tessa for the freak that she was. As she darted toward the closest exit, the counselor protested, "Where do you think you're going?"

Tessa was awkwardly loud in the otherwise hushed gallery, that nervousness popping out all at once. *"Bathroom!"*

Her echoes reverberated, burning her face crimson. *"Bathroom, bathroom, bathroom!"*

A few of the campmates hid their snickers. She'd be remembered as Bathroom Girl for the rest of the day, at least. But that was way better than the alternative.

Tessa rushed into a narrow hallway, but it only seemed to lead to the gift shop. Why were gift shops always easier to find than anything else in a museum? Still, she ducked behind a display of postcards and tried to calm her beating heart. She'd wait out the weird woman and that wolf for fifteen minutes or so—they tended to leave after a while—and find her group of friends, apologizing for accidentally drinking her sister's glass of milk this morning, instead of her normal almond milk, when she was lactose intolerant.

That would work, if only the woman in white wasn't standing in front of her, misty eyes staring straight back.

Tessa stifled a shriek. She couldn't let anyone see her freaking out from what everyone else saw as empty air.

At the mysterious woman's side, the enormous wolf let out a fierce growl. Then the woman spoke, with that voice like clashing swords: "Time is running out. You must heed my warning, or those around you will suffer the consequences."

Talk about *cursed*.

Tessa looked around. The gift shop was otherwise empty, except for the cashier who had headed to the other side of the store to restock a display of art prints.

"Just leave me alone, please," she whispered.

Hopefully, her older sisters weren't too close by—they were in the high school group of campers, in another section of the museum, but they always seemed to sense when Tessa was in trouble. A few months ago, Peyton and Cecilia had caught her trying to argue with the woman in white (though all of Tessa's reasoning hadn't encouraged her to stay away) in the parking lot behind their apartment. They thought she was talking to a *tree*, and they'd been worried about her ever since.

The woman's voice seemed different this time, almost desperate for Tessa to heed her words. "I am but a shadow messenger, one who comes before great change. This is the thirteenth and last warning. You must learn the ways of the past to fight the present—"

Tessa wanted to plug in her earbuds and listen to her favorite playlist, extra loud and on repeat. She'd tried that before, actually, but her misty visitor had somehow overridden Jungkook's vocals. She tried to wave her off. "Maybe later—"

There was a prickle on her shoulders, coming from the entrance. Tessa spun around.

It was one of the kids from her summer camp, with messy sandy-red hair and sharp green eyes, staring from behind the display of coffee table books. Worse, he had a phone in his hands, pointed at her.

She could already imagine what this looked like to him. Tessa staring into empty air, talking to herself, hand held out. Great first impression.

Tessa grinned. "Like my rehearsal? I'm planning on auditioning for my school play—"

"I heard about you," snorted the kid. "You know Allison Heinrich? She's my cousin. That video she took of you *slaps*. It trended faster than any other clip on Now-Look. One million views in an hour, a record."

The bitter ache of losing her best friend seared the most when she was walking behind a crowd of class-mates, and all of them were giggling at whatever Allison—now the most popular kid in school—had said. Or when Tessa tried to make a joke, and the teacher laughed, but all her classmates stared down at their desks, following Allison's lead.

From the moment Allison and Tessa had met in sixth grade homeroom, with matching *Aggretsuko* notebooks—they were both die-hard fans of the show—they had been inseparable. Tessa had moved from friend group to friend group before, never really belonging, but for once, she'd found someone who finally understood her. Allison laughed at all of her punch lines and told the funniest stories in return about the trips that she always took with her sales director father, and never asked awkward questions about Tessa's family being only her sisters and Gram. Allison even loved watching *My Hero Academia* and *Demon Slayer*, too, and didn't mind Tessa's trips to their middle school library to check out another pile of books.

They'd demolish the party-sized fries in the cafeteria, their heads bent together as they hashed out the latest episode of *Jujutsu Kaisen*. They were the unpopular kids, true, but they laughed about that, because they had each other. Still, Allison told her about how she'd been popular at her last school, and made it sound like it had been a world of difference. Back then, Allison's Now-Look account had even trended in her city, which had been perfect since she'd wanted to become a film producer and NowLook was *the* place to show off your talents.

So Allison and Tessa concocted wild plans to become popular: steal Mr. Hahn's famously ugly mustard tie and show it off; score backstage passes to the next BTS concert and become best friends with the members; invent a time machine to travel to the future and figure out all the trends before they started. But their plans were all for fun, because Tessa figured who needed other people when they had each other?

Allison did.

Thirty-six days after the start of sixth grade (not that she had counted), Tessa had been trying to dodge yet another "friendly" visit from the woman in white. She'd hidden behind the school buildings as she begged the woman and the wolf to stop bothering her; she'd tried shouting in English and Japanese just to make her point clear. She'd even typed out her message on her phone and waved it in front of their faces. Anyway, no matter what she did, the woman kept blathering on about some warning, and by the end Tessa was yelling loudly. But thankfully, no one paid attention to a nobody like her.

No one except the one other person who knew what it was like to be a nobody.

Allison followed her, recorded a video of her lecturing what looked to be the dumpster, and uploaded it onto her NowLook account. Tessa returned to a giggling classroom, their eyes glued to their screens, with Allison cozy in the middle.

The rest, as they say, was history. Especially since that video of "The Middle School Dumpster Weirdo" was living forever in everyone's view history.

Every time Tessa tried to approach Allison, she would disappear in a crowd of her new friends, laughing their heads off. Her ex-best-friend was good at jokes, and Tessa was the butt of this one.

"I wonder what this will do for my NowLook stats," the boy said, snickering, as he jabbed the phone screen.

Tessa could almost see the worry on Peyton and Cecilia's faces. The way her older sisters would look at her as they tried to get NowLook to pull down the video, as they told all their friends to stop watching. But even though her older sisters were popular in high school, once things went viral, it was beyond their control.

Then an idea flashed in her mind. Tessa turned to the misty woman, who was still going on about all sorts of timely warnings about doom and destruction.

"Please," she whispered. The cornered helplessness felt like she was stuck in slime, unable to move. "Help me. I need to make it so that video never existed."

The wolf growled, and the Tessa expected the woman to drone on about her cursed destiny, but—

"You will owe me a favor, then."

Tessa would have promised the world if she could just not be teased, not have to see her face show up on all her classmates' posts, and their laughing, laughing comments.

"What is it?" A shiver ran down her neck and along her arms.

"You must accept this." The woman reached her right arm across her body, toward the sleeve of her kimono—and the dagger sheath dangling from her waist—and Tessa tensed.

But the woman's long, graceful fingers swept up, to her mask. With a fluid motion, she pulled it off—only to reveal a face swathed in shadows, with misty eyes that glittered under the halogen lights—and held out the mask.

Tessa stared at the carved wood warily. Bold streaks of red paint lined the eyes and dotted its forehead. The mask was in the shape of a fierce ōkami, the legendary wolf said to be a messenger of spirits.

She had a feeling that things delivered by shadowy messengers weren't usually a winning lottery ticket or a get-out-of-school pass. "Um, what is it?"

"It will help guide you to your greater fate," the woman said.

"I don't want something to pick my fate for me," Tessa protested.

"The choice is *always* yours," the woman said. "However, to allow yourself a fighting chance, you must accept this before it's too late."

The boy was snickering. "Seventy-five percent uploaded!"

Options flashed through her mind in a split second. She could refuse the mask and face the ridicule of her new campmates. She could take the mask and *possibly* just stuff it under her bed and forget about it, right? Or burn it? How could a *mask* guide her toward her fate?

Or, maybe, if she accepted the wolf mask, this messenger might have answers. A reason for why she saw these things no one else did. A reason why she never fit in.

Tessa had a feeling she'd regret either option. But if Peyton and Cecilia had to see Tessa's face splashed on the homepage of the NowLook app again...The way their foreheads always crinkled with concern for Tessa burned at her heart.

Cursed or not, she never wanted to see her sisters look like that again.

"Yes, I promise. I accept the mask."

"Keizoku ha chikaranari."

"W-what?" Tessa's Japanese was pretty good after tons of Saturday classes, but this seemed to be a saying she hadn't heard before. Or maybe a warning. " 'Don't give up'? Give up on what?"

But there was no time to ask further. The mask appeared in her hand in a flash. The carved wood was slippery underneath her fingertips.

"This is the final warning," the woman repeated, her voice fading, as if the powers that had brought her here were starting to wane.

"But—this makes no sense—"

The woman and the wolf shifted, turning away. "We may—if you make the choice—meet again."

With that, the shadowy woman and her wolf began to move. Time seemed to speed up, and Tessa could barely breathe.

Metal on metal rang through the gift shop as the woman drew her dagger. A split second later, the wolf lunged forward. The boy, still laughing to himself, didn't see both woman and wolf move in a swirl of white mist, nor did he understand why Tessa gasped in shock, but he did look up—

Just as the wolf's sharp teeth tore through the phone and it burst into shattered pieces. The boy shrieked as he fell backward. His wide eyes swiveled around the gift shop wildly, not seeing the woman right in front of him as she disappeared into thin air. The only remaining trace of her was the mask in Tessa's hand—and the gigantic wolf.

It growled, looking down at the boy on the floor like it was about to eat him.

"Please don't eat him," Tessa whispered. "My sisters will absolutely *murder* me."

The wolf turned toward Tessa, eyes fixated on her.

"Oh, no, no." Tessa shook her head firmly. "Definitely eat the boy. He's way tastier."

The wolf pushed off his giant paws, lunging straight at her—

She couldn't move away in time, not fast enough for this. Tessa held out the mask in front of her, not that it'd be any protection, just as the wolf's fangs flashed—

But the wolf jumped *into* the mask, the wood warming under Tessa's fingertips. Before Tessa could drop it, the wolf-faced mask shrunk impossibly small, no bigger

than her thumbnail, and attached itself to the red bracelet. The tiny ōkami tapped against the kitsune charm, tin-
kling again like a warning.

Yikes and Yakult. What was that?

But Tessa couldn't inspect it now. She was in trouble.

"Freak!" the boy shrieked, rushing forward with fists
curled. "You broke my phone!"

"What in the world is going on?" From the far wall,
rolls of art prints tumbled out of the cashier's hands.

Tessa and the boy were ten feet apart. There was
no possible way she could've done anything....But she
knew things were never right or just, and when the boy
searched for someone to blame, it'd end up being her. He
pounded toward her, and Tessa threw up her hands to
protect herself—

A shadow darted between them.

The boy slammed into the interloper and tumbled
onto his backside, crying out in surprise.

Tessa was saved, but also in deeper trouble than
before. And so was the kid, who gulped as he stared up at
Tessa's older sister, taking in the black velvet choker, slick
braids wound into double buns (laced with scarily sharp
studs), and her hand on her black denim-clad hip.

"Think twice before you call my sister a freak," Peyton said, warningly, using her height to her full advantage. With her all-black outfits, she always looked way
older than her actual sixteen years.

Then Cecilia kneeled next to the boy. "C'mon. Let's go get you cleaned up. I'll make sure your phone gets fixed, too."

The oldest Miyata sister at seventeen years old, Cecilia was gentle and beautiful, and usually in a charming pastel floral dress that matched her sweet, kind personality. To the boy, she must've seemed like a guardian angel, swooping in to save him. He sniffled, and nodded.

"I was going to handle this," Tessa said. "You didn't need to worry."

"We've got your back." Peyton drew her gaze up from the shards of the phone, concern shimmering in her eyes.

Guilt weighed down Tessa's shoulders, with a heaviness she couldn't quite shake off. So quiet that no one could hear her, she said, "I *tried* to handle it myself."

"What's happened?" a voice snapped from the entrance.

The counselor stood there, with the other middle school campmates trailing behind her. Tessa's new friends peeked around the counselor, their eyes wide as they stared at the shattered phone and the angry boy, and then warily looked at her.

Tessa flinched.

"All four of you," snapped the counselor. "Get over here, now."

Peyton had to nudge Tessa toward the thunderous-looking adult. Cecilia guided over the boy; she was being extra kind, probably hoping it might help the boy or his parents from getting too mad at the Miyata family. Already, Tessa could visualize Gram—their late mom's mother, not to be confused with her grandparents from her dad's side in Japan—slumping over the kitchen table, trying to figure out who would take care of Tessa now that she'd been kicked out of yet another summer camp, while Gram had to work her long shifts at the grocery store. Peyton and Cecilia had offered to watch over her, but ever since Tessa had started getting in trouble for seeing things, their grandma had never let Tessa out of an adult's sight—what if the neighbor kids began bullying Tessa again, what if they uploaded another video—not that it had ever seemed to really help.

In so many ways, it felt like Tessa had cursed her family just by being alive. Her parents had passed away in a car accident when she was around a year old; Gram had saved Tessa and her sisters from getting split into different foster homes. But it'd come at a cost: Instead of enjoying knitting her way through retirement, Gram, her black hair streaked with white, was working until her knobby fingers and stooped back were aching, so that the Miyata sisters had an apartment to stay in and they wouldn't get separated. Her sisters, likewise, would protect Tessa to their dying breaths—and she wished that she could do *anything* for them. But she was the younger sister that they had to take care of, especially when she got into messes like these.

Later that night, if Tessa peeked into the kitchen,

Gram would likely be flipping through her checkbook again, murmuring to herself, worrying about how to repay the boy's family for the broken phone, and how to stretch out the money for the bills....

Someday, Tessa swore, her eyes burning as she slunk past her campmates, the counselor's hand like a claw in her shoulder, and the new charm heavy on her wrist. Someday, she'd no longer be a burden to Gram. Someday, she would be able to take care of her sisters. Someday, she'd finally be able to save those she loved.

Halfway across the globe, a long-shut door creaked open as an answer, like a veil parting between worlds. Whispers and wishes formed into puffs of air and began to slip and slither through the dark, creeping toward the light....

1

Location: Across the bay from Tokyo
in Kisarazu, Japan

THE FIRST TIME TESSA SAW A GLIMMER OF THE CITY OF
Legends was at the entrance of her paternal grandparents'
house in Kisarazu, Japan, and it should've been a sign to
turn around and hightail it out of the country.

But, moments before that, it was just Tessa and her
two older sisters, standing in front of the white gate with
their overstuffed suitcases, filled with dried fruit and
probably-melted chocolates that Gram had sent along as
thank you gifts to the other side of the family, for taking
care of the Miyata sisters for the rest of the summer...
and, for Tessa, possibly longer. She'd overheard a whispered conversation between Gram and her sisters the
night before: *This might be better for Tessa.*

From the shrine directly next door, the cicadas
chirped loudly through the thick trees, calling her closer.
But Tessa wasn't in Japan to visit some boring place like

that. She and her sisters drank in the sight of their grand-parents' charming two-story wood house, topped with rounded, shiny black roof tiles.

Even though the shrine was busy with visitors, there was something so peaceful and cozy about her grand-parents' home. Laundry fluttered cheerily from the second-story balcony, just like the way Cecilia and Peyton had described it after their past visit. All around the front, thick hydrangea bushes flowered like purple and white fireworks, with a faintly sweet scent. This was their glori-ous home for the next two months. This was going to be the start of the best summer for her and her sisters; Tessa was sure of it. She could take a bunch of photos and post them on NowLook to show that she wasn't hurt by her friends—okay, that was a stretch—*classmates* back home.

"I can't believe we're finally here." Tessa peered inside the gate, looking at the stone path that wound around the house. "The twelve-hour flight felt like a million years—"

Peyton, who had been just about to press the inter-com, paused, her fingers hovering in front of the white button. "Tessa...let's be careful about exaggerating things around Ojiichan and Obaachan."

Fresh disappointment wove together with a briny whiff of the fisherman's dock down the road; the bus had trundled along the sparkling bay, and it'd only been then when Tessa had realized she was still a major body of water away from Tokyo.

"We're counting on you, remember?" As the leader of the three, Cecilia was Tessa's idol. Cecilia's straight black hair was like hers, if Tessa's hair—with a tiny Miyata-sister braid on the side—hadn't somehow turned into a rat's nest during the cross-Pacific flight. Instead, Cecilia's braid above her forehead was delicate and perfect, just like the rest of her, as usual. No matter what Tessa tried, she never did look like her older sisters, who were gorgeous and nearly identical with their prettily freckled tan skin and bright, sparkling light brown eyes that made most people ask if they were twins. And then they asked if Tessa was their cousin, because clearly she couldn't be *that* closely related.

As soon as Gram had shared that their other grandparents had offered to take care of the three Miyata sisters for the rest of the summer, Tessa's sisters had jumped at the chance, their eyes shining. Tessa had sworn that this time would be different.

This time, it would be the ultimate Cecilia-Peyton-Tessa vacation.

"This is our summer," Tessa said, looking up at her sisters.

They smiled, ruffling her hair, and Tessa breathed in deeply, wishing that she could spend every day with her sisters, just like this.

"Ojiichan and Obaachan already have special plans for you, too," Cecilia said, her eyes crinkling in a big smile.

"What—?"

But Peyton had already pressed the intercom button and was calling loudly, "Ojiichan, Obaachan, we're here!"

A split second later, a shout of joy came from inside, and bare footsteps pounded loudly. The frosted glass front door slid open, and her wizened, adorable grandparents shuffled out in their sandals.

"Welcome, welcome! We've missed you," they cried, swooping down the second Tessa and her two older sisters stepped inside the gate and wheeled their suitcases into the entranceway. Thankfully, the classes had helped, and Tessa could understand everything her grandparents were saying in rapid-fire Japanese.

"Welcome to Japan, Tessa," Obaachan said, puffing up with pride. "I'm so glad your gram finally sent you over!"

Tessa had supposedly been to Japan *once*, when she was only a few months old, but she didn't remember a thing about that trip. Everything felt brand-new; she was truly building her first memories of Japan. She had seen her grandparents' house in video chats with her sisters when they'd come a few years back, but standing here felt almost unreal. Tessa hadn't been able to go because Gram had wanted to keep an eye on her, but all Tessa had wanted since then was to go to Japan. The house was old-fashioned and made of wood, unlike the fancy, modern apartment buildings in front of the bay. Tessa had loved everything about it—even the wall plastered with embarrassing pictures of her and her sisters—and always saved all the video clips and pictures from Cecilia and Peyton, looking forward to the day she'd be able to visit. Every corner was charming, from the tiny kitchen connected to a dining area with a low table to the tatami area where her sisters laid out futons and slept side by side, like a summer-long sleepover on the sweet-scented straw floor.

Ojiichan and Obaachan patted their heads roughly and pinched their cheeks as if the three Miyata sisters could be measured by how many times they could get squeezed before turning into puddles from Japan's midsummer muggy heat. Cool air from deeper inside the house brushed against Tessa's skin, with the lemon-like, woodsy mothball scent that always wafted out from her grandparents' suitcases when they visited Tessa's family.

"I don't know why you have to live in San Jose, it's so far away." Obaachan tried to take their luggage, but her two older sisters knew better than to let a seventy-five-year-old lift a forty-pound suitcase. Peyton dragged the beat-up suitcases off the tile entranceway and onto the wood floor, flexing her muscles. "I always tell your gram that you're welcome here, anytime."

The issue had always been the cost of the plane tickets—but thankfully, Obaachan and Ojiichan had

sent over prepaid tickets as soon as they'd heard that the
Miyata sisters' summer vacation plans had opened up.

Tessa's older sisters hurried past the glass curio cabinet inside the front door to sit on the bench and pull off
their shoes, but Tessa stopped. The cabinet had sliding
glass panels and four shelves filled with small wood statues, faded art prints, and a few older-style toys; it was
a homely looking, mismatched bunch of antiques. Tessa
had remembered seeing a few pictures before, and it'd
looked completely ordinary.

Except for now. A white glow flickered from the top-
most shelf. She stepped closer to look at the round doll.
"Did you—did you see that?"

Cecilia and Peyton shot each other worried looks,
and Tessa's stomach sunk.

"Tessa, are you feeling okay?" Peyton whispered when Ojiichan and Obaachan were busy enveloping their oldest sister in hugs.

Tessa swallowed. She *swore* she'd seen a strange flicker from the daruma, a one-eyed, bright red doll.

"Are you looking at our precious heirlooms, Tessa?" Ojiichan asked. "Your taste is great; you truly understand the Miyata legacy! Have you seen this miniature torii gate? It's based on the giant one at the shrine around the corner! My father made it himself; carved the wood posts and that beautifully arched top, and even painted it that exact red-orange, too. And—"

"What's that one?" Tessa asked, pointing at the fire-engine-red doll—it kind of reminded her of those nesting matryoshka dolls that one of her classmates had brought in for show-and-tell.

"You've got a great eye!" Ojiichan said cheerily. "That daruma doll had been handed down between generations of the shrine's caretakers. After a bad fire a decade or so ago, we brought it here for safekeeping."

Tessa had heard of daruma before. Tradition had it that whoever received one was supposed to make a wish. And once the owner reached their goal, they would fill in the other eye. But this daruma's goal was still unfulfilled, probably because it was an antique.

"In other words," Tessa's grandma interjected, "your ojiichan won't let go of anything, even if this daruma's old and dusty, and no one else remembers its real history." Obaachan nudged the glass case to show the lock on the back. She tugged at the wood panel, and it stayed firmly shut. "See? Sealed shut and we don't even have the key."

"I told you, I'll bring it to old Kikumoto and get him to *make* a key," Ojiichan said.

Obaachan shook her head. "Kikumoto? He'll charge us a fortune."

Ojiichan frowned, running his fingers across the front. "The case is cracking at the edge. We *need* to get it fixed."

Tessa murmured under her breath, "I swear I saw a light...."

"Do you feel unwell, Tessa-chan?" For an old man, Ojiichan had nearly perfect hearing.

It's just the muggy Japan heat melting my brain. Or probably the jet lag.

Tessa's heart sunk. She was no better at convincing herself than she was at convincing her family.

Peyton and Cecilia looked at her with concern, likely wondering, *Is Tessa really okay?*

She smoothed down a few strands sticking out of her long bangs. "It's nothing."

Tessa just wished she wasn't the only one, like always. She wished, just once, that someone would believe her.

"Come on, you all need to sit and rest," Obaachan

said, beckoning them forward. The rest of her family shuffled into the kitchen, and glasses clinked as her grandparents fussed over her sisters, probably shoving ice-cold barley tea and chiffon cake at them.

Tessa kicked off her gray Converses—remembering, belatedly, to line them up to point toward the door like Cecilia had told her was standard manners in Japan. Then Tessa headed into the kitchen. She grinned when she saw the stainless steel counters piled high with snacks for her and her sisters, and the frosted pitcher of barley tea. Her sisters were already sitting on the tatami floor around the low table, cooling off under the air conditioner. Everything was *way* better than the videos; somehow, it felt like things were finally clicking into place inside Tessa. Being in Japan, even though she'd only been here once before, settled into her heart like it was *home*.

But as she moved to close the sliding door, something stopped her.

A whispered sound, like the echoes of a faint, sharp voice. "*You...you...*"

Her hair prickled on the back of her neck.

She turned to look at the wooden doll. The daruma sat innocently, clustered next to a maneki neko, a cat frozen in the motion of waving its hand, beckoning in good fortune.

Everything was still. Tessa didn't know what she was thinking. It was probably just a draft from above the front door, letting in some light and that whistle of air. Maybe she *was* making things up, like her family kept saying.

The muggy heat was just getting to her head. Tessa needed a cold glass of barley tea, and tomorrow she would set off to sightsee Tokyo with her sisters, and she'd feel better.

She wanted a summer with her sisters, not endless days of sitting at her grandparents' house, staring at a strange doll. Maybe that woman in white didn't exist. Maybe, maybe.

She started to turn back toward the kitchen, back to safety, where her sisters chatted with their grandparents.

Then the round eyes on the daruma blazed bright as fire.

When she blinked, the figurine was all normal wood and paint.

2

"YOU'RE STAYING IN."

Tessa's stomach churned as if the breakfast of miso soup and rice and salmon had gone sour. She sat down hard on the wood bench in the entranceway, wishing she could disappear like that daruma's glimmer, wishing someone believed her.

Or that she hadn't said anything about what she'd seen.

Obaachan stared at her youngest granddaughter lacing up her shoes, and shook her head. She repeated her words. "You're staying home with us, Tessa. You had such a long flight yesterday, you're still jet-lagged. Cecilia and Peyton mentioned they've been worried about you these days—"

"I'm fine." The daruma was dull as ever, no light to be seen. But being near it gave Tessa a funny twisting sensation in her chest. She turned to her older sisters with a hopeful smile. "Plus, Cecilia and Peyton are going to Tokyo. I can go with them."

Peyton finished the knot on her boots, checked her backpack for her bus card, and slid on the straps. "Tessa, you need rest."

With hopes that felt as fragile as her sloshing stomach, Tessa tried to smile brightly. "I'm totally feeling great! Take me with you, please?"

Cecilia bit her lip. "I'm sorry, Tessa. We've got plans to visit Meiji Jingu with our friends, remember? Maybe another time."

Tessa's smile crumbled. "But—"

"Gram asked for you to stay with Ojiichan and Obaachan, out of trouble." Peyton towered over her, reminding Tessa how much older, how much more confident, how much more *everything* her sisters were. They didn't struggle to find the right words. They didn't sink into silence like she did, because the only words that she spoke, her classmates ridiculed and laughed at and made memes of. They didn't need someone to take care of them—though they always had to take care of Tessa.

Now her breakfast really was churning sour in her stomach. Tessa didn't have anyone like the friends her sisters had made while in Japan three years ago. Peyton and Cecilia were always video chatting with them like they were attached at the hip, even when they were an ocean apart. She knew they'd made plans to go to that old boring shrine, but why couldn't it include *her*?

"We'll bring you snacks, Tessa. Show Ojiichan and Obaachan you're doing fine, and they'll reconsider things," Cecilia said, looking guilty. The kindness in her voice hurt. They linked arms, and Peyton nudged her toward the gate. Cecilia's floral dress and gently curled hair clashed with Peyton's all-black clothes, metallic blue eyeliner, and knee-high boots, but they were best friends all the same. "Stay out of trouble, okay?"

They had that unbreakable sister bond. She'd always been the baby sister who didn't fit in. The one that they pitied and worried about, even if she was twelve.

But Tessa hadn't endured the turbulent flight, where the plane rattled her for eleven hours straight almost as soon as they'd taken off from San Francisco International Airport, and then an hour train ride to her grandparents' house on the *wrong* side of the Tokyo Bay, just to sit inside all day.

When Tessa had woken up this morning, she'd posted on NowLook about hanging out in Tokyo with her sisters for the best summer ever.

There had to be some way to get to the city. She'd take selfies and show Allison and the rest of the kids back home that she was having the coolest trip ever. It'd be something real for once. She could even get an Inumaki figurine—Allison's favorite anime character—and feature it on a NowLook video. She'd show her sisters how she could take care of herself, too.

Earlier, while Cecilia and Peyton were getting ready, Tessa's grandparents had refused to trade her dollars for yen, saying that they'd be with Tessa when they went out. In. A. Few. Days. For a *graveyard* visit to pay respects to her great-great-somebodies, around the corner from the shrine her grandparents took care of.

Tessa had waited her whole life for this, and all she'd get to see of Japan was the inside of her grandparents' house. Or some moldy graves.

"Now, let's go hang up the laundry!" Obaachan said cheerily as Peyton and Cecilia strode off to the bus station, and Tessa's stomach ached worse than ever.

The wind flapped the wet clothes as Obaachan handed Tessa clips and she hung each shirt, towel, and *ugh*, actual granny pants on the line. The dampness made her skin extra sticky in the heavy humidity. From the second-floor balcony, the town of Kisarazu spread out in front of her. Two-story houses and apartment buildings, capped with bright blue, red, or black tiles, led to the docks. Down the street, kids played soccer in an empty lot. Far, far in the horizon, beyond the sheet of blue-gray waters, the skyscrapers of Tokyo rose out of the clouds, like a jagged smile greeting her, and Tessa's heart fluttered.

She'd get into the city, soon.

Below, in the street, a man was scolding his son. The boy looked kind of like a younger version of the models she'd seen for Uniqlo or Muji or the other Japanese brands her sisters admired so much. He seemed to be about her age, with a long, lean frame. The father spoke sternly and the boy simply nodded, but his lips were drawn in a straight line.

Her chest tightened. Tessa had felt like that a thousand times before, when people—her once-friends—weren't listening to anything she was saying. She frowned.

"Aa, mou sono jikan dane!" Obaachan stood up with a happy hum, her eyes twinkling. "The Ueharas live across the street, remember?"

"Mm, you mentioned them in your emails. Anyway, I'm a little thirsty, do you mind if I check out the 7-Eleven down the block?" Tessa asked, clipping another towel on the line. At least the convenience stores were supposed to be neat in Japan.

"Don't worry," Obaachan said. "I've got something fun scheduled for you."

Tessa perked up. "Really?"

As Obaachan handed Tessa a pair of her grandpa's tighty-whities, the old woman smiled. "Jin's been looking forward to seeing you; we've been telling him so much about you. This is why it's better you didn't go off with Cecilia and Peyton."

He was *Jin?* Tessa stared down at the boy in surprise. As in the martial-arts-whiz Jin who came over every once in a while to hang out with Tessa's grandpa and spend an afternoon watching sumo wrestling matches together?

"*Demo...*" Jin's hair fell in front of his eyes. Though they were at least twenty feet away, the breeze carried the conversation up; Tessa could hear every word. In Japanese, he said, "But I don't know her. It's my last free afternoon before I'm at the dojo for the rest of summer break—"

"No!" His father had the look of a bulldog, with thick, hunched shoulders. His cheeks were cut in heavy jowls, and his voice growled like he was about to snap. Tessa could see how he could run a dojo; Peyton and Cecilia had tried one lesson last time and tapped out after fifteen minutes of nonstop jumping jacks. "You have to make something of yourself, learn some English from her. Do you want to be nothing, forever?"

The boy breathed in slowly, as if trying to reason this out to himself somewhere deep down inside, and finally he nodded. "Okay, fine. Where is she?"

Mr. Uehara pointed up at Tessa, with the underwear flapping in her hands, and she tried to duck behind the ledge, but there wasn't enough time.

Tessa's and Jin's eyes met, and the boy's dark eyebrows furrowed. With that glare, he looked like a miniature version of his father.

She glared straight back. *Excuse you, spending time with me is an honor—*

Just as the gust billowed, sending the wet underwear smack into her face, and the boy raised a sharply judging eyebrow.

Tessa peeled it off. "Darn it, Obaachan. This is *not* the adventure I had in mind."

3

"WELCOME, WELCOME!" OBAACHAN BUSTLED JIN INSIDE the gate. "Jin-kun, this is Tessa-chan. She's all the way from the United States. You two will have so much fun together."

For Tessa, "fun" was not defined by hanging out with someone who clearly already loathed her very existence. She opened her mouth to protest, but Obaachan's absolute assurance and happiness clenched at her chest.

When she glanced over, Jin's eyes narrowed as if he was thinking of all the better things he could be doing. He was just like the kids back in the US. Still, she shut her mouth as Obaachan patted her shoulder cheerfully.

Jin was a few inches taller than her, yet he was overshadowed by his father. They both had thick eyebrows and strong jaws, but Mr. Uehara had frown lines etched on his forehead, as if he was permanently in a state of anger.

"Thank you for watching over Jin." Mr. Uehara bowed toward Obaachan. He thrust out a wrapped box in blue paper with white snowflakes. "Please, have some Shiroi Koibito. From my recent kendo tournament in Hokkaido."

Tessa's stomach growled. Cecilia and Peyton had brought a box back for her, before. Shiroi Koibito were square cookies sandwiching a paper-thin cut of white chocolate. Just the thought of those treats made her mouth water. Maybe Jin wouldn't be so bad to hang out with if he came with cookies every time.

"Mr. Uehara, you are too generous!" Obaachan waved aside his proffered box.

"Please, please—"

"Oh, no, we can't possibly—"

He tried two more times before she finally accepted it. Standard Japanese customs that Tessa didn't quite understand. "Well, thank you. Jin and Tessa will enjoy this during snack time."

"Yes, he'll enjoy today, especially since he will be able to practice his English." Mr. Uehara sent one last warning look at his son before he turned, already dialing on his phone. Tessa couldn't help but notice the way Jin's shoulders slumped, like he was sinking under the weight of his father's expectations.

Obaachan beamed at the two of them as the latch on the gate shut with a metallic *snick!*

Darn it, am I stuck with him?

Jin glowered at her, and that same thought was basically written on his forehead in neon-bright letters: *Yuck.*

Yikes and Yakult. Clearly, he didn't want to be stuck with the weird American. He'd probably heard about her getting kicked out of summer camp.

Obaachan clapped her hands. "Well, Jin, did you already have breakfast?"

"Yes, thank you."

"Would you like some mugicha to drink?"

"No, thank you." He maintained a very polite facade, but Tessa could see straight through that. His eyes darted to his house on the other side of the street.

"Wonderful, wonderful!" Obaachan clapped her hands. "Just let Tessa know if you need anything, okay?"

Tessa and Jin looked at each other warily. He looked as cheerful as a boy who'd just opened his birthday presents to find a mountain of never-ending homework.

"So you speak English?" Tessa asked. They would be able to get along better if they were able to switch languages from time to time.

"*No English.*" He shrugged. In Japanese, he added, "My dad thinks I'll learn by being near an American." Tessa thought that label was a little funny—in California, she was always "Japanese," but here, she was "American." She never really had a place to belong; even if she spoke Japanese well enough, it seemed like everyone in

Japan could tell that she was *different*, and not in a cool way.

"See, you two get along so well already!" Obaachan beamed, patting their heads.

Ojiichan stuck his head out of the entranceway, dangling a tied-up furoshiki from his wrinkly hand. "This is all that I need to bring over to the antique shop, right?"

"Yes, yes, but hold the daruma carefully, now! I don't want to pay Kikumoto a yen extra," Obaachan scolded. "The padding I sewed into that furoshiki is strong, but don't *drop* it."

"What're you doing, Ojiichan?" Tessa asked.

"Taking in the daruma. It's due time that we get the lock fixed. Been jammed as long as I can remember. Kikumoto's a pain, but he's the best antique repairman in the city."

Tessa's ears perked up. "Where's his shop?"

The old man waved airily. "Near Asakusa."

Asakusa. Tessa searched her memory, but she didn't know much about that area...other than that it was part of Tokyo. An antique shop sounded boring. But if it meant she could get into the city... "I want to go!"

"Jin is here," he said, the tone obvious. *You can't just leave him here.* But Tokyo was where her sisters were; she wasn't in Japan to hang out with Jin.

Jin gazed wishfully at his house. "I don't want to intrude...."

She eyed the lumpy backpack on Ojiichan's shoulders and the furoshiki he was straining to hold up. "How about we help you carry your stuff?"

Ojiichan's eyes lit up. "Why, these old legs of mine could use some help."

He was about to put down the tied-up furoshiki when Obaachan swooped in. "Don't let that touch the ground! The daruma is far too precious."

Obaachan clutched the furoshiki to her chest and hurried across the street, calling, "Mr. Uehara, Mr. Uehara—"

A few seconds later, Jin's father strode out of his house, his dark eyebrows furrowed, his fists curled at his sides. "Is Jin causing trouble?"

Obaachan waved those words away with a laugh. "Your Jin? Never. We were just wondering if he can join Tessa and Ojiichan on a day trip to Asakusa."

"All the way across the bridge? I don't want him to be a burden...."

The buoyant air lifting Tessa up deflated. As much as Jin didn't care for Tessa, if he wasn't allowed to go, *she* might not be able to go, either.

"We'd love for him to join us!" Tessa piped up. "We can practice *lots* of English."

"Jin," Mr. Uehara said, the frown still etched over his eyebrows, "I expect you'll be on your best behavior, and be an excellent guide for Tessa, especially since she's new to Japan."

Jin jerked his head in a nod. "Of course. I promise."

That was a yes. A yes that made Jin somewhat responsible for Tessa, which she didn't care for, but a *yes*.

"It's not going to be that exciting." Ojiichan hesitated, like he was going to head straight out without them. "You'll have to wear exercise clothes, and—"

Tessa was already scrambling inside, flinging her shoes off on her way to her suitcase. "Don't leave without me!"

Ojiichan squawked, barely catching one of her flying shoes, but Tessa was in too much of a rush to line them up properly. Her heart thumped as she grabbed her cell phone—no international service, but she could still take photos. The lid of the clamshell suitcase nearly shut on her head as she dug for a pair of denim shorts and her white V-neck. It wasn't exactly the definition of exercise clothes, but it wasn't like walking around with Ojiichan was an intense workout; he was seventy-seven years old. If anything, he probably wanted to check out a golf shop to test out a new club.

As she shoved her phone into her pocket, something felt off.

"*Danger…a choice ahead…*" A soft, scratchy voice echoed around her. "*Be wary…*"

She spun around, but she was alone, only surrounded by her and her sisters' suitcases. It was just jet lag.

Tessa glanced down at the red bracelet, with her two

charms attached. The gold kitsune charm caught the sunlight streaming through the window, the fox flashing bright as a warning. And as if to answer, the white ōkami charm blazed hot as fire against her skin, for the barest of moments.

Tessa shook her wrist, ignoring the bracelet. Those charms didn't matter. She was going to *Tokyo*.

4

Location: Akihabara, Tokyo, Japan

TESSA COULD BARELY TAKE A SINGLE STEP. EVERYWHERE she turned, there was something new to look at, to breathe in, to experience. The midday sun was a familiar buttery gold, but the world around her shone brand-new neon.

They were in Akihabara—also known as Electric Town—and it beamed in fire-engine reds, highlighter yellows, and fluorescent greens. From the moment Tessa, Ojiichan, and Jin stepped out of Akihabara Train Station, there were too many things to take in—ramen restaurants and shouting storekeepers and adorable little stands for freshly made takoyaki, the scent of pan-fried batter making Tessa's stomach growl.

"*Onward…*" Again, that peculiar whisper in a sea of sound, but Tessa could've heard it anywhere, even in the middle of a BTS concert.

She tried to ignore that strange voice. Because this place was beautiful, it was chaotic, and it was Tokyo, finally.

Jin and Ojiichan didn't seem nearly as enthralled; they were talking about some manga that had just come out with its latest chapter. She'd watched a few episodes of *Detective Conan*, but she'd never really gotten into it enough to read its hundred-plus volumes.

Tessa clutched Ojiichan's backpack straps closer to her chest—she'd offered to carry the daruma, but her grandpa wanted to hold that himself—and glanced around. So far, other than the creepy voices, she hadn't seen anything odd. She tried to avoid looking at the scarlet bracelet; surely things were okay now. Maybe vanquishing the woman with the mask was all she had had to do. Sure, she'd have to carry around that charm, but other than that, now life would finally be normal.

Tessa's heart soared as she stopped in front of a five-story electronics shop. She'd never thought toothbrushes were exciting, but here, she *was* excited. And the rice cooker looked neat, too—when Cecilia wasn't drawing up orders for her custom bullet journals, she loved cooking, so she'd probably want to try it. Maybe she could borrow Ojiichan's phone and call her sisters to meet up—

"Tessa-chan, over here!" Ojiichan hollered from the corner.

"But, *look*!" Tessa gestured at the next shop. The

sparkling clear displays of the arcade games reeled her in, teeming with a special kind of magic. The machines were stuffed with all sorts of plushies and even themed chocolate and snacks from her favorite animes.

Ojiichan smiled. "We're going to be late. I still have to fill out the paperwork for you two."

"Why do I need to register for an antique store?" Tessa asked. Couldn't they spend time looking around Tokyo instead of just staying in a musty old shop?

Jin's jaw dropped, his eyes already glued to something. "Wait, we're going *here*?"

Tessa followed his gaze to the building Ojiichan was standing in front of. *Exercise Land?* That sounded like the polar opposite of cool. Slowly, she read the big poster board set in front: *Starting at noon! Move to the beat, and join us for our most popular senior aerobics class!*

Ojiichan grinned. "This is our first stop."

"*Senior* aerobics class?" Tessa and Jin spluttered.

"One, two, three!" called the instructor cheerily, bobbing her head to the beat, her ponytail pertly swinging along with the tune. "To the left, to the right, to the left!"

Tessa's face burned crimson, and it wasn't because of the intense exercises. She didn't even dare look at Jin, shuffling to her left. She had been *so* thrilled to finally, *finally* go into Tokyo, and look at her—*cursed*, as always.

Seriously, *who* else in the world went on a vacation to Japan and ended up doing shuffle-steps with senior citizens to the soundtrack of *High School Musical 3*?

Tessa threw her arms up—but only to match the perky instructor's next move.

Ojiichan looked so happy, his forehead gleaming with sweat, his eyes sparkling with delight. He'd brought Tessa and Jin around to meet all his other grandparent friends, which was basically the entire forty-person class. Tessa thought old people played pachinko or whatever it was that they found interesting when they got all wrinkly, but these wiry, bright-eyed grannies and gramps were Energizer Bunnies.

"This is my granddaughter. From the United States!" he'd said proudly, and Tessa had never been fawned over by so many people all at once. Then he'd waved at Jin. "And my neighbor! He's young, but he's a martial arts phenomenon! *And* he comes over to play Hanafuda with me every week!"

The sting that flashed through Tessa—*every week? Ojiichan barely figures out how to email me back once a month*—disappeared when she saw how delighted her grandpa was.

Still, that didn't make this class any less embarrassing.

There was a strange tug in her stomach, and the charms on her bracelet tinkled ominously, even as Taylor Swift's latest release started piping out of the speakers.

The air chilled; strange for the workout room, which had felt slightly warm despite the air conditioner cranking on in the corner. It felt like something was watching her, but clearly, no one in their right state of mind would want to watch *this*. She glanced around. It was just her, Ojiichan, and Jin in the back row, the line of stuffed cubbies behind them; everyone else was in some kind of sweaty euphoria, grinning their heads off while they bounced from left to right. *Everything is fine*, Tessa told herself, trying to follow the instructor's motions.

"This shall never be discussed," Jin muttered under his breath, as they dipped into a squat and then jumped up to reach toward the ceiling. They'd been doing this for what felt like hours, though only a few excruciating songs had played so far.

"Yippee!" The instructor was absolutely beaming. "Put your energy into it! Reach for the sky!"

"What happens in elderly aerobics class stays in elderly aerobics class," Tessa said gravely. Suddenly, she felt a set of hands on her shoulders and froze. The sensation disappeared when she looked behind them; there were only the cubbies filled with unattended backpacks and bags. Cold air wrapped around her skin, and she shivered.

"Do you not like the class?" Ojiichan called over the music.

"Oh!" Tessa was at a loss for words. "No, it's—"

Everyone was moving to the left, and she tried to keep up. Then she felt that set of ice-cold hands on her shoulders, but this time it shoved her to the right, pushing her off-balance.

She tried to correct herself just as Ojiichan twisted to avoid slamming into her, but his momentum was too much—

He stepped on his left foot at an angle and let out a choked "*Ara*."

Horror filled Tessa as Ojiichan tumbled to the floor.

The cheery music came to a screeching halt, and it felt like the whole world did, too, as her grandpa curled up on the ground, clutching his ankle, his eyes squeezed shut.

"Ojiichan!" Tessa gasped out. "Are you okay?"

The instructor swept through the crowd of gramps and grannies gathering around them. "Let me through!" She kneeled next to Ojiichan and gestured at his ankle. "May I?"

After his nod, she began expertly pressing lightly on his foot, and here and there, while Ojiichan kept shaking his head. "It's fine."

"She's a nurse at the clinic down the street," said one of the grannies, who'd told Tessa that all Americans looked like movie stars, including her.

"I'm a doctor," one of the grandpas replied, putting his hands on his spandex hips. "I will be able to determine—"

"You are a doctor of *tea*," snorted another of the grandpas.

"I am a specialist in *agriculture*, but my experience is vast and immense, greater than what you can even *fathom*."

Tessa tried to concentrate on Ojiichan. He was already sitting up, his left leg extended in front of him, with Jin hovering close behind. The nurse was moving his ankle around, checking for any pain, but Ojiichan kept shaking his head. "No, that's fine. No, it doesn't hurt. Hey, can we play that song again? 'School High'? What was it?"

"*High School Musical 3*," Tessa said.

"That one! 'Musical High'!" Ojiichan was getting cheerier than ever with every second.

"You seem fine," the instructor said, finally, and relief blossomed in Tessa's chest. "We're very lucky you didn't get hurt. But I still want you to get an X-ray, just to confirm, and after that, you're going straight home."

Ojiichan froze at that. "I have plans after this. I have an errand I must do. I cannot—"

"Then we'll find someone to do your errand for you."

"No, no, this must be protected by my family," Ojiichan said. "Until it's in the hands of old Kikumoto, it must be protected by a Miyata."

"You must rest," the nurse said firmly. Then she called out, "Emi-chan?"

A girl in her early twenties wove out of the crowd; she was one of the assistant teachers. "I'll bring you home, Mr. Miyata."

"But—"

The instructor sighed. "Remember, these classes are meant to be fun, but you're only supposed to do what feels comfortable. It's not like you can go running around Tokyo like you did in your teens. Unless you'd like me to share those stories with your granddaughter."

"I want to hear the stories," Tessa interjected, her voice light. Anything to get Ojiichan home safe.

"Well, another day." He hastily waved his hand, like he could fan away the memories of his past. "But...I have a more important question." Ojiichan cleared his throat, but his voice cracked, and nervousness shot through her veins, taut and chilling.

It'd all been her fault. And she'd never be able to make up for this. Cecilia and Peyton would be beyond disappointed that she'd hurt Ojiichan.

She kneeled next to her grandpa. "I'll do anything you need."

His wrinkled hand cupped hers. "This, dear Tessa, is something only you can do."

Tessa nodded. "Please, tell me."

"I cannot make it, so you must carry on." Ojiichan breathed out slowly.

Panic cut off her breath. *Oh no, he's going to croak—*

"Will you be able to go to the antique shop without me?"

"But are you okay—"

"You must carry on!" Ojiichan cried, throwing his arm out just *a little* too dramatically. "Dear grandchild of mine, I need you to carry on my legacy—"

She narrowed her eyes. "You're completely fine, aren't you."

The old man grinned cheekily, and Tessa let out a sigh of relief.

But it *was* her fault. Tessa had to make it up to him. "I'll do anything you need."

It was lucky that it was just a sore ankle. That was what Tessa kept trying to tell herself, as Ojiichan carefully gave her the daruma wrapped in the protective furoshiki; she tightened her grip around its padded cloth case carefully.

She tried not to think about how it'd almost felt like someone—or *something*—had pushed her into him. That was impossible. There was no one else behind Tessa's row; she'd seen for herself in the mirror.

Tessa glared down at her bracelet. Was this thing really a warning? Or maybe—considering how it'd attracted that woman in white—it was the cause of all of this trouble. She flicked the red string; the fox and the wolf charms tinkled merrily.

"What's that?" a voice asked, and a shadow fell over

her. Jin had wiped off his forehead, but a faint scent of sweat washed over her, woven with the warm smell of sun-dried laundry. She'd be the last person to admit that Jin kind of smelled good, though.

"What's what?"

"I thought I saw..." Jin's dark eyebrows furrowed at her wrist before turning to look over at Ojiichan, who was still being fawned over by the rest of his friends. "It's nothing. I've been staying up too late practicing karate."

Tessa frowned. Had Jin seen her bracelet? No one had *ever* seen it before. But she definitely couldn't ask. He'd tell her grandpa and then Ojiichan would tell her sisters, and Tessa would *really* be on lockdown all summer.

"Let's get Ojiichan on his train and then head to this antique shop," Jin said, and that was that.

Still, as Tessa helped her grandpa out of the studio, she wondered...what if he *had* seen her bracelet?

5

Location: In the backstreets of Asakusa
in Tokyo, Japan

CLEARLY, JIN COULDN'T WAIT TO BE RID OF HER AND
get on with his summer vacation.

"We have to drop this off at Kikumoto's shop fast," he
said, striding out of Asakusa Train Station. He muttered
something about a sparring session under his breath.

Tessa bit her lip. "If you have things you need to do,
I can go on my own." She clutched the furoshiki to her
chest. The daruma seemed to be only getting heavier and
heavier with each step; she had to keep a close grip, or
it felt like the box just might come tumbling out of her
hands. "You can just head off—"

Jin shook his head, as if that was unthinkable. "I
promised my father I'd ensure you returned to Kisarazu
safely. I can't break a promise to him, not after what just
happened."

Her stomach dropped, faster than the train that had

zipped them straight to Asakusa. *A promise.* Tessa hated those words. She hated being someone else's obligation, someone else's younger sister; a burden that others had to watch over and protect.

"Well," she said, trying to inject cheer into her voice, "we should get going, then."

Jin led them past a shrine with loads of tourists pouring through its huge gates; there was a line of shops that Tessa longed to visit, with freshly grilled rice crackers and pretty summer yukatas and tons of neat postcards. She tried pulling out her phone to snap a picture, but Jin was already twenty feet ahead of her, calling, with a hint of annoyance, "Come on!"

Tessa nearly dropped her phone. A group of kids hanging by the entrance to the shrine glanced at her and snickered; she could feel their burning eyes as she hurried away. *Great. Way to embarrass myself the instant I get into Tokyo.*

All she'd caught a picture of was a blur of red. She groaned as she followed Jin down another side street. This one was just okay. There were loads of shops selling dishware and old-people things like tea cups. Tessa could almost see Allison's NowLook sneering comment: *Wow. You make Tokyo look so fascinating.*

"How far is the antique shop?" she asked Jin, who was staring at his phone and looking around.

"It's a few more blocks away." Jin paused. Oddly, the

tips of his ears, peeking out from his messy hair, turned a little pink. "But can you wait here real quick? I have to run an errand over there"—he pointed to the small alleyway to their right, with a few stores—"but I'll return in five minutes, max."

"Fine by me," Tessa said.

"Just don't go into any stores," Jin called over his shoulder. "Stay at this corner, where I can find you."

Tessa bristled. *Sit, stay. Woof, woof.* What was she, a puppy?

But, twenty minutes later, Tessa was seriously wondering what had happened to Jin. He totally seemed the punctual type. Plus, that group of five kids that had snickered earlier were strolling along this side street, heading toward her.

She clutched the daruma closer to her chest, thankful for the thick padded case that kept it hidden, though that seemed to draw attention to it.

The tallest boy stopped. "What's your name?" He looked kind of like a bean sprout, all stretched out with nothing else to him. Even his face was a little long and indistinguishable.

Tessa stammered, "Tessa Miyata. I am here to visit."

The moment she spoke in her most formal Japanese, she knew she'd made a mistake. One of the girls smirked, and Tessa's heart thumped.

"Well, you know, since you're new to the area, we'll be nice," he said.

His tone sounded the opposite of nice, but Tessa didn't think she was in any place to comment. She gulped, backing into the alleyway that Jin had headed to. There was a slim, slim chance, but maybe Jin would see her through a window and get help.

Though Tessa knew from so many times before: She was likely very well cursed.

"Is there something you want?" Tessa asked. *Cut to the chase.* She had enough of getting bullied. Sometimes it worked to get straight to the humiliation.

The kids' eyes flicked down to the protective furoshiki, and Tessa took more steps back. She was almost halfway through the alley, and Jin hadn't poked his head out, even with as loud as the kids were being.

"What's in there?" the girl asked, her voice singsongy. There was something about her that reminded Tessa of the creepy animated figurines in the Haunted Mansion at Disneyland. Sweet-sounding, but clearly ready to reveal her true face of dried-out bones in the next second.

"Oh, this? It's some boring thing from my grandpa." Tessa tried to sound totally uninterested as she took another big step. "Like, I don't know why he's making me bring it to some place over here in Asakusa."

Tessa's back slammed into something, and for a split

second, she hoped with all her heart that it was an adult swooping in.

She peeked over her shoulder. A tall, gray concrete wall. She'd stumbled into a building, with no doors to be seen. The kids had cornered her in a spot so far down the alley that the passersby wouldn't see her, either.

Her heart sunk.

The kids eyed her package a little closer, and Tessa tightened her arms around the daruma. *Over my dead body.*

There was a flash of motion. "Ouch!" she cried out.

One of the kids knocked her off-balance with a sweeping low kick, making her slam her backside onto the ground. She gasped in pain, but that wasn't all.

The girl had grabbed the case and was peering inside.

"What?" Her nose curled up in disgust, just the way Allison did, that one day Tessa had tried to sit next to her at lunch. "A *daruma*?"

"An ugly, dusty one," spat out one of the boys. The kids had formed a circle around Tessa; the others snickered.

"It's my grandparents'!" Tessa cried out. "Please don't touch it—"

She could already imagine the look on her family's faces. She'd be letting everyone down after being in Japan for only twenty-four hours.

"Useless," the girl sneered.

"Give it back!" Tessa lunged toward the girl, but she threw it to her friend to her right.

The boy shook his head as Tessa darted toward him, his lips splitting in a cruel grin. "*Nice* try." He lofted it over her head.

"Please!" Tessa cried, as the kids began tossing it around.

"Faster, faster!" the kids chanted, laughing. "Faster!"

The daruma arced over her head, the top of the case flapping against the glass. She'd always hated being short; getting stuck in this situation made her angry, to the point of tears. She blinked those tears away as fast as she could, but they kept coming up, despite her efforts. Tessa needed to see clearly, to wait for the right moment—

"*What* do you think you're doing?" a sharp voice asked.

Jin glared at each bully in turn, and they stepped almost instinctively toward the right side of the alley as he stalked to Tessa's side.

"Well," the bean sprout boy said, clutching the daruma. "Jin Uehara. Look at who finally showed up."

Tessa blinked. Was it just her, or did they all look a little nervous?

"You saw me with this girl, so you wanted to mess around?" Jin spat out. "My *father* told me to watch over her, so bullying her means you don't just cross me; you cross my dad, too."

Would there ever be a day where she wasn't a burden for someone? Tessa's heart sunk.

One of the boys snickered. "Well, *you* weren't doing a good job. I bet Uehara Sensei would thank—"

"Oh, I'll thank you. When I beat you on the mats at the tournament next month, and take first place—as usual," Jin growled.

"But you don't have *this*," taunted the bean sprout boy, wiggling the daruma. Tessa let out a yelp, but the moment she inched closer, one of the girls narrowed her eyes.

Jin said smoothly, "Break it and I'll let your teachers know exactly how you spend your free time."

The kids glanced at each other, tensely. The bean sprout boy hissed, "You wouldn't dare!"

Jin stared him down. "Try me. Or would you rather try me right now?"

He slid one leg forward, ever so slightly. His body was poised in a fighting stance, like an arrow about to burst from its string. Wherever he aimed, Tessa had a feeling he *would* connect with his target. She gulped—as did the other kids.

The boy tightened his fingers around the daruma, and his eyes grew flinty. "Throw the match. Lose to us."

"Never," Jin said coldly. "You're so weak you need bribes to win?"

Then a peculiar sound—like dead leaves skittering across a forest floor—echoed through the alleyway.

"Did you hear that?" Tessa asked. No one paid her any attention; Jin was locked in a staring match with the other kids. She scanned around, trying to locate it. There were a few closed doors, the back entrances to stores that looked out onto main streets. A partly open door a little ways down the alley creaked, moving in an unseen wind.

Another noise, sharp and ringing, like metal scraping against metal, curdled Tessa's blood. Then the scent of rot, like damp leaves left unturned for far too long, filled the air. Something terrible was going to happen; Tessa could sense it in her blood.

"Stronger..."

Another scratching sound, like fingernails on a chalkboard—or...the daruma's case?

Was it broken? She hoped not, but Tessa had the *worst* luck.

Then the bean sprout boy's lips tugged up in a cruel smirk *No...* She'd seen that look before: on Allison, right when she'd shown that first video of Tessa to the rest of their class.

"Well, you'll have a lot to explain to Uehara Sensei," the boy said with a wide grin, as he tugged away the protective furoshiki. The black silk rippled like the night sky, the gold print shimmering brighter than pooled sunlight as it fluttered down.

Jin let out a garbled noise, and Tessa shouted, "Please—"

Bright flames flickered in the doll's eyes; the boy's eyes seemed to glow a strange red-neon color, too, as he opened up his hands to let the daruma tumble down, straight to the ground.

6

GLASS SHATTERED, A CACOPHONY OF SHARP, HORRIFY-
ing sounds.

"No!" Tessa cried out. All she could see was glittering glass. *Where is the daruma—where is it—*

"Uehara Sensei won't believe you over all of us," one
of the girls said smugly. "And—"

Her words cut off as a strange darkness fell over the
alleyway, like the furoshiki cloth had been thrown over
the sun.

But Tessa didn't care about what the bullies said. She
couldn't let her grandparents down, not like this. Her
knees scraped against the asphalt as she fell to the ground,
searching through the murky gloom for the daruma. *Let
it be whole, I know that's impossible, but please....*

A serpentine *hiss* filled the air, then—

"I've been waiting."

The stench of rot and miasma poured forth.

"There's—there's something weird about this place," the bean sprout boy said, trying to sound brave. But his shoes scuffled as he turned, his friends quickly following. He called over his shoulder, "Uehara, cross us again, and you can expect worse."

There was *definitely* something weird about this alleyway. On the dead end that had been to Tessa's back, a swooping arch seemed to paint itself into existence. It was one of the red-orange gates she'd seen in pictures of shrines, a bigger-than-Jin-and-Tessa-sized version of the miniature in her grandparents' curio case. But Tessa needed to find the daruma. *Where is it?*

Ding! Her bracelet chimed, and she heard that disembodied voice. *"Take the door before it's too late!"*

A howl of wind tore through the alley, like a pack of wolves, scraping like fangs against Tessa's skin.

Ding! Ding! Something dark and shadowy was growing taller behind Jin.

"Look out," Tessa gasped, pointing. Her bracelet burned with a sharp heat, but she'd pieced together this warning way too late.

Jin spun around, narrowly jumping out of the way as something came crashing down, splintering the asphalt.

A shadowy samurai, made of swirls of black mist, stood between them and the exit to the alleyway.

The figure was no more corporeal than a storm cloud—but a thousand times more deadly. This wasn't like the woman in white or the wolf she'd seen before. Though the figure was formed out of ether from the tips of the curved crest at the top of his helmet down to his armored boots, the katana he held glimmered bright and sharp—pointed at Jin's neck. The voice Tessa had heard earlier—then, faint as dead leaves skittering; now, sharp as blades clashing and deep as the roar of a river—spoke. "There you are. I've been waiting a long, long time for you."

Fear stole her words away as the samurai swung his sword straight at Tessa.

THE SWORD CAME DOWN, BUT JIN FLEW FORWARD, BARreling straight into the figure of mist. It shredded into wisps, the sword clattering on the ground.

Just as quickly as the sword fell, it shot up, pulled by invisible strings. Tessa screamed, ducking as the samurai lunged, slicing the wall right where her head had been. Concrete chunks sprayed over her; her heart thumped. Even if this phantom's body was mist, its blade was *very* real.

"We have to get out!" Jin shouted, pulling her to her feet.

"We *can't*!" Tessa cried. There was no way past this samurai.

"*Enter the torii.*" That voice. Surely...it wasn't from Tessa's *bracelet*, was it?

But, with another flash of metal, Tessa knew that there wasn't time to waste. She flung her right hand backward, to where there was solid concrete between the painted outline of the gate—

Or there should have been.

But her hand went straight through the wall.

A searing burn ran down her palm, tearing at her skin, and circled around her wrist where she wore the scarlet bracelet. The threads burst into life, burning like flames around the kitsune charm. The metal glowed; a dark outline morphed into the shadow of a samurai much larger than the one in front of them. Then the bracelet twisted, and pure light shot out in the shape of a sharp-nosed fox.

It landed on her arm, no bigger than two of her hands put together. The blaze cut out to reveal sleek white fur and a forehead marked with a crimson line, like a streak of blood. Its right ear was notched, like a beast had chomped out a nasty bite. Nine tails unfurled; this creature could only be a kitsune, the legendary mythological creature known for being a cunning yet faithful protector.

The fox looked at the shadowy figure.

And bounded away.

Tessa yelped. "Wait! You're supposed to save us—"

A golden thread flashed out of thin air—from Tessa's fingertips, stretching around the kitsune's body like a harness—yanking the creature straight to Tessa's side, splayed out on his belly. The once-scarlet bracelet burned with a gold light.

The kitsune growled, "We have to escape!"

"We're trying, please, help us!" Tessa gestured in panic at the samurai; Jin dodged another slice of that sword, but even Tessa could see that the boy was sweating in this close-quarters fight. "*Save* him."

"Well, I don't care for mortals dying so young, so I guess I can help." With a leap, the fox tore at the samurai, his sharp white teeth ripping the shadows. The tendrils of mist flickered weakly as it re-formed; this time, its body was more transparent and the curved crest of its helmet had disappeared. It took another step toward Jin, who let out heaving breaths, his back pressed against the wall, but the fox let out a warning snarl.

"*You.*" The samurai hissed. "I knew I had sensed you."

The kitsune perked his ears up. "You know who I am? I'd appreciate a hint in the right direction. A name, maybe?"

"I remember enough to know who you are and what *you* did." The dark figure swirled ominously, and his shadowy hand thumped his chest. "*You* murdered me, the one and only Taira Masakado."

Jin gaped. "Impossible."

The fox froze with one paw in the air. "*The* Taira Masakado?"

"Um, who?" Tessa asked.

Three pairs of eyes swung toward her in disbelief.

"You know, Lord Taira Masakado, the ridiculously strong samurai who almost *overthrew* the government in the Heian period?" Jin asked.

"I will not have my name thrown around by meager nothings," Lord Taira Masakado snapped. "I will get my revenge; on you, creature, and on the gods who never helped in my time of need." He aimed his sword straight at the kitsune; carved dragons and flames flashed on its hand guard.

"Godfire!" the kitsune exclaimed. "That samurai's got the Sword of a Thousand Souls. I knew I'd sensed something bad."

"The what?" Tessa echoed.

"You know, the sword that sucked up at *least* a thousand gods and spirits who tried to control it—" The fox took one look at Tessa. "We have a lot of catching up to do. Well, for now, I'd *like* to survive."

The samurai adjusted his sword to point straight at them. Tessa gulped.

"Yep. Most definitely. We're leaving." The fox's nine

tails flicked as he turned toward the wall with the gate. "This way!"

In a furious burst, the samurai dashed forward, flashing his katana. Tessa felt a tug on her wrist, where the fox charm had once been. In a fluid motion, like a burning-white star shooting across the sky, the kitsune shot toward the torii, and Tessa felt herself stumbling into—no, *through* the wall.

She lunged to grab Jin, barely grasping him by the wrist, and pulled him in with her, just before the samurai's sword clanged against the concrete.

There was a burning flash of light, searing her vision.

Tessa, Jin, and the fox sprawled on the ground, but a moment later, she looked up, expecting the samurai to charge through the wall.

Instead, she stared. "Where *are* we?"

II

You Have Arrived at the City of Legends

Location: Unknown

"WELCOME TO THE BEST HIDDEN SECRET OF TOKYO!" a voice said cheerily. "Whew! That took a lot of energy!"

Tessa groaned, pushing herself upright. There was a heavy weight on her shoulder. The fox was sitting on her right side, looking happily around.

Jin's eyes narrowed. "Wait, what's this place?"

Oddly, they were on a dirt path, dust coating Tessa's gray Converses. Then she looked around and gaped.

They were definitely not in Asakusa. Moments ago, they'd been a stone's throw away from the busy streets leading up to Sensō-ji temple, crowded with vans and cars. But there wasn't a single car around. A clean, pure breeze swirled, brushing her cheeks more softly than an early spring day. True, the wall they'd come through was still here, framed in a wood torii, and behind a strange hunk of rope that was almost taller than Tessa, but that was it. The path they were sitting on led through a meadow and over a gentle hill.

Lining its sides, there were a few cherry blossom trees in full bloom—though they should've stopped flowering months ago—with petals swirling through the air. Tessa peered closer. It was beautiful and all, but that wasn't what made her know that something was off....

It was the sky above, blazingly sunny and a clear blue.

And not a skyscraper was in sight.

The issue was, they should've been in the middle of Tokyo.

The kitsune's ears twitched to and fro. "I never expected to see this again. I don't know why I left, but *no one* could forget a place like this. Thank goodness I was here to vanquish that guy. The Sword of a Thousand Souls is really something, though. Spirits, what a gorgeous design on that tsuba, the dragons and—"

"Um, since when does Asakusa lead to a meadow? Aren't we supposed to be in Tokyo?" Tessa tried to shake him off her shoulder, but the fox seemed to defy gravity. "And are you really a talking *kitsune*?"

She frowned. Also, was it just her, or did his shadow not quite look like a kitsune? When she squinted, it looked like a samurai, pointy helmet and all.

"Well, I guess," the fox responded. "Except, before I was in that charm of yours, I'm pretty sure I *wasn't* a fox. I was a god." The fox shook his head in an assured nod.

"Definitely a god. But, ah, you wouldn't happen to know my name, would you?"

"*No*, how would I know that?" Tessa asked. Jin shook his head, too.

The fox looked oddly sad. Kind of like the way Tessa felt, when no one knew who *she* was at school—except to laugh at her.

"Kit!" Tessa blurted. "We'll call you Kit!"

"Well, that works."

"A talking kitsune. Sitting around in some place that definitely doesn't exist on any map of Tokyo." Jin slumped forward, his messy hair falling in front of his eyes. "This has got to be a bad dream. Dad's going to come wake me up and tell me I'm late for practice any minute now."

"That Lord Taira guy would've guzzled you up like a bottle of ramune," the fox continued. "I mean, *you* saw that sword."

Tessa blinked. "I *have* to be dreaming, too." Her heart thumped. *No. Way. Jin can actually see what I'm seeing?* Tessa's mind flashed back to the aerobics class, when she'd sworn Jin had seen her bracelet. "So, I'm not the only one, right? Have you seen weird things like this before? Like, maybe a woman in white who *definitely* was supposed to only be part of an anime?"

"Like *what*?" Jin stared. Kit stared, too, scratching his notched ear.

Tessa's cheeks burned red. "Ha ha ha, that was just a

joke." But her stomach felt like it'd been pummeled by that samurai. "Um, right, so what was that torii, anyway?"

"It's a gateway into the City. I used basically *all* of my ku—that's energy—to open it up so you shrimpy mortals could survive, so be grateful," the fox grumbled. He unfurled his nine tails; one, oddly, was white like the rest of his fur, but slightly transparent. "See? Cost me a bit of my godforce to summon it up. Thankfully, you're both god-blessed, so you were able to enter with me."

"And I'm the empress of Japan," Tessa said. As if *that* made any sense. *Godforce? Ku?* And what the Yakult was being "god-blessed"? A sneeze? She had to be super jet-lagged and was likely hearing things. The fox's shadow still looked weird, too, stretching out into the shape of a samurai, not a fox. Jet. Lag. It had to be jet lag.

"Guys, what's that?" Jin gestured toward Tessa.

"What? *Me*?"

"No," Jin said, pointing behind them, "*that*. It looks like a gigantic shimenawa."

"A shime-what?" Tessa glanced up at the enormous woven rope she was leaning on. It was so big that she could barely see the wall on the other side.

Kit gave it a cautious sniff, his black nose wiggling. "Definitely a shimenawa. This one's oozing with power. I don't have a good feeling about it."

"It's a purification rope," Jin explained. "At least, the shimenawa I see at shrines are. But those are like the width of my arm, wrapped around the front of the temple or trees or sacred things like that. Not bigger than hundreds of these scrawny kitsune put together."

"I am not scrawny, human. I am a *little* low on power after saving your lives," Kit sniffed. "Anyway, we have to find the Seven Lucky Gods."

"No, thanks," Tessa said. "I have to get back to my grandpa. And somehow explain how our family heirloom daruma turned into a murderous samurai."

"My father is going to murder me, period," Jin muttered. "Miyata, let's go."

The fox shrugged. "Suit yourself. I'm sure you'll be able to make your way home eventually. It may take a few years."

"What?" Jin yelped.

Tessa shook her head. "That's impossible, we'll just go through the torii—"

The kitsune gave them a sharp-fanged grin. Belatedly, Tessa remembered that the mythological foxes were notorious tricksters. A peculiar feeling tickled the nape of her neck.

Tessa and Jin scrambled to their feet to look around the shimenawa for the wall with the gate. Only, it had vanished into thin air, and all that remained were wide, open plains.

They were surrounded by softly whispering grasses, the tall cherry blossom trees...

Without a way home.

9

Location: A hidden suburb of Tokyo, Japan

"A DOORWAY TO THE CITY OPENS TO THOSE IN NEED," Kit said, his bushy white tail flicking to and fro. "It's been great meeting you face-to-face finally—thanks for taking care of me all these years, Miyata, and for freeing me. Wasn't fun being stuck on a bracelet, but you made it work out okay. See you in another lifetime."

The fox saluted them and sauntered along the dirt path toward the hill, his nine tails flicking merrily. The moment he got to the bottom, Kit stumbled, scrabbling for footing. "Godfire! What's going on?"

"Um…" Tessa gestured at the gold glow circling Kit's paw, faintly illuminated even in the bright midafternoon. It led straight to Tessa, where the bracelet turned into molten light, and where the ōkami charm still dangled, same as ever. It seemed that, perhaps, the kitsune wasn't able to go anywhere without her.

Kit groaned. "I thought you'd released me."

"You were freeloading on my *arm* for years. You were a parasite."

The fox yelped in wounded horror. "I'm the one who was saving your butt all the time. You heard that tinkle, right? That was me clanging as hard as I could to get your attention, so that you'd be more careful! I'd be having a nice little nap, gathering up my energy, and I'd be shoved awake by the worst feeling in my nonexistent stomach, knowing you were in danger!"

Tessa had always noticed that the bracelet *had* seemed to chime right before she got in trouble. But it hadn't helped. She'd still messed up anyway, getting friend-dumped by Allison or letting down her sisters. Even that strange warning, earlier—had that been from the ōkami charm?—warning her of danger or choices, or whatever. Judging by what had just happened, *that* message definitely hadn't done any good.

Jin was looking between the two of them and their connecting golden light. "Kit. Fox. Whatever your name is. Do you know how to get to Kisarazu?"

"Wait, wait, wait." Tessa froze. "Does this mean I have to take you to my grandparents' house?"

"Who said anything about me going with *you*?" Kit shot back.

Tessa and Kit tried walking in opposite directions, but the light grew taut and pulled them toward each other, with an angry, ear-pestering buzz. They *were* stuck together.

Kit swatted at his ears. "Great, I've always wanted to be glued to a human for eternity. When you die, your bones will rattle along with me like you're *my* bracelet."

Tessa seethed. "Your bones will be rattling first, shrimpy fox."

"You mean powerful, all-knowing—"

"Calm down, you two," Jin cut in placatingly. "Fighting won't help—"

"I am going *home*!" Tessa declared. She needed to check on Ojiichan. She started marching through the grass, looking left and right for another doorway.

Her wrist tugged; the fox was lying stubbornly on the path, his paws crossed. His nine tails flicked with annoyance. "That's not how getting out of the City works."

"Tell us, then," Tessa shot back. "If you're some magical bracelet fox thing, help me get home, Toto."

"I thought my name was Kit," the kitsune responded. "Well, anyway, the entrance to the City is always in plain sight for those who are allowed in. At least, the way I remember it. Sometimes it's a doorway in an abandoned building. Or it's a closet that doesn't quite lead to a closet after all. You might be somewhere sacred, like one of Tokyo's best shrines, and walk a little too far into its most holy areas and step into the City. For some, it's a train ride where you get off at a stop that no one else realizes exists. Even that department store—what's it called, Takashimaya?—and Kinokuniya, the bookstore, have doors to the City in their shops. The telltale sign is that glowing light coming from the door, so bright that it seems like the sun is right on the other side. When a torii opens, it means the City has been calling you, asking you to come. But no matter how you get here, the City becomes home."

"Home." Jin looked flatly around them. "This is *not* home."

"That's impossible," Tessa added. She tried to ignore the nervous butterflies in her stomach, even though what he was saying exactly matched how they'd gotten in. Realistically, how could a *city* bring someone to it?

"If the door to the City lets you in, it means you should be able to open the door again." Then Kit frowned. "Unless some sort of magic's blocking it."

"Oh, wise and magical fox, how about *you* open the door?" Tessa asked.

Kit sniffed. "That's the thing. Usually, when I'm trying to leave, there's a door that's already here, waiting to take me wherever I need to go. *Clearly* you're not meant to go home, human."

Tessa and Kit glared at each other, the buzzing from the golden link making her head hurt even more.

"Whoa, you two," Jin said. "This obviously isn't ideal, but arguing—"

"You're a *charm* that belongs on my wrist," Tessa snapped. "A charm that's *anything* but charming. I am going home, whether you come with me or not."

"Okay, we get that it's complicated and all, but can we find a way out?" Jin asked.

"Shush it, model boy," Kit growled.

"What he said," Tessa echoed. "Fox, Kit, whatever your name is—"

"Is arguing going to help us find a doorway?" Jin snapped, his brows angled into sharp lines. "Or get you two separated?"

Kit and Tessa reluctantly shook their heads.

"That's right." He glared sternly. "Now, stand next to each other. That'll probably stop the buzzing from that bracelet, at least."

It was starting to sound like hornets were living in Tessa's head. Kit complained with every step, but when they walked closer, the light disappeared and the buzz faded away. Though Tessa would never admit it out loud, Jin was right.

"Let's get this removed. How do we make this happen?" Tessa groaned. "Right, you don't remember anything."

"Hey, be nice to me. It's not every thousand years that I have an identity crisis and forget my whole existence. I know I used to be *somebody* that could've done something about this with a snap of my fingers." Kit rubbed his notched ear with a paw. "There are some powerful folks that might be able to help....Maybe Fukurokuju? I bet he can get you two home in an instant. He serves pretty good tea, too."

Jin stared at him a little funny. "Fukurokuju. As in the God of Wisdom? Um...do you see any gods here?"

"*I* am a god." The fox puffed up his chest.

"Uh huh," Tessa said. "And I'm the queen of Tokyo."

Kit glanced around. "Don't let Bishamonten catch you saying that. After all...there's a reason why she's called the Goddess of War."

"I don't believe you," Tessa said. "The only Bisha-monten I know is in an anime, and it's an anime because *it's not real.*"

Jin nodded. "History? That's real. Gods? Nope. Lord Taira trying to kill me? Just a nightmare."

"Know another way for us to get separated? The Seven Lucky Gods are the only ones who can help." Kit shook out his fur. "C'mon. They're just on the other side of this hill, in the City. Some god between the seven of them will be able to separate us."

With that, the fox pranced toward the hill with his nine tails flicking in the breeze, without a worry to be had.

However, Tessa and Jin glanced at each other.

I don't have much of a choice. Tessa grimaced, but out loud she just said, "Well, one cup of tea can't hurt. Even if it's not actually from a god."

When they met this Fukurokuju—who was probably

named Fred or Fuyumi or something, well, *not* a god's name—then clearly they'd know that this talking fox was beyond ridiculous. Then Tessa could drag Kit to Kisarazu and check on her grandpa. Knowing him, Ojiichan would probably enjoy this odd creature as a pet.

"I'm not sure about this...." Jin chewed on his lip.

From the bottom of the hill, the small white fox hollered, "I don't have all day to just sit around! I've got tea to drink! You two coming with me?"

"We can do this," she said, squaring her shoulders. "Kit will show us to this fake god-person, we'll get someone to cut this bracelet off, and then we'll head home. Easy."

Jin stepped to her side. "Okay, let's do this."

They hurried along the crest of the dirt path stretching up the hill, maybe a staircase or so high. As they reached the top, a warm summer breeze swirled around them, with dancing cherry blossom petals. Tessa's hair flew in front of her eyes, so she couldn't see.

Then the wind stilled, and so did Tessa and Jin.

Underneath the thickly blooming trees, the dirt path became a cobblestone street full of visitors, with shops and stalls on either side, but beyond that, there was just a strange, pure white mist. Tessa could hardly take a moment to study that, not with everything else to see.

Figures that looked like they had stepped out of a storybook strolled about, draped in sumptuous kimonos or noble suits of armor. Cafes were crammed with patrons eating dainty pastries and sipping cups of tea; at the corner restaurant, a bowing waiter pulled covers off plates, the food so bright and fresh that it looked unreal. The shops seemed like they'd been pulled directly out of the past—a clothier, an armory, two cobblers, even the entrance to what looked to be a natural hot springs. At the far end of the road, a hotel rose out of the mist, next to a trickling stream, its doors wide open for guests. Kids were laughing and playing games, weaving in and out of the crowds. The bubbling sounds of conversation trickled like a stream of noise, beautiful and lively.

If Tessa could have chosen anywhere in the world to take a vacation, it would be *here*.

Jin nudged her, and she glanced to her left. His jaw was gaping open; he gestured wordlessly at the boulders near the beginning of this magical street.

But it wasn't a lump of rocks.

Under a cherry blossom tree, a dragon with pearly scales napped, petals dusted across its thick hide. At its left, a set of tiny animals that looked similar to racoons played with its claw; the dragon shifted, and the air before it shimmered with heat. The little tanuki scampered away with fright; the dragon lazily opened an eye to glance at them. In a few moments, the troublemaking creatures crept back to play with the dragon.

Kit's eyes were misty. "I never thought I'd see this place again."

"Where are we?" Tessa whispered reverently. This was the stuff of dreams. She didn't want to speak too loudly, for fear it would all disappear in a flash—or that the dragon might wake up.

"Welcome," Kit breathed out, "to Takamagahara, the most magical spot in all of Tokyo, where gods and enchanted spirits dwell. Or, as most call it, the City of Legends."

10

Location: The City of Legends,
a hidden suburb of Tokyo, Japan

CHERRY BLOSSOM PETALS FLOWED THROUGH THE AIR, scented sweet as honey. Tessa, Jin, and Kit (happily sitting on Tessa's shoulder) strolled down the central lane of shops and temples and shrines—there were a *lot* of them—at least one temple or shrine every few shops. And Tessa, who never thought she'd be interested in a boring temple, was certain that her new goal in life was to visit every sacred spot in Japan.

"Act *godly*," Kit whispered. "It's hard to tell who's a god or spirit, but...it's strange, there don't really seem to be many humans around."

"How can you tell?" Jin asked, in an undertone.

"They gape like Tessa. Thankfully, I've put up a barrier around you two that hides your lifeforce, so no one can tell you're mortals."

She stuck her tongue out at the fox. Then a peculiar, cooling breeze tickled her nose.

"What's that?" Jin rubbed his face.

"Ah, you felt it? That's a good sign; that was a prayer, coming straight in from mortals like you." Kit scanned around again. "Chin *up*."

"It *is*," Tessa protested.

Contrary to what Kit said, the gods paid them no mind; they were too wrapped up in their shopping or tea (which smelled so good that Tessa wanted to drink a gallon of it). Instead, she tried to memorize every detail of this world around her, to tell her sisters, to explain to Allison if they ever talked again so that she'd be able to use it for one of her film projects, to tell Ojiichan as she helped his ankle heal.

Though no one would ever believe her. She shut those thoughts away. First, these Seven Lucky Gods—whoever they really were—had to help her get separated from Kit. She glanced down at the bracelet on her wrist, with the charm still attached. The string between her and Kit had faded from view, but it seemed to reappear—and keep them stuck together—whenever the fox got interested in one of the shrines or stands and jumped off to look.

"That's not how I remembered this tea spot." Kit sniffed. "Since when do they serve boba? It looks pretty good, though—"

"We're not here for a snack." Jin shooed the fox onward.

"What's the difference between a shrine and temple?" Tessa asked, looking at the buildings left and right.

"Shrines have those torii at the front and are Shinto; temples are Buddhist," Jin said. "Some people practice both religions, like my dad. He'll drag me around to ask for blessings at a Shinto shrine the day before one of my matches, and head to a Buddhist temple the morning of."

"That's a lot of praying."

"Yeah, especially with how many tournaments he signs me up for." Jin shook his head. "I tell him that me spending time practicing matters more, but he's stubborn."

Farther down the road, a gold-tipped temple peeked out of the mist. But to their right, next to a shop selling neat-looking haori coats and pretty kimonos, there was a huge shrine.

"Look at that!" Tessa's eyes grew big and round.

The shrine was an enormous fortress on its own. But, more than that, it was *on fire*. No...it was *made* of fire. White flames roared, edged in impossibly neon colors, with a bitter, incense-like scent, forming in the shape of a torii gate, the entryway to a typical shrine. But nothing, *nothing* about this monument was ordinary.

Kit shuddered. "That's Kagutsuchi—the God of Fire. Don't get on his bad side."

"But it looks so beautiful—"

"See the neon edges of those flames? That's godfire." Kit curled close to her neck. "Us gods...we're immortal.

We can't die, other than getting killed by another god. Most of us favor katanas and daggers, maybe poison or spells...godfire is a burning fire that isn't clean like the slice of a blade. Just the smoke paralyzes a god. Then it fills your mind with nightmares as it consumes your immortal body, limb by limb. It's a fate worse than death."

The flickering flames didn't look so pretty anymore.

"Are those the Seven Lucky Gods' shrines?" Jin asked from where he'd stopped.

Tessa dragged her eyes away from Kagutsuchi's shrine to glance at what Jin was pointing to. It was a gigantic carved wooden sign next to a gold gate, tall as a billboard, as if the Seven couldn't *dare* let a soul miss how important they were.

THE CITY'S MOST HONORABLE LEADERS

Ebisu, the God of Prosperity

Daikokuten, the God of Business and Trade

Bishamonten, the Goddess of War

Benzaiten, the Goddess of the Arts

Kichijoten, the Goddess of Happiness

Hotei, the God of Fortune

Fukurokuju, the God of Wisdom

She glanced around the sign. Surely nothing could be more impressive than a building constantly on fire—

The Lucky Gods' shrines were *beyond* Tessa's wildest imaginations.

She moved as if she was in a trance, pressing her face into a gap in the gold gates, her breath shallow and in disbelief. Seven buildings surrounded a peaceful garden of raked sand, sparse trees, and moss-mottled rocks. Each and every shrine made Tessa's jaw fall more and more; she was sure it was going to come straight off.

From her shoulder, Kit murmured the names of the gods, using his paw to point them out, but Tessa only gurgled a non-response.

To her right, Jin said in wonder, "Can that even be real? In my classes, we learned about the gods, but... nothing like *this*."

According to Kit—he could've been one of those audio tour narrators—the shrines were arranged from left to right from least to most powerful.

Fukurokuju, the God of Wisdom, had a shrine made of books; the pillars were gigantic calligraphy brushes and the carpets were rolls of thick parchment. Hotei, the God of Fortune, had a path of lucky five-yen brass coins leading up to a bright red temple edged in gold. Kichijoten, the Goddess of Happiness, seemed to favor gemstones; the silver walls and even the curved roof tiles, all the way to the third floor, were studded with sparkling jewels. Benzaiten, the Goddess of the Arts, had a shrine that Cecilia would have loved; she'd probably make a whole bullet journal spread inspired by the art all over the white stone walls and pillars. These were not normal paintings; they *moved*. A rabbit danced through sheafs of rice and up to the moon. On another pillar, colossal painted waves crashed against the rocks and drew up again, to their full height.

"That's ukiyo-e style art....My mom used to collect these pieces, before..." Jin cut himself off, peering at another shrine.

Bishamonten, the Goddess of War, seemed to have an ordinary enough place, until Tessa squinted and realized everything was made of sharp weapons, starting with daggers that formed the steps. Daikokuten, the God of Business and Trade, had a shrine of silver within a field of swaying rice. Ebisu, the God of Prosperity—and seemingly the most powerful—basically lived in a fortress of pure gold, glinting in the early afternoon light.

"Wow," Tessa said.

"Wow," Jin echoed.

"Wow," Kit repeated. Then he barked, "Are we going to just gawk here all day?"

Tessa nodded through the gates. "Is *that* one of the Seven Lucky Gods?"

A figure was stepping gingerly through the sand garden, careful to keep on the stone steps. "Oi! Oi, anatatachi! Get away from the gods' fence."

As he drew closer, Kit bounced excitedly on Tessa's shoulder. "Hachiman, God of Fighting! I'm your old friend!"

The man was in a hakama, the shortened version of a kimono-like robe, in all black with the design of small katanas woven in gold. His tanned face looked like he'd met a few of those katanas head-on; scars traced along his eyebrows and along his jaws. When he tried waving them away with his hand, even his fingers had thickly raised scars. "Visitors are not allowed at this time."

"Don't you remember me?" Kit said. "Your powerful friend, um, currently going by the name of Kit? We fought a crew of rebel gods a few hundred years or so ago, or something like that. I'm positive of it."

"Who?" Hachiman scrunched up his face to look at Kit through the gate.

Tessa and Jin exchanged looks. Clearly, Kit hadn't been a kitsune in whatever form he'd been before—if he *had* actually known someone who was connected to the Seven Lucky Gods.

"I'm now Kit!" The fox flexed his scrawny arms. "Super strong, you know?"

Hachiman shook his head. "Never seen you before."

Tessa kind of felt bad for the way Kit tucked his head down. Quickly, she cleared her throat. "Excuse me, we're hoping to get some support from the Lucky Gods. Kit and I got cursed to be connected by this"—she gave her wrist a good shake to show off the gold bracelet—"and we're hoping they might be able to help get us home."

"Sure, sure," Hachiman said. "During receiving hours."

"When's that?"

"Don't know, they haven't had a session in a decade or so." Hachiman shrugged, with a clank of armor. "I don't mind. All those people? Having to *talk* to them? Awful. I get so drained. I wish they'd show up with weapons and I could fight them instead."

"Right, well, we need to see the gods today," Jin said. "Can we get a special exception? We'll leave the moment these two get separated."

Hachiman turned his head to the side, like he was listening to an invisible phone. "Mm...Mhm..."

"Are the gods talking to you?" Tessa asked.

Hachiman sighed. "I don't have to talk to them to know their answer. This gate's got the gods' magic, and it won't let anyone in unless they will it. Seeing as the latch is still locked, the answer is *no*."

"Can't you let us request this in person? Please?" Kit asked.

"There's no way they'll let a spirit like you waste their time, you should know that." Hachiman frowned. "Who did you say you were, again? Everyone in the City knows the rules."

"I lost my memories," Kit said cheerily. Then he shoved his muzzle through the gates and hollered, over Hachiman's protests, "Let me in, Honorable Seven Lucky Gods! I have a spirit, wait, *two* little spirits you can keep!"

Tessa's jaw dropped. "You're god-meat first, *minor* spirit."

"I'm not a spirit! I swear, I am all-powerful—"

The ground shook under their feet, and then stopped.

"What is that?" Tessa yelped.

Jin looked unconcerned. "A small earthquake. It happens every once in a while."

Hachiman shook his head. "We don't have earthquakes in the City. You should know that, spirit. The only time we have an earthquake...But, no. It's impossible...."

A chime rang through the air. It sounded like the way Tessa's bracelet had clinked, right before misfortune was about to happen.

Hachiman started shuffling away from the gate, visibly paling. "I...This can't be..."

Around them, the passersby that had been going on their way had turned to stare, too.

The clanging grew louder and louder, and then Tessa noticed that there were wind chimes, attached to the front of the Seven Lucky Gods' shrines; each matched the gods' homes, from a gold-laced chime for Hotei, the God of Fortune, to razor-sharp shuriken for Bishamonten, the Goddess of War.

A rumble echoed through the ground, and the air crackled with static. Mist unfurled from the seven fortresses, and Hachiman whimpered.

"The Seven Lucky Gods. *How?* Did you summon them?" Hachiman gasped and ran for cover—and not a moment too soon—

A lightning bolt struck the gate, piercingly bright, resonating with a roar of thunder.

When the searing bright light faded from Tessa's eyes and the mist disappeared, seven glowing figures stood where the gate once rested. They were dressed in sumptuous clothes and dripped with gold and katanas, sharp enough to kill, and all seven of them were glaring down at Tessa, Kit, and Jin.

They were face-to-face with the Seven Lucky Gods.

11

In the center of the Seven Lucky Gods, a tall woman stared down at them. Tessa tried not to quake at the sight of the goddess towering above her with long, dagger-like heels and the staff-like naginata in her left hand, complete with a sharp, curved blade. The goddess looked disgruntled, like someone had spilled her morning cup of tea on her scarlet kimono, and she was ready to skewer whoever crossed her path next. Tessa breathed out in relief as the goddess's gaze swept to Hachiman. "*Yes?*"

Her voice was so powerful it sounded like a drum pounding in Tessa's brain.

"Bishamonten," the guard cried, falling to his knees. "Goddess, I tried to—"

"What's with all the ringing?" she snapped.

Kit explained quietly, just for Tessa and Jin, "The

City receives prayers through the wind; the biggest, most dire of requests ring at the doors of the Seven."

A man sitting, no, *lounging* on a floating cloud, waved his long fingers at the chimes, silencing them throughout the City. "There's a disturbance." The man had a long forehead, and something about his serene movements reminded Tessa of a crane, along with his all-white robe embroidered with shimmering cranes in flight.

"Fukurokuju," Kit whispered. "The God of Wisdom. Kuju's a pretty good guy."

"Can you all take care of this so I can return to reading in peace?" the god asked. With a snap of his fingers, a cerulean-colored book appeared out of thin air, and he stuck his nose into it. Tessa sighed with longing. She wished she could be in the library back home.

Kit stared. "Well, he *used* to care about mortals."

"Kuju, show us, then, good fellow," the god to the far right said with a jolly grin. This god was dressed in a flashy, flamboyant red-and-gold suit, with a tall hat. Tessa had seen him in loads of animes before. Ebisu, the perpetually smiling God of Prosperity, and according to the leaderboard, the head of all the gods in Tokyo.

But Kuju only grumbled. "Really? I'm at a great part, there's a storm and—"

"*You* won over the Yata no Kagami," Benzaiten, the Goddess of the Arts replied; she was stylishly dressed in dark capris, a white blouse, and a painter's smock. Her dark hair was swirled up into a bun, with a paintbrush stuck into it. Smears of ink splotched the gold fabric of her smock like she'd been in the middle of painting. "So *you* get to use your mirror to show us why we're getting summoned."

The other gods chorused in agreement, and Kuju threw up his hands. "I thought that shimenawa meant we'd be at peace! There are so many books, and so little time."

"You're immortal, aren't you?" Kit asked. "These people need you, and you all are just hanging around arguing? What about your duty?"

Seven pairs of godly eyes swung toward the fox hanging out on Tessa's shoulder.

"Apologies, apologies!" Hachiman squeaked, shoving Tessa and Kit away. "These little spirits are just disturbing the peace. Scat, minor spirits, scat!"

"We're stuck together!" Tessa said, louder than the guard, showing the gold bracelet on her wrist that led to Kit. "Mighty Seven Lucky Gods, can you please separate us?"

"We have *important* things to discuss. Come during receiving hours." Kuju sighed, waving at the arguing gods and goddess. He returned to his book, flipping another page.

"The receiving hours that haven't happened in a decade?" Tessa gaped. On her shoulder, Kit was silent with disbelief.

"You *said* this would work!" Jin hissed. "Say something to them."

"I swear, it didn't used to be like this...." Kit let out a low growl. "Is this why the mortal side of Tokyo reeks of misfortune? Because the gods are only focused on themselves?"

The wind chimes started ringing insistently again, and the Seven looked around, pausing mid-argument. Along the main street, the crowd of minor gods and spirits gossiped with each other in surprise, eyeing the leaders of the City.

Ebisu cleared his throat. "Well. Kuju, if you please—"

"Fine, fine, *fine*!" The God of Wisdom snapped his book shut. "It's likely some silly argument amongst the humans, slinging insults on that social media chicken-app they use."

The god tossed his book up into the air; it disappeared in a flash. Kuju's forehead furrowed as he swirled his fingers in the air, muttering to himself, "I must disable my shields first...."

From behind the Seven Lucky Gods, Kuju's shrine—the fortress made of books—shimmered in the light, glowing brighter and brighter. Then the biggest book that made the top of the roof flipped open, pages fluttering, and something shiny rose into the sky. The watching crowd *ooh*ed in delight.

"Show-off," sniffed Hotei. "Just because you read

so much doesn't mean you have to show off your Divine Treasure, too!"

"Reading is a Divine Treasure," Kuju shot back. With a snap of Kuju's fingers, the object zipped in front of the god, and the crowd dropped into a reverent silence.

The gleaming pane of glass was cut into eight sharp points that looked like they would shear Tessa's fingers if she tried even brushing them lightly against the edges. It rippled with a rainbow of colors, brighter than the god-fire Tessa had seen earlier.

"Consider yourselves blessed, humans," Kit whispered. "Only the Emperor usually gets to see any part of the Divine Trinity. It's rumored that a powerful god lives within, only responding to its true owner to show a glimpse of the present."

Over the mirror, Kuju paused ever so briefly. Had he heard Kit call them humans? Tessa gulped, but the god returned to swirling his hand over the mirror, which now hovered in the air.

"Don't they need a wall? You know, like 'mirror, mirror on the wall'?" Tessa asked.

"They're *gods*, Miyata," Jin whispered.

Kuju dipped his head, chanting something soft and low. Misty tendrils flowed up into the air, glowing, glowing—

Then a miniature version of Tokyo unfurled from the mirror, with even Tokyo Skytree so perfectly made that the tip looked like it'd poke Tessa if she tried to touch it.

"Wow, okay, sure," she croaked. "Yeah, let's make a city appear out of thin air."

Then Kuju clapped his hands twice, and the misty apparition wove into place around them, so they were standing *in* it.

Jin spluttered. "Wh-what—"

Kit kept his voice low. "This is just *part* of the power of Kuju's Divine Mirror."

"But, *how*?" Tessa asked. "Like, I've never seen any kind of technology like this."

"You mean that wee-fee thing you mortals rely on?" Kit snorted. "Our godly powers are *very* different."

"Wi-Fi?" Tessa echoed.

"Wee-fee, yeah, that thing. Gods receive prayers as energy; magic, I suppose you'd call it. The more wishes and hopes from supplicants, the more power the gods have. And, being the Seven Lucky Gods, well, they get a *lot* of prayers. Who wouldn't wish for fortune, wisdom, or happiness? So, that's why the Seven Lucky Gods would have ample powers to do whatever they want." Kit flicked his nine tails. "Unlike some of us."

But, it seemed, people in Tokyo could definitely use the gods' help. The chimes rang louder and louder.

Kuju's thick brows furrowed as his eyes scanned the skyscrapers. "What is it—what's going on.... Show me, Divine Mirror."

The city spun around them, curving down alleyways

and major streets and over trains, zipping to a spot where smoke unfurled from pale green roofs. The commotion was coming from a beautiful shrine, with stately, dark wood buildings. Masses of people—tiny as ants—were running out of a building; the echo of their screams was enough to chill Tessa's blood.

"Meiji Jingu," Jin gasped.

Tessa's blood turned into ice. "My sisters are there. Right now."

A misty figure in black strode behind the crowds; they zoomed closer. Then, all of a sudden, they were too close. The samurai shimmered in front of them, his katana flashing in the light, his hollow eyes not seeing the Seven Gods, Tessa, Kit, and Jin, who watched him face-to-face. Though Tessa knew she wasn't actually there, it was like all of her nightmares had come to life.

Taira Masakado was very much alive.

And he burned with a vengeance angrier than ever.

12

CECILIA HAD SHOWN TESSA PICTURE AFTER PICTURE OF Meiji Jingu on the plane ride over. Everything from the smooth wood stands to buy an omamori, a protection charm (Tessa could really use a mountain of those, right now); the white-and-red outfitted shrine workers; and the gigantic torii gate at the very front.

"I can't wait to go back," Cecilia had said brightly as the three of them demolished their airplane-sized Häagen-Dazs cups. Tessa, who had been queasy from the turbulence, hadn't been able to turn down ice cream, of course. "There's something about Meiji. At first, you're in a busy city like Tokyo, and then...*wow*. With one step inside the shrine's gate, you get immersed in this bright, beautiful forest. It's the first place I want to go to."

Peyton, who would've rather played arcade games or gone on a ramen restaurant hunt, had smiled from the window seat. "We'll go there tomorrow. I'll ask our group chat the moment the plane lands."

From below those seafoam-green roofs that Cecilia loved, a samurai dark as midnight strode forth, toward screaming crowds. Tessa searched frantically for a flash of Peyton's metallic blue eyeliner or Cecilia's flowing hair. "Please don't be here, please be somewhere else, please, please, *please*."

Jin's fists clenched. "Your sisters *have* to be safe. They were so nice to me the last time they visited Japan....I'm sure they're fine...."

But Lord Taira Masakado was life-size and real in his fury, down to the shiny, gleaming points of his armor.

The curved crest at the tip of the dark helmet glinted under the sun. Indeed, it was the same fighter who'd attacked—and almost killed—the three of them. Even worse, he seemed to have become stronger, more corporeal than the figure of mist they had fought off.

Hachiman spun around and glared at Tessa, Jin, and Kit. "This stinks of the three of you."

"Funny you should say that." Kit coughed, looking pointedly between Tessa and Jin.

"Kit, don't say anything," Tessa pleaded. She had a foreboding sense that these gods weren't exactly as Kit had remembered them to be. What kind of god that was supposed to help had their gates closed and their receiving hours canceled for more than a decade?

The fox was earnestly saying, "These two measly souls let out that vengeful spirit—"

But Tessa took one look at Hachiman's deepening frown and paled, grabbing for the kitsune to quiet him. "Shh!"

Hachiman glared between Tessa and Kit. "If I find this is your fault, by the laws of the City, inga ouhou."

A bad cause; a bad result.

Bishamonten pointed her naginata at the illusion of the samurai, ten feet away. "I'd recognize the Sword of a Thousand Souls anywhere. The dancing flames on his tsuba, the rival dragons...I thought Lord Taira had disappeared."

"That *is* him. Back, somehow," Ebisu gasped. "No one else could wield that vengeful sword." The jolly look wiped off his face as a woman screamed. Tessa's brain couldn't keep up with what was unfolding before them—

This was worse than any anime Tessa had ever watched. One minute, a woman was clutching a bright red omamori in her hands...the next, Lord Taira's shadows washed over her, until only her purse was left tumbling onto the gravel path as the samurai continued forth toward the rest of the crowd.

"Did he—did he just *swallow* someone up?" Benzaiten gasped, fanning her face. "He...he just..."

"This is yet another reason that the Seven Lucky Gods should not help minor spirits," Hachiman said. "The Seven Lucky Gods banned fighting amongst the gods and spirits almost a decade ago, to keep balance within the last magical city, raising the shimenawa to protect us all from the mortals' greedy wishes. And you've flagrantly disobeyed the treaty by allowing this to happen. If our beloved leaders step outside of the City, they'll have to use their powers on *humans*."

"This samurai *attacked* us, unprovoked!" Tessa cried. "It is *because* you have power that you should help those in need. Look at what it's doing now!"

She knew what it felt like to be at the bottom of the "cool kids ranking." When Allison could've held her hand out and waved her over to the nice table in the cafeteria. When each kid made the choice to press upload.

"In other words," Kit explained, low so only Tessa and Jin could hear, "the gods are keeping their strength to themselves for immortality."

Petrified, horrifying screams rang in her ears. The gods were everything Tessa was not: They were powerful, the ones who could wave their hands and magically change things.

"I am not dealing with that." Ebisu shook his head. "One of you must deal with Lord Taira."

"And leave the City?" Hotei gasped, clutching his bronze robes close, with a clink of coins. "Why, I'd be leaving my fortunes!"

"My book is calling to me; I'm at a cliffhanger," Kuju said.

"Well, *I* must complete my painting." Benzaiten flicked her long hair back and stuck her nose in the air. "While inspiration is fresh."

"Battling Lord Taira should be left to those who created this mess," Bishamonten huffed, pounding her naginata on the ground. "I'm not using my powers on *this*. The mortals will rebuild Meiji Jingu, anyway."

Tessa's eyes stung. How could the gods do this just to keep their own immortality?

"Any takers?" Ebisu, the leader, glanced at the other six gods. But their answer was already clear.

Jin looked like someone had sucker punched him in the stomach; he hissed to Tessa and Kit in disbelief, "After all the prayers my dad does, he swears it's what gives me the ability to win my tournaments...the gods don't even *do* anything?"

Kit's voice was low and sad. "They are—or, once upon a time, *were*—Tokyo's leaders."

"My sisters," Tessa whispered, her eyes clinging to the memory of Lord Taira, stepping menacingly toward another group of tourists. "I have to make sure they're safe. Cecilia and Peyton—even through all the trouble I've caused them, they still love me. They still support me. *They* see me." She swallowed down her tears. "I *can't* let them get hurt."

To her surprise, Jin tucked his head down. "I understand that feeling."

Kit growled, looking over his shoulder at his transparent tail. "I'm still too weak. If I had my normal powers, I wouldn't even be in this kitsune shape. *And* I'd do more than any of these gods." But it seemed even he knew better than to challenge the Seven Gods outright. "Where's the Unlucky God when you need them?"

"The who?"

Hachiman's wiry eyebrows shot up, and he looked around to make sure the Seven hadn't heard. "That's just a rumor. The Lucky Gods don't need to be kept in *balance*; they are perfectly fine as is. We don't need some god that doesn't even exist."

Kit rolled his eyes and muttered, "Things are going well for mortals and spirit folk alike, obviously. Tokyo under destruction? No big deal."

Tessa's hopes plummeted. *Who* could help Tokyo, if the strongest gods didn't?

"Well, time to go home now," Ebisu said. "Nothing to see here."

Kuju snapped his fingers; the mirror shimmered, reverting to its book form, and soared to his shrine. And with that, the gods had the mortal area of Tokyo out of sight, like the destruction didn't matter.

"I'll take care of it."

The gods froze. But the voice had definitely not come from amongst them.

"Who said that?" Hotei asked.

Tessa stepped forward. "Me."

The Seven Lucky Gods leaned forward, inspecting her. Tessa jammed her trembling, sweaty hands into her pockets and tried to meet their gazes. She failed miserably. The most she could bear to look at was Bishamonten's heels, and that was even *more* frightening.

"You, again." Daikokuten, who was glaring from underneath his bushy eyebrows.

"I'm Tessa Miyata."

"God of?" Bishamonten waved her naginata toward her, and Tessa felt her life nearly disappear before her eyes.

"God of..." Tessa floundered.

"Don't let them know you're a mortal!" Kit whispered, jumping onto her shoulder. Louder, he said, "Minor God of Rice; that's why her name is Miyata. *Miya* as in temple, and the *ta* for rice paddies. And I'm her companion, a minor spirit."

Tessa muttered under her breath, "*Rice?*"

"Fair enough. *Tessa* is an awfully strange name," Ebisu commented.

"What do you want in return?" Bishamonten jabbed her naginata toward Tessa; she yelped, stumbling. Jin caught her, helping her stand upright.

"In return?" Tessa echoed.

"No one will put themselves at risk without a cost," sneered Hotei. "It would do us Seven well not to have to bother with this nuisance. However, we need to know in advance: What's *your* price?"

"If I stop Lord Taira, all I ask is that you remove this." Tessa raised her wrist to show them the glowing bracelet.

"And get my memory back," Kit piped up. "So I can return to my former glory."

"I'd like to get home, too," Jin added, crossing his arms.

Kuju peered closer at the wolf charm that still dangled from the band, and steepled his fingers. "Strange. A powerful magic. It would take some effort." Then he took a look at Jin and Kit. "A trip home? Your memory and powers? That could be managed.... Though, you might not want to keep some recollections. Perhaps it's good that you don't remember your past."

"Having another god take care of this would be more convenient, though," Hotei murmured; the other gods nodded. "We can allow this minor goddess and her followers into the boundaries of Greater Tokyo."

"Just for them?" asked Daikokuten.

As an answer, Ebisu clapped his hands together, sounding like the pounding of a taiko drum. A sleek wood gate appeared out of thin air, taller than Tessa's three-story apartment building back home. The inside of the torii showed Meiji Jingu, smoky and real.

"Wait." Kit frantically pawed the ground. "We need weapons! You can't send me with two little weak kids—I mean, minor gods—straight into the fray. You've got to actually give us some help. Lord Taira will just swallow our lifeforces up—I don't have enough power to take him on, not in this form! You will have our lives marked on your souls!"

"Bah, better yours than mine," Ebisu grumbled. For being the god of all things jolly, he looked particularly doom-and-gloom. "I have a TV show to finish up. *Spy × Family* doesn't wait for just anyone."

"Isn't there some godly power we can borrow?" Jin asked.

Tessa nodded. Getting swallowed up by an evil god definitely wasn't part of her summer goals. "If they're that strong…"

Kit's nine tails flicked as he thought. "There has to be something… *Oh*, why can't I remember…."

"You're…" Jin stared between the gods. "You're being dishonorable. For every fight, it should be between equals. I've never chosen to fight a match against someone who is far below my strength, and anyone honorable would never do the same to me."

"Honor, schmonor. It's what you deserve, honestly," Hachiman sniffed. "*You* dared to bother the Seven—"

Tessa spoke up. "You can't leave Tokyo like this. Everyone out there? That's *someone's* somebody. Someone's sister, someone's grandpa, someone's best friend. Even if I'm not an all-powerful god, I'll fight Lord Taira however I can. *That's* why I"—she glanced over at Jin and Kit, who both nodded—"*we* need your help, Seven Gods. Please."

The Seven Gods paused, studying her. A very peculiar sensation ran up her arms, like the wind was spinning in circles, ruffling her clothes. Like fate itself was twisting and changing from her very actions.

"This minor god is a pain," Daikokuten whined, but the other gods looked a little bit curious.

"Send us to the Dojo of Many Doors!" Kit burst out. "We'll be able to get hinoki weapons to fight Lord Taira there, strong enough to purify his evil."

Jin frowned. "I've never heard of that dojo—"

"It's a place that only the Seven Gods can send you to," Kit murmured.

Kuju stroked his chin. "A rather interesting proposition, indeed. But are you willing to pay the cost?"

"How much is the entry fee?" Jin asked.

"It's not paid out in yen." Kit swallowed. "The Dojo of Many Doors exists on a different plane of time and space; a day in there is a minute in this world. But there's a cost. If we don't pass the two torii in five Dojo days—" He hesitated.

A strange feeling filled Tessa's stomach. "What is it? What happens?"

"If you don't pass the Dojo's two challenges within the five-day period, you'll be stuck," Bishamonten cut in.

Jin gurgled. "Stuck?"

"Stuck like a passenger perpetually circling on the Yamanote train line." Kit grimaced. "But it's worse, because your life energy will become part of the City. And, puny mort—ah, gods, as much as I want to be separated from you, even I don't want you all to experience that fate. Over the next few days, your bodies will start turning into ether—nearly transparent, like you're disappearing. If you're still in the Dojo by the five-day mark..." Kit's eyes slid to the ground. "You'll never be able to leave."

Forever, without being able to see her family again. Without even the chance to fight Lord Taira and protect them.

Tessa breathed in deep.

If she didn't do something now, her sisters might get hurt. If she didn't do *anything*, something worse could happen. Tessa could see gods, which, according to Kit, was more than most humans, and she'd never known of anything actually special about herself before. What if this was something that no one else could do, and no one else could help her family?

She had to take this chance.

"I'll do it," Tessa declared. "I'll take whatever risks it comes with. Let's go."

After a moment's hesitation, Jin nodded, too. "I'm ready."

A *boom* shattered his words; smoke rolled up into the sky visible within the torii. Even though it was just a mirage of what was truly happening, sweat prickled at Tessa's neck.

Lord Taira was inching closer and closer to Tessa's sisters. Too soon, he would be beyond anything Tessa, Jin, or Kit could handle—if he wasn't already.

"You two may be Tokyo's last hope." Kit's tails flicked. "I just pray we can make it out of the Dojo alive."

The air burned hot, a dry blast that made Tessa's skin feel like it was shriveling up. In front of them, the image between the two posts of the giant torii shifted from the elegant Meiji Jingu to a long hall with a tatami floor and a high ceiling. It seemed unassuming, but a trickle of dread pooled in Tessa's stomach. Wherever she was going, it was cut off from the rest of the world. If she didn't make it out of there, she'd never see her sisters again.

"Jin, keep a hand on Tessa; she's connected to me. We're going to the Dojo of Many Doors," Kit said.

Tessa wasn't sure about the idea of Jin holding her hand. Instead, she offered a bit of the string connecting her bracelet to Kit's.

"Three...two...one...," Kit chanted. *"Open, Dojo of Many Doors!"*

This is a chance to save my sisters, like they've always saved me. Her heart pounded with unsaid fears and hopes, tangling into each other.

They stepped through the glowing gateway. Tessa expected to land on the tatami floor on the other side of the gate, but lightning flashed, followed by a roar of thunder. Gears creaked, like time itself was slowing. Winds blew out of nowhere, making her eyes water to the point where she had to close them.

When she opened her eyes, she *definitely* wasn't standing in front of the Seven Gods—that was all she could be sure of.

13

Location: The Dojo of Many Doors

THE SWEET SCENT OF TATAMI ENVELOPED TESSA. FOR A brief, blissful moment, she thought she was at her grandparents' house. Tessa, Jin, and Kit stood in a tall, wide building, with shuttered windows built up high in a sloped ceiling overhead. The light was dim, with only a few lanterns dangling from the rafters.

"We just walked through a torii and ended up in a dojo." Jin gaped. "I still want to believe this is just the weirdest dream ever."

In one corner, there were three futons, a low table, and two doorways leading to bathrooms. Tessa could feel dried sweat and grime coating her skin, and the beds looked all too tempting. Then she blinked, noticing the center of the Dojo. "Um, is it normal to have a tree here?"

A willowy cherry blossom tree, its trunk gnarled in twists, stretched up from the middle of the straw floor.

"Ah." Kit padded closer. "Come here, shrimpy mortals."

The air was perfumed with that faint honey-like scent that had danced on the breeze when they'd first entered the City of Legends. Each pale pink blossom was thick and heavy, the spindly branches sagging toward the ground from the weight. The branches shifted in an unfelt wind, as if acknowledging them.

Jin squinted as they stood underneath. "Are those five branches connected to how many days we have left?"

Kit let out a whistle. "Observant. Indeed, meet the Tree of Time; each blossom counts as an hour. Right now, you have five full branches, with twenty-four blossoms thriving on each. The god who made this Dojo created the Tree of Time to measure minutes and hours; its ten petals make each blossom look beautiful...."

"But they don't last." Tessa gasped, pointing at a cherry blossom close to them; a petal was shriveling, as if burning up. Five days was basically the same as a whole school week; when she was sitting in homeroom on Monday mornings, it'd felt like the Friday dismissal bell was so far away that it could've been in another universe. But she had a feeling that time in the Dojo was going to fly by.

The fox barked, "That's right. Five days is barely enough to learn how to even *hold* a sword. Much less forge the right weapon. But you two have potential, and hopefully that'll pull us through."

"How are we going to do *enough*?" Jin spoke up as they continued to look up at the heavy blossoms. "If Lord Taira keeps on his destructive path, he's going to be headed straight toward Kisarazu. I can't let anything happen to my dad. He's the only family I have left."

Even though Tessa's stomach was freezing up with fear at the thought of failure, something about the way that Jin's hands protectively curled into tight fists propelled her to say, "We won't let that happen. We'll get through whatever challenges are in this Dojo."

She met Jin's eyes; he nodded. It felt weirdly nice to agree with someone.

Kit flicked his tails and started toward the pile of futons. "Okay."

"Okay, what?" Jin asked.

"Okay, it's time to start off with Plan A: Go to sleep. We've got a lot on our plate tomorrow. And I am *tired*. Good thing I don't have to keep up that shield on you two. There's no one around to tell if you're mortals."

"*Sleep*?" Tessa spluttered. "I mean, I'm jet-lagged and all, but you just told us we've got a ticking clock, and—"

She frowned. Under the golden bracelet, her wrist was...

"Am I already becoming part of the City?" Tessa lifted up her hand. Her wrist was there; she could feel it. But when she looked down, it was almost like she was becoming see-through.

Jin gaped. "If I squint, I can see the outline of your wrist....What's going on?"

Kit whistled, his eyes wide with shock. "I've never seen it begin so fast. Usually, the Tree is the primary reminder for challengers to know how much time is left. Lifeforces don't start fading until close to the second day, at the earliest. The City likes you, Miyata. Which may be more dangerous than good...especially if it wants you to stay. Regardless, you need a full night's sleep before training starts. Let's get to bed."

Maybe it was the inter-time travel or meeting the Seven Gods or a murderous evil samurai rampaging through Tokyo, but Tessa barely could recall polishing off the bowl of rice and natto that magically appeared on the table, or the shower that scalded her skin. Within seconds, Kit was already curled up on a futon in the middle of the room, sound asleep. Jin plucked up a book from a stack on a low table and then plopped down on the futon closest to the wall. He lay on his side and opened it a crack, his eyes drooping wearily as he flipped through the pages. In the time they'd simply gotten ready for bed, an entire blossom had fallen, petal by petal. As Tessa lay out on her buckwheat-hull pillow, staring at her disappearing wrist, the weight of the exhaustion seeped out of her bones, despite the pitter-patter of her heart: *Five days. Five days. The petals are falling.* Within a few seconds, she was asleep.

The sweet scent of the cherry blossom petals infiltrated her dreams. In her deep sleep, she was sitting on her grandparents' porch and eating juicy slices of watermelon. Strangely, the cool liquid dribbling down her chin felt sharp, with a metallic scent, rather than candy-like juice.

"If you didn't have me, you'd be dead right now," a deep voice growled. "And this is exactly why you need training if you *think* you're going to even land a scratch on Lord Taira."

Tessa woke with a yelp.

High above the rafters, a window cut into the rooftop

was cracked open with early hints of dawn glimmering through, but a figure stood above her, with his face covered in shadows and a sword pressed to her neck. *No.* A katana. The curved blade of a samurai.

She wrapped her blanket around her hand, knocked the blade away, and tumbled unceremoniously out of the futon.

But it didn't matter. The attacker changed his focus to Jin, shearing his blanket in two. "You are *not* prepared to fight!"

The boy shouted as his sleepy eyes opened to the sight of the blade. He rolled to his side and jumped to his feet, shifting into a fighting stance.

Quickly, Tessa dove for a vase sitting on a table near the entrance to the bathroom, holding it up threateningly.

"Whoa, whoa," the figure said, and lanterns flashed on in the rafters of the Dojo. "I actually like that vase. I think it's made by an ancestor of mine."

"Kit?" Tessa exclaimed. "Why are you trying to kill us?"

The bigger-than-life shadows seemed to recede; it was only the fox, though he was holding a rather sharp katana in his mouth. "It's time for training."

"We get to use katanas?" Tessa perked up.

"Hello, did anyone notice he sliced through my *bed*?" Jin asked, lifting his blanket up. It fluttered in ribbons.

"What's up with all of you gods and tearing things apart? How does a *fox* know sword fighting? And that vase is from the Heian period. Like, a thousand years ago. Exactly *how* ancient are you?"

"I've been thinking about things, and I just might be a minor god of scholars; that's why it was easy for me to come up with a solid plan to teach you two. But enough about me." The fox gestured at their neatly folded clothes at the foot of their futons. "Get dressed and meet me in the courtyard."

"Already?" Jin asked. "I barely slept—"

With a flick of his nine tails, the fox disappeared out the front door.

Tessa and Jin exchanged glances and picked up the piles of clothes the fox had left for them. They were their outfits from the day before, magically freshly laundered, but Kit had added something new. Tessa still had her denim shorts and white T-shirt, but there was also a short-sleeve coat that opened in the front. It was a bold red, with tigers dancing over the pattern, with a darker red trim.

"A haori," Jin said, answering Tessa's questioning look. He picked up his; it was a dark blue decorated with fierce dragons, breathing out streaks of gold fire. "Pretty neat."

"I've got a feeling we'll never be prepared enough for

what Kit has up his sleeve," Tessa said. She was surprised when Jin cracked a smile instead of frowning with worry.

He nodded, rolling his shoulders back. "Let's learn how to fight a god."

Kit paced in the middle of a packed dirt circle that was surrounded by an open grass park. The air was noticeably cooler. Like the City, thick white clouds covered anything beyond the next hundred or so yards.

Behind Kit were three red-orange arches, side by side. They were brightly painted torii gates like the one that had appeared to let them into the Dojo of Many Doors. The torii in the middle was the biggest, with long columns twice Tessa's height. The one on the right was a little smaller, and the torii on the very left just about the same height as Tessa's sisters.

Curiously, through each gate's opening, she could see different scenery. The one on the left led to a lush forest, and the one to the right *burned* with dancing and flickering flames.

The most enthralling gate was the largest one in the middle. Dry, desolate hills were studded with countless blades, bows, and all sorts of weapons. She took a step closer. It seemed to let out a soft, haunting melody. Tessa couldn't quite catch a grasp of it, but it left her with a sense of melancholy and made her ache to see more of what lay inside.

"We're in Shibafu Park," the fox said, and the music cut out. "It's part of—"

"Meiji Jingu?" Jin asked, eyes wide. "That means we're right next to Lord Taira."

"Exactly. Holy places within Tokyo are connected to the hidden City. This Dojo faces Meiji Jingu's mortal training dojo," Kit said. "Ordinary humans can practice archery, judo, kendo, all kinds of martial arts. But *our* Dojo is hidden from mere humans' sight; they just see this place as an empty patch of grass. And that means the second you finish these two challenges, we can immediately fight Lord Taira."

"So, these are the challenges? Why are there three of them?" Tessa pointed at the torii.

"I thought you'd never ask," Kit said primly, and Tessa fought the urge to roll her eyes.

The fox trotted to the very left, his white fur glimmering under the weakening moonlight. His shadow stretched out, unusually long, into that shape of a samurai. "Normally, the Seven bless mortals, minor spirits, and lower-level gods with the chance to come here, the Dojo of Many Doors, as a way to test their worthiness for the Academy of Gods, a school for future legends. The Torii of the Forest leads to Nikko, where you must survive amongst its hills and thick trees for an hour."

"That doesn't sound too bad," Tessa said, encouraged.

"Only half of those who challenge this torii succeed. Monsters lurk in the forest, attracted to the blood of young challengers. If you cannot pass the first torii, you truly will be stuck in the City, your life becoming part of its magic."

"Let's sacrifice the fox. He's a spirit or whatever, right? Gotta be worth about two human lives," Tessa muttered to Jin.

She wasn't completely sure, but she *swore* he let out a snort.

"How's running through a forest supposed to help us with beating Lord Taira?" Jin asked.

Kit raked a paw in the ground. "If you can't survive through the first torii, that means you won't stand a chance against an evil god. What's inside that forest may not be nice, but it's still weaker than Lord Taira. See? Aren't I doing well? I must've been a god of scholars; I know my stuff."

"So we have to be strong," Tessa muttered. She glanced at Jin, who, despite his lean frame, had chased away a group of bullies with just a scowl. She tried to frown, too.

"Are you trying to cross your eyes?" Jin asked.

She spluttered. "No. Just, uh, thinking. What's the second torii, Kit?"

The fox leaped to the far right. "Here is the Torii of Flames, where you must show your spiritual strength. Nine out of ten who undergo this trial simply turn into dust, becoming part of the City, because they are not strong enough to pass within the five-day window. If you can survive, this is where you will forge your worthy weapon. With this, a god-blessed mortal will have a minuscule chance against Lord Taira."

"Reassuring," Tessa muttered.

"A minuscule chance is better than none. Anyway, that's why there are three of us," Kit informed her. "A powerful god like me, who needs these five days to regain enough power—which I used a *lot* of to summon a torii out of nothing to get us into the City, thank you very much—and two shrimpy mortals to help fill out my ranks, with enchanted hinoki weapons to combat Lord Taira's evil."

"Um, if we're not helpful, maybe we shouldn't be here," Jin said.

"You two have potential, or I never would've put mortals like you in danger like this in the first place." Kit narrowed his eyes, as if he could see some part of them that Tessa couldn't. "Being god-blessed? That's rare. And, honestly, being able to stand up to the Seven Lucky Gods? That's something that I doubt has happened in over a decade, by the sound of things. That's potential, and I can sense something else, too...." He turned his head, hopefully seeing something really amazing that Tessa couldn't, because all she felt like was pure chaos (and jet lag), right now. Then the fox shook his head. "But it's a matter of whether you're both strong enough to live up to that potential. Especially since no other gods would dare go against the Seven and fight with us."

Having potential sounded more promising than any NowLook video recording Tessa had seen of herself. Knowing they didn't have any help, though, did *not*. Tessa nodded at the torii in the middle; she could hear the faintest hint of music, gentle as cherry blossoms brushing against her skin. "How about that last one?"

"*That* torii is strictly out of bounds," Kit said, shaking his head as he trotted in front of it. "It's not needed to exit the Dojo."

"But aren't those weapons in there?" Jin asked.

"The Armory of Fallen Souls only has weapons fit

for the strongest of souls, forged from the spirit energy of fallen gods, spirits...*and* god-blessed humans. You are not ready to even enter it; a mere mortal won't survive a minute of trying to win a weapon from there. The Armory extracts a harrowing sacrifice from those foolish enough to attempt this."

Tessa protested, "But we have to forge something, right? The ones in the Armory are ready-made, like picking up a box of Cinnabon. Why go through all the fuss of trying to make perfection happen when it already exists? If we have something strong to fight with, we have *power.*"

"Power isn't everything," Jin shot back.

"He's right." The fox's nine tails curled tight around his body. "This power comes at a terrible cost, especially for mortals. That sacrifice often takes the very thing the challenger holds most dear. What if the Armory asked for your mortal life in exchange for a weapon? Would you truly be able to make that trade?"

The mesmerizing music cut out. Tessa swallowed; there was something urgent yet sad about Kit's words that stopped her from voicing any rebuttals. Jin bit his lip, too.

The kitsune's focus drifted, like he was trying to recollect a thread of his past, but the details weren't quite clear. "I...I can't remember exactly what happened, but I think I lost someone dear to the Armory."

"I'm sorry," Tessa said softly.

Jin nodded, his eyes shadowed. "We didn't mean to push you. That was too far."

"No, you two need to know the danger." The fox shook out his tails, continuing on. "Even if there was a way to train you two to be ready for the Armory—no matter your potential—it would take *years*. No weapon is the same as the other, whether in looks or abilities, and as such, each bears a different trial to win it over. Some study all their godly lives for the chance to acquire a weapon from the Armory...and still don't make it out."

Tessa frowned. The warnings were dire, and she wasn't sure that she wanted to sacrifice anything....But what was that music that had beckoned her closer, then? Besides, wouldn't the Armory be the only place to find a weapon equal to Lord Taira's legendary sword? Maybe this was what the woman in white had meant about a chance....If there were a bunch of weapons right inside, maybe she could jump in and pick one up, and actually have something to fight Lord Taira with.

"How do we know how much time we have left?" Jin asked. "It's not like we can go into the Dojo every time we need to check on the blossoms."

Kit flicked his nine tails. *"Summon the Tree of Time."*

The air shimmered; a miniature version of the tree, like a bonsai, hovered in the air. It was like Kuju's illusion that had showed them Tokyo, but this time the blossoms were thick and full. Except the lowest branch was half-bare.

"One power of the Dojo of Many Doors. You can easily see how much time is left," Kit explained.

She gulped, looking at the ground. *And how much time is already gone.* Deflated petals, like scraps of rippling silk, rested at the roots.

Then the fox looked between the two of them, his body looking small against the tall torii. "Because our time here is limited, I wouldn't offer this choice if I didn't think it was possible... but there's a chance you can get through the first torii, as you are. Do you want to try—"

"Yes," Tessa spoke up. She had to be brave. She had to do anything possible to save her sisters. "Let's go."

"—Uehara?" the fox finished, his eyes looking up at the boy.

Tessa's heart sunk.

Kit turned to Tessa. "Miyata, you want to go, too?"

"I can survive," she said.

The kitsune studied her with a long, long look and muttered, almost to himself, "Time *is* limited....But if you fail, it's a huge step back...."

Jin glanced at the Tree of Time and said, "I'm ready."

Kit nodded decisively. "I saw you fight Lord Taira. You have a solid chance; there aren't many spirits that could fight in the way you did, Jin."

Tessa nodded eagerly. "We'll watch each other's backs."

Kit looked at her. "You *can* try. After all, you do have potential; I wouldn't have even thought of this Dojo if I didn't think you were up to it. But I can train you, Miyata; it's okay if you wait—"

Jin started walking toward the gateway, and Tessa's heart thumped. *I need to stick with him. I am not going to be left behind.*

"If Uehara-kun is going, I'm going in, too." She took a deep breath and strode forward, getting to the gate first; her skin felt like it was painted with ice as she stepped inside.

14

SHADOWS WEIGHED DOWN ON TESSA THE INSTANT SHE walked into the forest. She blinked and looked around the dark, tall trees, with the trunks wrapped in thick vines. Fingers of mist crept along the brush low on the ground. It felt like she'd dove underwater, or maybe into Gram's closet, where things were dusty and nothing had been moved around in a long time.

Still, it wasn't anything *too* scary.

But the forest was way, way too silent. There should have been birds chirping. But there was just a musty scent and a strange stagnancy to the air, like no one had been here in a long, long time. There was also a rumbling sound, kind of like rocks tumbling around.

"This isn't bad," Tessa said. To no one.

She glanced around. Jin, strangely, was nowhere to be seen. Nor was Kit—

Something landed on her shoulder, and Tessa let out a shriek.

Kit stared at her, his tiny nose nearly tip to tip with hers. Jin was standing next to her, looking around warily.

"Geez," the fox complained. "Yell louder, would you? All I wanted was a ride."

"I could give you a ride straight to the third torii so we can get a weapon worthy of fighting a god," Tessa retorted.

"Hah. I told you, that one's off-limits. Anyway, you'll get the weapon you need in the second torii."

Jin cleared his throat. "Kit. Miyata—"

"Uehara-kun, your dad wanted English practice, so here's a phrase: *Wait a minute.* I need to enlighten this fox. Look, Kit, it sounds strange, but I *swear* the Armory was beckoning me—"

"*Miyata,*" Jin said, louder. "There is no time for *Wait a minute.*"

She spun around to follow the point of his gaze. A boulder was *stampeding* toward them.

"WHO DARES ENTER MY FOREST?" a voice pounded.

An enormous rock materialized out of thin air, right above their heads.

"Ah!" they cried out, scrambling backward. The rock dropped where they'd been standing, sending dirt flying.

Tessa only had a second to look at their attacker who loomed as tall as the trees, before another boulder flew out from the left. Unlike the shadowy samurai, this one was *very* real. Her breath froze in horror—it was a giant monster of solid rock, standing on two feet, with its emotionless eyes focused on them.

It held a hefty, unbelievably huge rock in one hand and a rotten tree stump in the other.

"Any chance we can say *Wait a minute*?" Jin asked hopefully.

Whoosh.

Tessa screamed, barely dodging the flying boulder.

"They're the ones getting tested!" Kit shouted, jumping off her shoulder. "Not me! I'm an all-powerful god—"

Another rock came their way, and the fox let out the most ungodly of squeaks.

The tree stump sailed through the air toward Jin, who disappeared behind a thick set of bushes to their left; the prickly leaves let out a toxic-smelling rot. Tessa and Kit ran down a path, toward the sound of a rushing river. She chanced a glance—but the beast was still heading straight toward them.

"Get on my shoulder," she called to Kit, who was floundering in a pile of leaves. Sure, she'd be faster on her own, with a better chance of surviving, but she wasn't the type of person to leave someone behind. *I'll never be like*

Allison, she thought grimly. Plus, the fox had done too much to keep her safe, even through all the trouble they'd gotten into together.

The fox leaped up, and Tessa cut a fast turn toward the right.

"But the water!" Kit protested. "I thought we were going to the river!"

"And figure out if we can swim through it?" Tessa asked. "Not on my watch. Can foxes even swim?"

"I can if I'm not wearing full-plated armor, but I don't *like* water." The fox stuck close to her neck, his nails digging into her shoulder as he clung on for dear life.

"You have *fur*, not armor."

"I would like you to know that my fur is one of a kind, very—"

"When I tell you to be quiet, don't let out a single peep. Our lives depend on it. Trust me?" Tessa asked.

The fox mimed clamping his muzzle shut, even though from the corner of her eyes, Tessa could tell he looked a *little* skeptical, to say the least.

"Over here!" she cried. As she ran, she leaned down to grab a hefty stick. When she circled around a thick gnarl of bushes, she banged it against a boulder to the right, shouting louder. "Come and get me!"

Then, with the kitsune on her shoulder, she dove into the thick bush, crawling on her stomach along the bare foot or so of space she'd noticed earlier, her heart in her throat, trying to silence her jagged breath as the rock creature stomped close.

Through the gaps in the leaves, she could see a bit of it; the beast paused in the middle, looking toward the direction of the boulder she'd banged the stick against, and toward the bushes.

Please, please, she begged silently. Long, thin thorns pricked at her skin, but she didn't dare move.

The rock creature took another step toward the bushes. Kit's nails dug in sharply.

She tensed, getting ready to sprint for their lives, no matter how many thorns were between them and the open path.

Then, slowly, the beast turned away and lumbered off.

She and Kit melted to the ground when it disappeared into the shadows of the forest. A little scratched up, but still all in one piece, she crawled out from under the bushes and huddled in the shadows of a tree.

"We just have to stay here until the hour's up," she whispered.

Kit hopped onto the ground. "Take a breather, relax, maybe catch a nap. We'll be onto the second torii soon enough. Honestly, the rest of the forest seems quiet. I'm thinking that beast gobbled up whatever other curses the gods left behind. Hope Jin survived."

A sharp hiss broke the silence. "I'm here. I can't believe you guys didn't notice me."

Tessa and Kit whipped their heads to the left. Jin was sitting on a branch about twenty feet up, looking comfortable and calm.

"Did you just sit there and watch us struggle?" Tessa gaped. "Don't you care about others—"

Then a loud *crunch* broke the branches to the right. All of Kit's fur stood up.

"NO ONE IS ALLOWED IN MY FOREST!"

Boom! A rock slammed down where the fox had been sitting.

Kit shrieked, rushing toward Jin. "You almost got my precious tails! I'm the teacher here, not a student!"

The monster let out a colossal roar, and the fox squeaked.

Tessa darted behind a tree, but that wasn't enough. The boulder-creature slammed right through, sending splinters and branches flying.

She fell flat on her back. *Boom, boom.* Tessa's heart jumped to her throat. The boulder-creature stood with a stone foot about to crush her, when something tugged at her mind. *You're not seeing everything, are you?*

Tessa gasped, pointing up at a slip lined in red, with scribbles of black ink, stuck to the chest of the rock beast, right where its heart should have been. To her (and her sisters' shock), she always did well in her Japanese school kanji tests—even though it wasn't easy trying to remember a thousand characters—and she saw that it read *Great Misfortune*.

"It's cursed!" She rolled out of the way just as its foot slammed down. "It's an ofuda!" If she took it off, maybe the curse would be broken.

"Run!" Jin screamed, jumping down from the branch.

Still, she reached out, trying desperately to grab the paper.

"A curse doesn't matter if you're *dead*!" Jin was at her side, his face beaded with sweat, pulling her away. "We'll never even get to face Lord Taira again—"

"No! I've almost got it!" she cried.

Kit grabbed the ends of her haori, helping Jin yank her backward, but it was too late.

The monster's arm raised up and—

Boom.

A searing blaze of white; her ears rang with the screech of gears.

Then—silence.

Tessa groaned, looking around. She'd been somehow teleported to the front of the Dojo, facing the three torii, her body aching like she had been crushed into a thousand pieces. The taste of dirt filled her mouth, bitter and earthy, from where her face was flat against the ground.

If only to grind salt into the stinging wounds all over, the first torii flashed with neon letters.

COMPETITOR TESSA MIYATA
THE FIRST TRIAL: FAILED

Failed. *Failed.* She had failed.

Her bracelet was warm on her wrist; the white ōkami charm seemed to stare back at her, and a strange sound filled the air. She blinked, then rubbed her ears.

Did she just hear it *howl*?

Tessa examined it carefully, even gave it a shake, but it was as flat and lifeless as before.

"Can't you help me? Tell me something useful?"

No answer.

Instead, she turned to the torii, frustration simmering in her until—what felt like a year later, though she was too scared to check the Tree of Time—a new message glowed within the gate.

COMPETITOR JIN UEHARA
THE FIRST TRIAL: COMPLETE
You may now challenge the second torii.
The gods wish the winds of fortune upon you.

The light shimmered, breaking up as Jin and Kit strode out of the gate. The boy anxiously looked over her. "Miyata. You're *alive*." He slid to his knees in relief. "I thought I'd have to explain to my dad that you'd died on my watch."

"You passed," Tessa said, her voice a tiny whisper. "Congratulations."

Kit, however, gnashed his fangs. He was furious. "You *failed*, Miyata. In case that wasn't clear. You could've passed, and you threw away that chance, completely. In reality, you would have *died*. The magic of the torii was the only thing that kept you alive and whisked you out. Not only that, you threw away your ticket into the next torii, but most of all, the opportunity to *save* Tokyo."

"There's got to be a Plan B or something. There is, right?"

Kit cast his head down, his nine tails flat against the ground, and Tessa's stomach sunk.

"Is that it?" Tessa asked. "It's . . . over?"

15

TESSA'S HEAD POUNDED, BUT SHE DIDN'T HAVE TIME TO drown in her regrets. She picked herself up and strode toward the torii, toward the forest that glimmered without any sight of the rock monster.

But the moment she tried to step inside the first trial, a force shoved her away. Between the poles, neon numbers shimmered in the air: *23:58:01.*

Tessa gasped. Jin stepped up next to her and put his hand in; his fingers went straight through, and a message formed: *Competitor Jin Uehara, please proceed to the second torii.*

"I can't get in," Tessa said softly. "Not for another full day."

She turned to face Jin and Kit.

"I don't like that look." Jin eyed her. "Whatever you're thinking, *no*—"

"We need to remove that curse," Tessa said. "In twenty-four hours, when I can get into the torii—"

"I *knew* you'd say something ridiculous! We're not here to save the world! First, you want to go to the Armory, and now *this*?" he huffed. "I *told* my dad I was going to bring you back. Obviously, talking foxes, revenge-bent samurais, and rock creatures were not what he or I were expecting, but I am going to live up to my word!"

"Then *help* me. This creature needs our help."

"Is that what you think about the samurai, too, that you have to save him or something?" Jin snapped. "Just *survive* an hour. You don't have to stick your head out and ask for it to get crushed, or try to solve problems we really aren't here to help with. I passed the first test. I didn't need to help anyone other than myself."

He didn't understand. He didn't know what it felt like to be cursed.

"Are you really just going to do nothing?" Tessa snapped.

She knew the truth: When things came down to the wire, she was always alone, always cursed. Dealing with her classmates had shown her that. People watched her pityingly—if she was lucky—and turned the other way as the bullies closed in.

Pity never made her feel better. She'd just wanted a real friend.

But Jin was shaking his head. He wasn't going to help.

"I'm not leaving until I get that curse off! It's not like that creature asked for this." Tessa blinked back her tears. "We can't leave someone who's hurting. How could you do that?"

"*We* need to survive." Jin's eyes were cold. "The reason you failed is because you wanted to *help* the enemy! Don't you care about your family? Don't you care about getting home? Or are you okay with just fading away and becoming part of the City?"

Tessa stared, stunned into silence.

With that, Jin turned, trudged to the second torii, and stepped inside.

"That's not true!" Tessa shouted, rushing after him, but she bounced off the face of the torii, landing hard on the ground. The same timer showed up, glimmering tauntingly in thin air: *23:56:48.*

"I want to be able to save them, too," Tessa whispered, her eyes stinging. Her words were a shrunken whisper. "But they'd never want me to save them at the cost of letting someone else suffer."

Tessa wasn't able to get inside either of the trials until that countdown was up. She stared down at her right hand, under the glowing bracelet. The touch of the City was obvious; her arm had become transparent, all the way up to her elbow. She ground a fistful of dirt in her hand, sharp and pebbly. *I'm not going to disappear, I'm not.*

Kit, who had been looking between them like a spectator at a tennis match, simply sighed. "You can try again. You can try as many times as you want, but it's not going to get any easier. I should've thought through this before allowing you in."

Jin doesn't want me here. Neither does Kit.

"Summon the Tree of Time," she said.

Honey laced the air; the tree shimmered into sight. Almost an entire branch was withered; the last few blossoms clung onto its tip. Only four full sets of cherry blossoms—four days—remained. She stared at it until the mirage faded away.

"What if I train?" Tessa asked, finally, her voice scratchy.

The fox's dark eyes settled on her. "You lack fundamentals. Jin is strong; he's practiced martial arts since he was in diapers. But you..."

"Tell me what I need to do." Tessa pushed herself off the ground and breathed out. Dust swirled around her, a fitting match for the insignificance that she felt right now. But she refused to be left behind again. "I'll do whatever it takes."

The kitsune took a long look at her; surely they didn't have the time to deliberate like this. "I said something like that myself, a long, long time ago."

He turned and headed toward the Dojo, and Tessa's heart sunk—

Kit looked over his shoulder. "Well, are you coming with me or what?"

She grinned, racing to catch up.

At the doorway, Kit tapped on the frame, muttering to himself about the specifics of what he wanted—something about endurance and dodging and jumping—and with a push of his nose, slid the door open.

"What is this?" Tessa gasped. The Tree of Time had shifted to the far corner; in the center, a two-story course rose *out* of the floor, stretching up to the rafters, which seemed to be oddly higher than before.

"A custom-made obstacle course, courtesy of the Dojo. From the brilliance of my mind, as a god of scholars, as well. If you pass this, you'll have the skills to survive that beast rampaging through the Torii of the Forest—but most of all, tactics to fight Lord Taira."

"Um, do you expect me to beat *this*?"

"Easy peasy," Kit said, and shot forward to demonstrate.

"Endurance!" the fox shouted. With surprising ease, he hopped over a set of fallen tree trunks.

"Agility!" In the next minute, he dodged punching bags that swung at him, one after another, so fast that she could barely keep track of them.

"Strength!" With a solid headbutt, he burst his way through a wall of wood, which quickly re-formed itself.

"Mobility!" Kit hopped from branch to branch of a pine tree that had sprouted out within the straw floor, grabbed a ring that was on the top between his teeth, and sprinted to the end zone, putting the ring onto a small platform. There, purring with success, he curled up in a circle, looking ready to nap.

"But...what's this got to do with Lord Taira?" Tessa grumbled. "Isn't there something else—"

"Are you doubting the God of Scholars?" Kit looked left and right, sniffing the air. "I know there's something...." The fox walked over to the sliding paper door and scratched one paw on a panel.

"It's going to tear—"

The paper fluttered, and Tessa gaped. Ink swirled along the soft grains and darkened intensely, turning into a familiar scene.

Lord Taira was drawn in strokes of midnight-sky ink, with his dark armor and fierce stance. He moved with his sword in a motion of attacks against shadowy victims, so fast that Tessa's eyes watered trying to keep up.

"Those who train in the Dojo can study their opponents," Kit explained. "There's some fancy modern word for it—simulator? Anyway, this takes records of recent memories from the person who activates the screen, and extrapolates the strength and abilities of the target. For example—"

The screen flashed into creamy paper-white, then ink splattered in the middle and stretched out. Tessa could recognize that scowling, serious-eyed boy anywhere.

"Jin!"

The inky version of Jin fought with grace, dancing out of the reach of a sword, then using his bare hands to deflect a flurry of punches.

"I'll put you on here—"

"Yeah, we can pass on that." Tessa didn't really want to see her paper-self fall face-first and then get walloped by the ink.

"By making mistakes, you'll become stronger—as long as you learn from them. Look at your potential, Miyata."

With another tap of Kit's paw, the ink swirled into the form of Lord Taira. This time, a small figure—Tessa's size—fought against him, with a blade in her hands.

The girl jumped over broken pieces of buildings as the inky samurai chased her down—*endurance.*

But Lord Taira caught up; even worse, he summoned strange bits of shadows in the shape of fighters.

"Shadow warriors," Kit growled. "Deadly spirits controlled by the will of the summoner. Wouldn't be surprised if he throws those our way."

Still, the inky girl dodged his blade and those of Lord Taira's minions. *Agility.*

Until she hit a dead end, just like the alleyway Tessa had been stuck in. But, instead of panicking, the girl spun around in a solid roundhouse, and the wood shattered under her kick, allowing her room to jump through. *Strength.*

Finally—Lord Taira chased the girl toward a shrine;

instead of getting caught inside, the girl scaled the outside wall and climbed onto the rooftop. With her sword
raised, she jumped down, just as Lord Taira approached,
slicing the inky evil god into two. He faded away, as did
the girl—but not before giving the real Tessa a cheeky
wink.

Mobility—and *victory*.

Tessa stared in silence at the paper screen, now blank,
her head buzzing with thoughts. If she could learn how
to fight Lord Taira like that inky version of Tessa...she
could do this. Tessa looked out at the obstacle course, her
heart beginning to hammer.

"You *can* learn to fight like this. In fact, I'll make a
few updates for you. To your point, you don't just need
to survive through the forest." With a flick of Kit's nine
tails, the logs shimmered away, turning into pieces of
broken buildings; the swinging punching bags became
shadowy forms with sharp katanas.

"There, just like the streets of Tokyo," Kit said. "Finish it unscathed, and you'll be ready for the first torii in
no time. And on your way to meeting Lord Taira."

The fox made weaving through the obstacles look
easy; she wasn't sure she could even make it over the first
slab of concrete.

Still, she teetered on the start line, ready to begin.
When the fox yapped, "GO!" she burst forward, ready to
test herself on the obstacle course—or fail trying.

16

It didn't take long at all for Kit to find out what Tessa was made of. Whoever that inky girl was, it was likely Tessa in some alternate universe, a version when she had grown up next to Jin and gone to his dad's dojo every day.

Her shoe caught on the edge of a concrete block, and she sprawled forward, *again*. "Yikes and Yakult!"

The first few tries, Kit had been hopeful, pacing back and forth. "Run faster!"

"I've got this!" she'd shouted, even though that was *clearly* not the case.

Sweat poured down Tessa's face, but she seriously couldn't run *any* faster. After trial run eighteen, the fox had let out a loud sigh and curled up in the end zone. "I'm wondering if I should've really sacrificed my godforce to get you into the City. Wake me up when you finish."

So Tessa plunged onward, pretending she was actually in the City and Lord Taira was coming after her. It wasn't difficult; after scraping her shins during the first jump, she'd found that the concrete was *very* real.

There were seven blocks of concrete. Easy enough. Tessa had to leap over them to get to the next obstacle, the mercilessly fierce shadow warriors.

With the first block, she jumped, her heart pounding in her chest. *If I can do this, I can fight Lord Taira.*

For the second block, she kept her mind focused, too. *If I can fight Lord Taira, I can save my family.*

The only issue was that some of these blocks were almost as tall as her, without a good place to grip. Tessa fell flat on her face—*again*. A loud buzz sounded and a wall appeared in front of the entrance to the shadow warriors area. She had to start from the beginning.

"Yikes and Yakult!" she cried out. "Is this even legal?"

"You think that rock creature will follow your rules? That Lord Taira will twiddle his thumbs and wait for you to stand up?" Kit's tails flicked from side to side and then curled right around him again, so only his nose showed. His shadow receded, from that samurai-shaped figure into the form of a tiny fox.

She sighed. He was right, even though it felt like her sisters were getting farther and farther away, like she really would be stuck in the Dojo forever.

Tessa lined up again, sweat stinging at her eyes. She wiped her face and breathed in deep. Somehow, it felt like energy from the air poured into her lungs, giving her stronger focus. The first two concrete blocks were easy enough. She would jump higher for the next five. The last one, she had no choice but to climb—fast—before she fell unceremoniously off.

She could do this, she totally could. This was the start of getting strong enough to beat Lord Taira, and she needed all the training she could get. Slowly, surely, she was getting stronger.

With that, Tessa shot forward.

Only to trip and tumble upside down, landing with her heels on the first block. Her legs reverberated with pain.

"Argh!" she cried out, pushing herself upright. Moments later, she melted to the floor in front of Kit. "I need your help. Running around like a hamster on a wheel isn't going to get me ready to fight a boulder monster in a day, much less Lord Taira. *How* can I do this? We're in the land of gods and spirits. There has to be something I can do."

Kit measured her up.

"C'mon!" Tessa pleaded. "The faster I get through this, the faster you can get split up from me, and we'll be able to go our separate ways."

"I don't want to get rid of you *that* badly."

"You can be honest. I...I don't want pity," Tessa said.

That was what had hurt about her sisters' glances. They didn't see her as an equal. And Tessa had never wanted that. She wanted a friend, not to be an obligation or get a pat on the head to feel better. "I need a way to stand up on my own."

The fox sniffed. "I guess, seeing as this is something you'll learn in the second torii, it won't hurt to introduce it to you a bit earlier."

Tessa's ears perked up immediately. "Count me in."

"It's not going to be easy," the fox warned. "But sit. Listen."

She arranged herself cross-legged in front of the fox, and he paced back and forth as he spoke.

"The way that you—a shrimpy—"

"Speed it up!"

"Anyway, as someone lacking basic skills—"

"Do *you* want to start an insult war?"

"Okay, okay. Not to be dramatic or anything, but *power*. It's used for good and for evil." Kit flicked his tails. Like magic—no, Tessa realized, it *was* magic—illuminations popped up out of thin air, like Tessa was living inside a Pixar movie.

Four globes of light—emerald, sapphire, ruby, and white diamond—shimmered around Tessa, each burning with a pure white, flame-like core. But, behind them, there was a darker spot. She squinted, though she couldn't quite make it out.

"These are the traditional elements. Earth, water, fire, and wind."

"What's that blob?" Tessa asked, pointing at the one in the back.

Kit's eyes widened. "Well. Maybe we have a fast learner, after all." Then he nodded at the bracelet connecting the two of them. "Or maybe you get a little bit of a leg up with our connection."

"I'd like to think it's my natural talent." Tessa grinned.

"Use all the talent that you have, because we need it," Kit responded.

He was right. *Tokyo* needed it. Her family needed it.

"Now," Kit added, "behold the greatest lecture from the God of Scholars." The five blobs began to circle around them, moving like planets in orbit. "That *blob*, as you call it, is ku. Humans are obsessed with mortal energy, ki, but always forget about the power that really matters: ku. The sky is what mortals think of as ku, or sometimes you all call it 'the void' in your fancy video games. What you all think is nothing? *That* is the energy of the gods. What the Seven Lucky Gods get so much of, since so many pray to them. But there are always prayers sent into the sky, wishes and hopes and such forth, that any being, lowly as they may be, can access."

"Ooh. So, anyone has access to the unnamed prayers? Like, for example, *me*."

"Now we're getting somewhere." Kit gave a toothy

grin. "Here's your chance to grab it, god-blessed mortal. You can use that extra spirit strength to help you get a leg up—literally—on those logs. The power of ku is only limited by what you can harness and what is available, of course."

"How do I get started?" *This* was something Tessa could get behind.

"Feel for the energy and power within the air."

"Like, by waving my hands around or something?"

The fox snorted. "Think of it as strings, almost. A harp, maybe. A giant, celestial, around-the-world harp. You've heard the phrase *everything is connected*, right? That's the truth of it. We're all connected through ku."

Kit paused. "If I transfer some ku to you, it'll help you sense it, kind of like glasses. It'll only last for a few minutes; after that, you'll have to gather ku on your own. But if you want to try—"

She scooted closer to the fox. "I'm in."

The fox tapped her hand with his paw. "Close your eyes. That'll make the switch easier. And work fast. It takes a lot of ku to do this, you know. It's not every day that I have to train a completely shrimpy human like you."

A gentle warmth flowed through her, like a sip of hot chocolate on a chilly day.

"Now, take a look."

Tessa's eyes flew open, and she stared in shock. Tiny

glowing lines shimmered all over in a web. When she moved her fingers forward, the lines thrummed, like she'd plucked the strings of a harp, just like Kit had said.

"Take one," Kit said. "Bring it to you, then direct the energy to where you need it to go. Watch." The fox reached out and caught a thread between his teeth. With a gentle tug, he pulled it toward him, and it unraveled, making his fur glow a bright white for a moment, before fading. "Ah. That felt nice. I wanted it to ease my headache, and it did a good job. Now all I need is some sleep. And for you to figure this out, too."

Tessa's fingers closed around the thread resting on her palm, and she gave it a tug. It broke off into a tiny piece. Kit grumbled. "Well, that snack-sized bite won't do much. Focus. It's not going to be easy to get the hang of managing ku, so I'm not expecting it'll happen fast."

"Can't you just transfer me a bunch of energy—"

The fox scowled. "Do I *look* like I'm brimming with free ku? Definitely not after I saved you and Uehara from Lord Taira. Anyway, no one's strong enough to just endlessly pull energy out of thin air. If it's sent directly to you, it's easier, sure, but the unnamed stuff requires your own strength. You still have to rest, to eat—since you're mortal, or if you're a nobody-spirit, like me."

"So I can use this to help me get through the obstacles or even to help the rock creature, but it won't make me stronger all the time?"

"Exactly. Tough, right?" Kit sighed. "If you were a major god with loads of shrines, you'd have a daily flow of power, but even then, there are limits."

Tessa soaked this in. There was no instant, magic answer. But at least ku, the spirit energy, would hopefully be enough to get her through the obstacle course today... and the torii tomorrow.

In front of her eyes, the threads faded.

"Wait, wait," she protested. "Help me see—"

"I can't give you energy forever," Kit responded. "Search for it on your own."

Tessa reached out and waved her arms.

Nothing.

Kit chortled. "Remember, it's like a harp. There are prayers, thin as a line, filled with emotion, just within reach. Breathe it in to pull them out of the air and circulate it through your body and blood, to make you stronger and faster. The strongest gods can do this *as* they fight, so they have a constant source of energy. It's not wise to store up a bunch you can't use, though. It leaves soon after you access it, if you don't channel it into something."

"Then is this bracelet made of ku? How can it stay put?"

Kit nodded. "My lifeforce in the form of ku keeps it powered; that's part of what's draining me now, especially with not having a lot of energy to begin with."

Tessa hadn't thought of the bracelet hurting Kit. This was yet another debt she owed him.

This time, she focused harder, reaching out for an invisible thread of ku. *It's there, but I can't see it. I can believe in it, because it can help. I will believe in it, because I will help.*

She heard a faint, aching melody as she grasped onto the ku, pulling it into herself, feeling her body burn with renewed strength.

Kit squinted at her with surprise. "You did it. Maybe we'll survive after all. You did that pretty well." Then he yawned. "I'm...I'm tired. But I have to go check on Jin. The second torii must be keeping him busy if he isn't back yet, alive or dead." He gave a sharp grin.

"I want to go with you," Tessa said instantly. She wanted to be side by side with Jin. Not always lagging behind, like the way she trailed after her sisters.

Kit shook his head as he trotted out the door. "Finish your first torii, Miyata. You can't leap for the finish from the start line." Then he paused, looking at her quietly. "You've got this."

Moments later, Tessa teetered at the beginning of the obstacle course. The Tree of Time loomed in the corner; even when she had her back to it, she could smell its honey-like aroma and sense the withering, dying petals. *Time is limited.* She spread her fingers out, searching for the ku.

Her lips curved up as her fingertips snagged on a thread. There. All she needed was a little boost to get her over the concrete blocks; she was ready to go.

Tessa grabbed the ku, bringing it into her body, feeling her energy spike, and focused on her feet.

Her toes and soles tingled.

"Ready, set...," she said to herself. Then she shouted, "Go!"

17

Tessa shot forward, leaping higher over the concrete than she ever had before. Adrenaline surged even as she felt the instantaneous drain of ku, and she searched for more. A deep breath in, focus, and *boom!*

She leaped on top of the blocks, from one to another, her heartbeat pulsating like flickers of fire. She *could* do this. She *could* fight Lord Taira. She *could* save her sisters.

There were no other alternatives.

Okay. Pull in the ku. Channel the energy. Focus. *That's all it is, really.*

Tessa studied the shadow warriors, wishing she could slow down time with ku. The ōkami charm pressed against her skin, and she gave it a shake. "Can't you do something?"

No answers there.

She stepped forward, ducking and twisting between the jabs of the warriors' swords. If she pulled on the ku, she could get a split-second warning of danger and sidestep—

A shadow warrior came flying out from behind her, faster than the others.

Tessa fell like a rock, thumping against the wood platform's sides on her way down, and unceremoniously slid to a stop with a squeak of rubber.

A sigh came from the doorway. She spun around. Kit and Jin stood in the entrance; the fox's ears were slightly droopy with fatigue but otherwise fine. Jin, on the other hand, was ruffled and his hair was messy, with sweat tracking over his face. "You're the one that's going to save Tokyo. *Really?*"

Ouch. Someone needed to tell Jin that his sarcasm was a little too on the mark.

"I'll be fine," Tessa snapped. "This is just to keep myself occupied until I can get into the torii and remove that curse."

"I told you, we need to focus on winning, not helping out that rock monster. We owe it to Tokyo, first," Jin protested, but he seemed slightly distracted, fiddling with his hands.

Tessa eyed him. Was it just her, or did it look like his fingers were starting to become transparent? "How was the trial? So, you passed?"

"I'm not done. This one's different though, I can go in and out of the second torii," Jin said, and then clamped down on his lips when Kit gave him a look.

"Miyata needs to focus on the first challenge. But, for now, it's time to eat," Kit said, pulling her attention away. "C'mon, I'll show you the best restaurant in the Dojo."

Tessa protested. "But I can practice some more—"

The fox shook his head. "You barely touched the onigiri we ate for lunch. Fuel is part of training, too. Follow me."

With that, the fox loped out of the Dojo and around the corner.

"Was there a restaurant outside?" Tessa frowned. All she'd seen were the smooth clouds; sometimes, they thinned to reveal a peek into the rest of Meiji, but it was strange to see people moving in slow, slow motion.

"Not that I remember," Jin said, echoing her confusion. "But I'm starving, so I'll take anything at this point."

Tessa trailed after him, her body aching from her bumps and bruises. The pain momentarily dropped away when she saw what was around the corner, and they both stopped short.

A wood cart was backed up against the clouds. Three seats were set out in front; it looked like one of the stands Tessa had seen photos of in busy cities like Osaka.

"Whoa," Tessa whispered.

"Seriously." Jin glanced at her, as if he was surprised that they were agreeing on anything. Tessa gave him a small smile; to her surprise, the corner of his lip twitched. *Well, that's an improvement.*

"The good part of being a god," Kit said from his perch on one of the stools. "The Dojo's diner serves up some of the best; the god that created the Dojo added this so anyone can get a meal at the end of their practice session."

Jin gave Kit a curious look. "How do you know that if you don't even really know who you are? Do you know where you live? Like, you should have a shrine, too, right?"

The fox pawed his ears, giving a big sigh. "I don't remember where it is. I keep thinking it's outside of Tokyo, though. Somewhere leafy and green, maybe? Totally magnificent, too."

"So, basically anywhere."

"We can't get out of the Dojo, so trying to look for Kit's shrine would be a total dead end," Tessa said. She'd had enough of those after Lord Taira had broken out of the daruma in the alleyway. "Anyway, where's the food?"

"Grab a menu and make your choice. Once you have dinner here, you'll be grateful you're god-blessed," Kit said. Tessa picked up the menu that was as thick as a book. Each meal—from yakisoba to Japanese-style hamburgers—had a matching hand-drawn illustration. Tessa checked her chin for drool; she could almost smell the sizzling gyoza with a side of fried rice.

"What *is* god-blessed, anyway?" Tessa asked, pausing in the desserts section. "Like, you said it means we can see stuff, like Lord Taira. But doesn't that make me stronger or something? Ooh…look at this shaved ice…. No, dinner, I want dinner…."

" 'God-blessed' means that you have awoken a power in you that few mortals ever access, sometimes through birth, but usually through a vital event where, without the god-blessed powers, you may have very well ended up dead," Kit said, flipping pages between a bowl piled high with crispy tempura shrimp and veggies and a set of sushi. "Being blessed gives you the power to see gods, but you cannot become one straightaway. But you can begin to work with ku, and someday, maybe you will be Chosen by one of the Seven Gods to go to the Academy and start on the path of actually becoming a god. Though, you should know, those chances are thinner than *me* being Chosen, a major-god kind of slim. Better than being completely not-god-blessed though, because those people who can't see Lord Taira? They think a fire started, or that there's an earthquake, or something. They don't know the truth."

"But how'd I become god-blessed?" Jin asked, peering at a picture of sushi; the glistening cuts of fish looked absolutely drool-worthy. "I never saw anything magical before."

"It must've happened when Tessa's bracelet summoned me," Kit said.

"Have I been god-blessed since birth, then? Because I've been able to see your charm, like, forever." Tessa frowned. Not just that, she'd seen the woman in white—who definitely had some sort of magic, like Kit—way before coming to Japan. When she was younger, it had shocked her when she'd realized Gram and her sisters couldn't see the bracelet, and things had only gotten more confusing with the woman in white.

Kit scratched the notch on his ear. "I guess it must've been whenever you got the bracelet and were blessed with my presence, whenever that was."

The cart let out an impatient rattle of dishes, and the pages of the menu fluttered back and forth.

"Ah, it wants to start cooking. Choose your meal or the cart will close up shop. Sakini taberuyo." Kit tucked his head down in a quick prayer and tapped a picture with his paw.

"Wow." Tessa gaped, totally distracted from all things god-blessed. It was like the illustration had hopped straight out of the book; an enormous bowl of rice laden with just-fried tempura shrimp and vegetables appeared in front of the fox. There was a whiff of smoke that reminded Tessa faintly of the incense Peyton had brought back from her sisters' previous visit.

"It's a book version of a restaurant's vending machine," Kit said.

Jin nodded. "Oh, like the ones in front of ramen restaurants!"

Tessa added it to her mental post-save-the-world bucket list, right between "hug her sisters again" and "go to 7-Eleven." She'd always wanted to go to a real ramen restaurant.

"Just tap the photo and say a quick prayer of thanks to Ukemochi—she's the God of Food." Kit paused in the middle of chomping down a crispy battered shishito pepper. "Maybe I'm her. I've heard she sometimes takes the form of a fox...." Then he frowned, shaking his head. "No, that doesn't feel right. Being the God of Scholars sounds like a better match."

Jin flipped through the menu. "I've studied the gods before, and there are a few books about the gods in the Dojo that I read the other night, but you being Ukemochi doesn't add up. You said your family made that vase in the Dojo, so that makes me think maybe you were a mortal who went through that Academy for the god-blessed that you were talking about. That kind of stoneware with an ash-style glaze is from around the Heian period, so that's more than a thousand years ago."

"What else did you find out?" Tessa asked. "I've never really learned anything about Japan's history in school."

"Well, I do know that Lord Taira was almost assassinated when he was a human, so he *did* have enemies. How'd you become one of them, Kit? He was pretty powerful then, and I guess that didn't change when he became a god. I wish I could go back in time and see what it was like then, to be a samurai trying to rise against the government...."

"You know your stuff," Tessa admitted.

"Assassinated?" Kit chomped on a tempura shrimp with scorn. "I wouldn't go around *assassinating* Lord Taira. I don't do sly things like that. I'd challenge someone face-to-face."

Tessa shook her head in awe. "Jin, I can't believe you remember all this from history class. It sounds like your courses are more interesting than mine."

"I...I like history." Jin ducked his head to mutter a prayer, too quietly for Tessa to hear, and then hastily jabbed his finger at the menu. There was a puff of smoke, and then an intricately arranged plate of sashimi, so pretty that it looked unreal, appeared before him.

"That's incredible!" Tessa gasped. "That looks just like something Kimagure Cook makes!"

Now it was Jin's turn to look at her in confusion.

"He's a Japanese chef who makes loads of delicious seafood at home, and I *love* his YouTube videos....I've been waiting to come to Japan for a long time, okay?"

Tessa muttered into the menu. She was getting too excited about something Jin clearly wasn't interested in. She expected a sharp laugh, like when Allison didn't see quite eye to eye with her. Like that time they'd played truth or dare, and for "dorkiest confession," Tessa had revealed that she'd been so obsessed with *My Hero Academia* that she'd built a whole world on *Minecraft* to look like UA High School, during the summer her sisters had gone to Japan without her. Allison had featured *that* on another NowLook video, and their classmates had stuck the anime's school crest all over her locker the next day.

Tessa chanced a look at Jin. Rather than raising an eyebrow, he had his head tilted to the side. He wasn't laughing. He was thinking over her words. "That's cool; I like watching process videos by this artist called May-chan. She makes great digital art. No narration, nothing, just the art. I'll show you one of her videos...well, after this." He waved his hand vaguely around at the Dojo and the torii.

Tessa's heart jumped. Weird. She never would've thought Jin was into history or even drawing, not with how he was super into karate. Anyway, would they really be friends once they stopped Lord Taira from destroying Tokyo? *If* they could manage that?

She glanced down and pressed her finger to the picture of a bowl of ramen, murmuring a quick word of thanks. With a puff of white smoke, a pretty red bowl filled with freshly made noodles appeared in front of her, complete with steaming-hot, rich broth.

Maybe after all of this, she and Jin could get ramen together—as friends.

After her stomach had digested the tastiest noodles in the universe, Tessa returned to the obstacle course. Kit had moved it in the front of the torii—"so I can sleep in peace without you falling off all the time," he'd said. Jin had also headed straight to bed, yawning, and in seconds, the two of them were snoring on their futons.

One, two. Tessa jumped over the first two concrete blocks.

Three, four. She leaped from block to block. Slowly but surely, she was getting the hang of this.

Then a shadow warrior flew in from the left, and Tessa went flying, landing face-first into the dirt. She groaned, unable to move. Dirt coated her face, and she brushed it off. Imagine what Allison and her friends would say if they saw Tessa now.

She sighed, gripping the dirt between her fingers. It wasn't much, but she needed to feel something, something *real*.

Then she looked down, closer. Dirt.

Small and insignificant, like her.

A soft melody wove around Tessa, lifting her head up and turning her toward the torii.

Or, to be exact, the Armory of Fallen Souls. Above, the dark skies hinted at it being almost midnight, and the Dojo's courtyard was dim and quiet, but the land within the third torii gave off an ethereal glow. Sure, it was the one torii that Kit *may* have mentioned was off-limits....

But the music seemed to beckon her forward, thrumming with words she couldn't quite make out. She shifted forward with interest. In the strange moonlight that shone over the dried, cracked dirt plains, weapons glittered, ready to be picked.

Dirt was insignificant on its own. But if you put a lot of it together with a bit of something special, maybe it became something.

She couldn't get into the other torii just yet, but what about this one? What if this music was a sign? An invite from the Armory, even?

Tessa would be able to finally pull her weight, with a weapon that could actually do something.

She sat up and glanced over her shoulder.

The Dojo was filled with silent shadows. Kit and Jin were both sound asleep. It was just her and the entrance to the Armory of Fallen Souls.

Tessa stretched out toward the torii...

...and her fingers went *through*.

The air within the gateway thrummed with energy as words shimmered into existence, like written moonlight:

If you choose to enter the Armory of Fallen Souls,
know that a weapon will require a sacrifice.
One cannot leave until the debt is paid.

YOU HAVE BEEN WARNED.

Tessa knew. She knew the danger of this, but wasn't there danger everywhere? In the first torii, in the second… in Tokyo, with Lord Taira.

That strange, haunting music, like fingers faintly brushing against piano keys, encouraged her to inch closer. *This* could be their way to fight the evil god. If Tessa had a weapon worthy to fight against Lord Taira's legendary Sword of a Thousand Souls, she'd finally be able to take care of those she loved. Kit had said that the Armory required a sacrifice, but wasn't she more than willing to sacrifice anything for her family, after all that they'd done for her?

Tessa couldn't seem to resist; it felt like she was in a trance as the music pulled her, like a magical beckoning, straight into the Armory of Fallen Souls.

18

TESSA STOOD IN AN OPEN PLAIN, WITH A DARK, STARRY sky above and endless parched dirt hills, rippling as far as she could see. The final torii, the Armory of Fallen Souls, was no ordinary place; shiny weapons impaled the earth, with insidious glimmers that dared to match the searing glow of the stars.

"Who dares to step inside?" A voice reverberated through her skull, coming from everywhere and nowhere all at once. Tessa yelped, stumbling over her feet. *"Are you willing to pay the cost?"*

"I am Tessa Miyata, and I'm here to win a weapon from the Armory!" Tessa cried. Her fingers shook, revealing her nerves. Hadn't—hadn't the torii been inviting her in with that melody? Her skin prickled. Or—was this a trap? Kit had said that the City had taken a liking to her....

But...why had the music cut out? She turned, straining to hear it again.

"*You are too weak,*" the voice responded. "*Remember I gave you warning, when you surrender to your fate.*"

"Surrender?" Tessa echoed, her heart pounding. It felt like she was standing in outer space, or somewhere outside of the world she'd always known. The City was tucked within pockets behind other buildings of Tokyo, hidden yet still there. If the City was hidden, the Armory was truly on another level.

Packed dirt crunched under her shoes when she shifted her stance. Her sore legs protested, but she focused on the world around her.

Moonlight splashed on the hilt of a curved sword; the blade was embedded deep into the dirt. It'd take some effort to pull it out. She had a feeling she had to pick the right weapon; she couldn't pluck them up like she was grabbing apples at the grocery store.

She looked closer; there was something strange about the sword, but maybe this would be her weapon—

Tessa stumbled backward, stifling her scream.

It was not a blade.

Curved rib bones stretched out toward her. Her eyes adjusted to the semi-darkness. There were katanas, there were bows, true. But there were also dried-out bones everywhere. In front of a sword to her right, a skeleton reached out toward the shiny metal, forever stuck.

This wasn't just an armory; it was a battlefield filled with the dead.

"*See what you will become?*" the voice taunted. "*These are the lost souls who could not meet their end of the bargain, so they stay here, fueling the power of my treasured weapons instead.*"

To her left, she saw a throwing star with four sharp points. The shuriken gleamed luminescent gold under the moonlight, jewels studded into its sides. It was as beautiful as it was deadly.

She leaned closer, and her blood chilled. Whisper-like noises came straight from the weapon.

"You shouldn't be here," someone else added from behind her, and she nearly grabbed the closest sword to protect herself. Then she saw the sleepy boy, pushing his messy hair out of his face.

"Uehara-kun!"

Tessa was *very* much caught. He shifted from foot to foot in his pajamas, his shoulders weary with the need for sleep, with his eyes focused on her. Those forever-frowning eyebrows hadn't changed a hair.

"Did you come to get a weapon, too?" she asked hopefully.

His frown only deepened. "I'm here to get you to *leave*. We make our weapons in the second torii. The Armory is strictly out-of-bounds. Let's go, Miyata."

"Do you trust a homemade weapon compared to

these?" Tessa spluttered. "Just look at what's around us, the best the City has to offer! These are what *real* gods use. Any weapon we make isn't going to get us far if Lord Taira's blade is legendary. It'll cut through ours like butter." Tessa started trudging up the nearest hill of sharp weapons, humming one of her favorite BTS songs under her breath, even though her heart was pounding in her ears. She knew this was risky. Surely the Armory had been calling to her; what else could that music have been? But why had it suddenly cut out?

"Didn't you hear Kit?" Jin hissed, treading close behind. "I read one of the books in the Dojo. This place is named 'Fallen Souls' because if you can't control the weapon, it controls you. As in, you'll *die*. This is a sure-fire way to get stuck in the City forever before the five days are even up."

His words felt like a strange buzzing in her ears compared to the music that had started up again, ever so faintly. Where was it coming from? As she turned, trying to find the source, she kept a careful eye on her bracelet to make sure it wasn't getting too taut. That'd send her tumbling back toward Kit, and more than that, it would wake up the fox. Over the past hours, it felt like the string between them had become looser, but maybe it was just because they were at the Dojo and it was a place that bent time. The ōkami charm was still and cold against her wrist; not for the first time, Tessa wondered, *What* does *it do?*

Then the melody grew louder. As haunting as fingers brushing against harp strings, it was like ku that she could hear.

Tessa scanned the rolling slopes. The sound was coming from just beyond the hill to the right, not very far away at all. The golden bracelet could stretch out just enough for that.

Jin protested, "Where do you think you're going—"

Dirt crunched under her feet. She twisted around the weapons and piles of bones, careful not to look too closely. At the top of the hill, she looked down at what could've been a long-lost battlefield. Countless skeletons had collapsed around a single weapon. A small path wove through the bones.

There were more urgent whispers, but these were just from Jin, who spluttered behind her. "Miyata, this is way too dangerous. Do you see these bodies?"

"I've seen the wreckage of Tokyo," Tessa replied, her eyes set on the blade. "And that is reason enough to pick up this weapon."

She made her way to the sword. The melody curled around her, pulling her closer. The tsuba, the hand guard where the hilt met the blade, was covered in rust, thick and heavy, almost unassuming.

Tessa took a deep breath and reached out to wrap her fingers around the sword. It was freezing cold to the touch, like she'd plunged her hands into an ice bath.

The melody increased in pace, with musical delight.

She pulled the sword from the packed dirt. The blade slid out easily, smooth as butter, and she let out a cheer. "This one's meant for me, Uehara-kun!"

He didn't respond.

She turned around. He wasn't there.

19

Tessa stood in a white chamber, clutching the sword—but it was back in the ground and didn't budge a centimeter. Tall, rectangular mirrors surrounded her, reflecting a dusty, small girl with trembling hands yanking at the hilt.

But it was not quiet here. That strange melody rose into a crescendo, and her heartbeat slammed against her chest.

It wasn't a melody. Her blood ran cold. It was voices.

"I fought you with everything I had!"

"Why did you take away my soul?"

A sob. *"I want to return to my family."*

The voices shouted and demanded and pleaded, and her head pounded.

Invisible hands grabbed at her, and she let out a scream as they shook her arms, nails clawing into her skin; it felt like these bodiless voices were about to pull her apart.

Was this the sacrifice that Kit had warned her of?

But she couldn't let go, though her body burned with pain. "I must use this sword! I have to fight Lord Taira!"

Familiar voices echoed against the mirrors.

"Tessa won't help us. She only thinks about herself. That's why she makes up those stories about things no one else can see." Cecilia's voice was like a wind chime made of daggers, each word piercing.

Cherry blossom petals fell around her, withered into ashy darkness.

"She isn't going to be able to save us." Peyton was matter-of-fact. "Tessa is not a hero."

Her sisters.

Tessa Miyata is not a hero.

She was no hero. It was true; when she tried to save her family, it ended up like this. Someone else always had to save her. With the NowLook videos that Peyton and Cecilia always tried to take down. With the way she hid in the library during lunch, sheltering behind stacks of books, waiting for Allison to notice her again. With Gram working day in and day out to keep a roof over their heads.

A sob wracked her chest. "Cecilia. Peyton. I wanted to make you proud."

Pure white light flashed; the sound of gears creaked, like time was shifting.

Tessa's twelfth birthday, all over again. The twenty-ninth day of sixth grade.

She knew this not because of the calendar tacked up in the bedroom that she shared with her older sisters, but because of her new socks.

The real Tessa stood like a ghost, watching the past-Tessa. "Hello?" she tried calling out, waving her arms. "Can you see me?"

No answer. The past-Tessa was sitting on the edge of the lower bunk bed, wiggling her covered toes with a big smile.

The socks were decorated with little pink bunnies sporting an energetic grin, a character that Tessa loved, so her sisters had surprised her with them this morning, over her birthday breakfast. "Allison will love these, too!"

The real Tessa's heart stuttered. It really was *that* morning.

Happily, the past-Tessa hurried down the hall to find her sisters; they were going to walk with her to school today, and—

The past-Tessa slowed in front of the kitchen door. It was cracked open. But something kept her from bursting inside; the air felt thick with some strange emotion, and not the bright grins that her family had glowed with during their stacks of confetti pancakes, minutes earlier.

"I miss them, too." Gram's husky voice was soft as

she set a hand on Peyton's slumped shoulders. Tessa loved Gram's gentleness; it was a balm after a long day when her head was all jumbled from sixth-grade math, or from the weird way Allison had been acting recently.

The real Tessa pushed into the room and waved in front of her family's faces. "Cecilia! Peyton! Can you see me? Hello? Gram?"

No answer.

The lump in her throat grew and grew, until she couldn't speak. She stood there, frozen as them, stuck in sad thoughts. Even though Tessa knew now what they were thinking about, it didn't make the pain burn any less.

"I can't believe it's been eleven years," Cecilia said. "I just remember...those last Fridays of the month, when Mom and Dad would take us all to pick up freshly made rice cakes from the corner manju shop to demolish the moment we got home, and then we'd spend the evening watching a movie, curled up on the couch, with sushi ordered in, and bowls and bowls of the butteriest popcorn Dad and Peyton could pop up on the stove, and—"

Eleven years.

They had died eleven years ago. Could that mean...

She couldn't breathe.

"I wish they'd listened," Gram said, her voice strained. "They had wanted so badly to see Tessa on her birthday that they were in such a rush to the hospital, and..."

Faintly illuminated through the crack in the door, past-Tessa's face shifted through emotions, like fractured light trying to shine through deep waters, the colors distorted and the subtle waves adjusting her frown, her wide eyes, and the burn of tears close to tipping over. Her *birthday* was when—no, *why*—her parents had passed away?

She'd known that she had been hospitalized—just for a few days—as a baby, when she'd gotten a bad case of pneumonia. That was why Gram fussed over the slightest of Tessa's colds.

But she'd never known this.

It was because of her.

And the real Tessa wanted to reach out, to comfort her past self, but she knew there were no words, no hugs, nothing that could ever heal that ache in her soul.

The past-Tessa tiptoed to her room, where her sisters found her, scooping her up in big hugs and laughter, like they hadn't been sitting in a mournful despair minutes earlier.

Tessa played along. She couldn't make her sisters feel hurt, knowing that she'd found out the truth when they'd tried so hard to protect her from it for so many years.

This was her burden to bear, a curse marking her soul.

The memory shattered around her like glass, piercing her skin, and she cried out with all the pain from the freshness of reliving the memory.

Lights flashed. She was in a crowded room, filled with people she knew. They kept walking past. Peyton, Cecilia. Her parents. Ojiichan and Obaachan. Gram. Allison. They strode on by, not seeing her. Not knowing how much she cared about them.

Because she wasn't strong enough to save them.

"Mom!"

No answer.

"Dad!"

Nothing. They were long gone, and it was because of her.

"Peyton! Cecilia!"

Her sisters walked right on by.

"Allison! Can't we still be friends? Remember all our jokes and the shows we watched together—"

The girl shook her hands off. "Who are you?"

The truth was that she was alone. Alone, alone, alone.

Weights sunk her arms down, and her head screamed with a hundred taunting voices: *Who are you? You are a nobody. I don't know you.*

The nightmare never ended, the people never stopped walking on by, not when her loneliness was carved deep in her heart, forged to her soul in its truth.

Tessa tried to shake herself out of this. *I need to save Tokyo—to save my sisters—I have to—*

She tore herself out of her memories, back to the Armory, a scream on the tip of her tongue. When she looked down, her body was fading, being pulled into the sword like vapor—

Tessa fell to her knees, still clutching at the sword and trying to yank it up, as the claws dug deeper into her skin, pulling down.

Then the sword attacked deeper into her soul. Pulling all of Tessa out of her to show how truly worthless she was. It tore at her, showing time after time of Gram crying in front of her parents' faded photographs. The news article she'd found later, about her parents' unfortunate deaths: nothing more than a paragraph in the local paper. That time, a few years ago, when Peyton and Cecilia had braided each other's hair and it had become *their* thing, until they finally noticed her longingly looking at their matching braids and remembered to include her, too. Taunting laughs from flashes of the videos her classmates had posted—she'd watched them late at night on her sisters' computers, like a train wreck she couldn't look away from. The laughter rebounded, getting louder and louder with every replay.

"Don't leave me, Cecilia. Take me with you, Peyton," Tessa cried, her heart burning. "Gram! Mom! Dad! I'm so sorry, I—"

Then—someone wrenched her hands away from the sword, and light burst in her eyes, searing with pain—

Tessa cried out, her throat aching from screams. Her head hung down; her hands were still clutched around the hilt of the sword. She couldn't let go. It had been just an illusion testing her, but it pierced her with how real it could be. Those were words that she could imagine her sisters saying. She was so close to failing them, just like that vision.

Another terrible image filled her mind.

She was nothing more than a baby, swaddled in blankets on a cold, shadowy night. Then there was a husky whisper—*I will watch over you, always.* But, moments later, when she cried out, the person looking down at her wasn't her father, wasn't her family at all....

Someone stood over her, shouting her name. But her mind didn't clear; the words from the sword echoed in her brain. *You are not ready.*

When she looked down, her body was almost all faded, sucked into the sword like vapor—

"NO!"

A flash of white, and shadows raged forward.

Kit's teeth landed sharp on the blade. "Her life is not yours to take!"

Tessa fell backward, Jin pulling her farther away. Kit fought the sword, his eyes sharp, his fangs snarling. She focused her eyesight; ku shot out in the form of blades, trying to stab the fox.

Kit's shadow, in that samurai form, seemed to pull a sword out of thin air and battled the ku, alongside the fox himself.

"She *is not yours*," the fox snarled, biting at the ku. "Tessa Miyata will choose her own path. I will guard her with my godforce!"

With one last flash of teeth and the shadow samurai's blade, the ku seemed to dissipate. *"Then that is your sacrifice to make."*

Kit breathed heavily, his back to Tessa and Jin.

Finally, Tessa could look around. Her body was numb and her heart aching with an unspeakable pain. But she was no longer caught in the web of nightmares, and the starry sky glimmered hauntingly above. They were in the Armory of Fallen Souls, and she was mostly intact. Her body was much more transparent than before, with that see-through shimmer stretching all along her torso and down to her fingertips.

"You do not attack Tessa Miyata." Kit glared at the tarnished sword, his hackles raised, with one final warning. "She is not yours to control. Tessa is all her own being."

The roaring winds had quieted, along with the voices of the Armory. Still, Tessa had a feeling they continued to watch.

Kit craned his neck to stare at Tessa. His dark eyes were sharp blades, piercing her to the spot.

Tessa was in trouble. *Deep* trouble. She gulped and forced out, "Um, hello, Kit."

"Don't you dare *hello* me!" Kit roared. The fox was

furious, his shadow stretching into the image of that tall man, kneeling next to her, worry straining every line of his body taut. "This is why you are undergoing training. You are not ready! You almost died. How can you ever survive fighting Lord Taira?"

The fox was paler than before, almost like he was going to slip away into the moonlight. Tessa stared, trying to wash away the thoughts that the sword had brought up. She was getting better and better at forgetting her past, even though it felt like forgetting a part of who she was. "I'm okay. Are you okay? You're looking...fainter."

Jin's lips tugged down. "He used his ku to save you. Didn't you, Kit?" he asked. "I'm guessing he lost all the power he's been trying to collect."

The fox growled, looking away. "More...more than I wanted to."

Oh. Regret burned at Tessa's throat, making it difficult to squeeze out her words. "I'm so sorry. I didn't mean for you to use your ku to help me. We needed a weapon, and—"

"I had to choose between using my energy or letting you sacrifice your mortal life to the sword." Kit pawed the ground; his shadow returned to the form of a kitsune. Then, finally, he met Tessa's eyes. "I *know* you can beat the two torii. With what you learn from those, you will be able to fight Lord Taira. Evil corrupts him to his core.

If he was ever good as a god, like others have said, then your human ways will be what will purify him."

Then the Armory spoke: "*Through the kitsune's sacrifice, you may have survived, but we will not let you stay any longer. Unless you, too, want to join these bones.*"

Tessa dragged her eyes to the nearest skeleton, brittle bone hands clutching their neck. She could imagine herself right next to them, reaching out for her family to notice her, forever, until all her flesh faded away.

"We will not be joining the Armory," Kit snarled. "Never as a pile of bones."

He nudged Tessa and Jin. "C'mon. Let's return to the Dojo."

Kit seemed to know the way instinctively, like he had passed through the Armory many times before. Tessa's head throbbed, echoes of shouts still pounding in her skull.

They wound around another skeleton, this one with a plump coin purse attached to its hip, and Kit sighed, looking at the pale, long bones.

"I know the allure of the Armory is hard to resist," Kit said. "But so long as I'm alive, can you promise me you won't come back here?"

"Yes, of course," Jin said immediately.

Tessa bowed her head in shame. "I'm sorry you had to use your ku for me. I won't come here again. I...I promise."

The fox tore his gaze away from the skeleton and gave them a sharp, sad smile. "If something happens to me, you can do whatever you want. You can go home. The bracelet won't connect us if I'm dead, after all."

Tessa grasped for words. She *knew* how important this was for them; that this was life or death. But she hadn't thought about what she would do if she made it out alive and Kit didn't. She'd imagined that the feisty fox would always be snapping at her, making up these silly rules that she didn't understand, but still guiding her through the City.

"You won't die," Jin insisted. "That's...No, you're our guardian, Kit."

"There's only so much I can protect you from, whether within the Dojo or the Armory, or within the rest of the last magical city." The fox padded toward the archway to the Dojo.

Tessa gulped down the lump in her throat. "I'm sorry, Kit. I really am. I—"

"I'm not letting you get hurt." Kit stared her down. "I was helpless in your bracelet when you were getting bullied. But your pain felt like mine, and even if you're possibly the shrimpiest human that has ever challenged the torii, I'm going to do something to help you now. I hated not doing anything, and that's not the kind of person I am."

She understood. That was just like her, her heart

aching as she watched Tokyo burn. Maybe she didn't belong because she was Japanese American and not "full" Japanese. But...wasn't her blood still from this country? Didn't that make her worthy? Shouldn't she try her best to save it, too?

When Tessa stood in the clearing in front of the three torii, her heart raced. She looked up at the stars. Somewhere, outside the barriers of the Dojo, her sisters were close by. They were still in danger. She had to fight. If it meant the two torii instead of a legendary weapon, then so be it. She *was* going to win.

For the sake of everyone she loved, she had to.

20

Tessa inhaled her breakfast of buttered toast and eggs like it was one of the breakfast bars Gram stuffed in her mouth on the way out the door to the grocery store. She had a job to do, too.

She'd had a poor night of sleep after her botched visit to the Armory. The sting of her failure had felt even worse when Jin had glanced up at the Tree of Time, huffing when he saw that the blossoms on the second branch were withering away. When she'd tried to say good morning, he'd only given her a grunt in response.

Sure, last night hadn't gone well, but seeing him had given her a great idea.

If only he would agree to it.

Tessa glanced quickly at her companions, both of whom were too focused on their meals to talk.

Kit was chowing down on a bowl of cereal. She'd

thought everyone in Japan ate rice or bread for breakfast, like her grandparents, but the fox was enamored with the granola that the magical cart had served up. The string connecting them was invisible in the morning light, but his bracelet still remained around his paw, shimmering soft and golden. Still, he looked a little paler than yesterday, and guilt burned at Tessa. It was all because of the ku he'd used saving her from the Armory.

Jin was eating his rice balls with a particular fury that seemed to be directed at Tessa. She could almost see the storm of thoughts that was clouding his mind, which made her uneasy. To get him to agree to her plan, Tessa would need a shrine full of luck.

The moment Jin set his dish on the counter and stood up, Tessa was ready. She hurriedly put her plate away and chugged down the rest of her water.

He began stalking toward the second torii, but she called, "Uehara-kun. Please, wait."

Formalities. For a boy as rigid as Jin, being proper was the first step.

He didn't turn to look at her. He only barked, "What, Miyata?"

Kit stopped crunching on his cereal to shoot her a skeptical gaze.

I've got this, she tried to tell the fox, with a reassuring smile she definitely *didn't* feel.

She had to lay it all out.

"I need your help. Please." Her heart thudded in her chest. "I'm figuring out the obstacles as best as I can, but I still have seven hours until the first torii."

"Yeah, you'll need all that time—if not more—to prepare," Jin remarked over his shoulder. "My father always says that's what happens when you're not strong enough."

"Can you help me train?"

The boy finally turned, looking like he'd never seen her before in his life. "I'm not a good teacher."

"You breezed through the first challenge," Tessa said. "I don't have your years of experience, but I really need all the help I can get. I want to do something for Tokyo. My sisters. My grandparents live just across the bay. If Lord Taira gets out of Tokyo, there's no way my seventy-year-old grandma or hurt grandpa is going to outrun those shadows or his sword. I *need* to do something. But to get through this, I need *you*. If you train me, if you can give me tips, I bet I can clear the obstacle course in seven hours. Besides, I think if I break the curse on the rock monster, I might even get to go to the next torii without the full hour countdown, so it's worth a try. I just need a *little* help."

Jin looked down at her. "I have to finish up the second torii. I'm not—"

"One hour—one cherry blossom of time—at most. That's all I'll ask," Tessa said. "I won't ask you to help me with saving the creature from its curse, or anything else. I'll do that on my own, I promise."

The boy frowned, his face looking like he was eating a sour plum. "It makes more sense for me to focus on my work so that *I* can get us home."

He was right. Jin was a martial arts master, and Tessa was only, well, Tessa.

"Um…" Tessa hesitated. "Ten minutes, then?"

Kit cleared his throat, taking a long, measured look at the boy. "No one is the same as another. Our lives and experiences all mark us differently, giving us separate strengths and weaknesses, joys and sorrows that we carry in our hearts. Something to keep in mind."

Jin glanced over at Tessa quizzically, as if he couldn't see how she was strong. "Fine. Let's talk strategy."

Tessa's breakfast sloshed in her stomach as she followed Jin into the Dojo. When she caught up with him, she said, "Thanks, Uehara-kun."

He paused at the start line to the obstacle course. "I don't know if you're going to thank me once we get started. You know, I don't train newbies at my dad's dojo for a reason. None of them can keep up with me."

"I will," Tessa promised, even as the eggs in her stomach churned. "I'll do whatever it takes—"

He bellowed, at an ear-piercing level, "Okay, start running in place! I'll talk you through each obstacle, but you better listen carefully!"

Oof. Tessa's head rang, but she only nodded. *Game on. I've got a chance now.*

Jin knew his stuff. Kit had introduced ku, but Jin helped Tessa click together how to fight, dodge, and *survive* with—or without—ku.

Training with him was a whole different experience from Kit. The fox had barked out commands here and there, but he didn't seem to have enough energy to go through the paces with her or make her do laps around the Dojo at the slightest of mistakes.

Jin did.

This was the fiftieth or hundred-and-fiftieth practice run; she'd lost count after the first ten. Along with all the Lessons (capital *L* where rule-following Jin was involved).

Lesson #1: How to *breathe*.

Kit, Jin, and Tessa sat in front of the Dojo and practiced matching their breathing patterns to the soft clouds rolling on by.

Then Jin sent her onto the obstacle course, armed with this new tactic. It helped her draw in more ku—she'd never really noticed her breathing much before, but she still went flying from the second-to-last shadow warrior.

Lesson #49: Memorization.

This wasn't the cramming-before-a-test kind of memorization. Kit let them use the paper screen to view past flashes of Meiji Jingu itself. Jin had Tessa peek for a split second, and then he had her recollect what she'd just seen.

"What color were their robes?" Jin asked.

Tessa didn't even remember; she'd been too busy gawking at the tall wood building, the crowds of people flocking to ring the prayer bell.

"Um, orange?"

"Nope." Jin motioned for her to turn toward the paper screen. "Look."

"Oh. Red. Close enough."

His look was so withering, Tessa almost shriveled up. But after a few more tests, Jin seemed satisfied, and they headed to the start line.

"I got through!" Tessa cheered, at the end of the shadow warriors. She'd made it, finally. Jin was right—even though she was reluctant to admit it. Focusing on having better awareness of her surroundings *did* help her notice the approaching shadowy fighters.

She turned to face the solid wall and geared up her arm for a strong punch. *Ready, set—*

A merrily swinging warrior swooped in, sending her flying.

"Ouch!"

"TOO SLOW TO PUNCH!" Jin bellowed the obvious.

So they started Lesson #298: How to punch and kick.

Jin had her practice kicking only about fifty million times, adjusting her posture centimeter by centimeter. He showed her how to follow through with her punches, aiming at going through the wall instead of just hitting it.

After Tessa was able to punch and kick Jin's hand enough to satisfy him (he never winced, not even once, even when Tessa got annoyed and kicked with all her strength), he even let her try a roundhouse kick.

This didn't keep her from getting more simple lessons.

Lesson #358: How to *jump*. Hadn't she been doing it just fine all her life?

She was trying to show Jin how she was going to climb the wall of the obstacle course's mini shrine (even though she'd already fallen down a few times, surely this last obstacle was doable; she'd climbed the tree behind her apartment building before). She was mimicking the way she'd leap from side to side, using ku to help her move faster. But he merely raised his hand when she was mid-jump and said, "Stop. Freeze."

So she paused, one foot in the air, and in seconds she was ready to fall over.

"Look," Jin said. "Move your feet in more. Yeah, you're going from ledge to ledge, but you have to continuously remain mobile in order to avoid Lord Taira or the rock creature. You're taking way too big leaps that are beyond your control."

"The way I jump isn't going to save me, is it?" Tessa asked with a laugh.

Jin looked at her quietly. "In a past sparring match, it wasn't raw power that helped me win. It was my technique and strategy. My opponent was known for a wider stance; he liked to use it to look bigger than he actually is, but it was all for show, and he didn't have the speed to stabilize himself after I did a low sweeping kick."

"Where was this? Your dad's dojo? Maybe they're just being nice because they don't want to get your dad mad."

He looked away self-consciously. "The National Karate Tournament. I placed first for the twelve-year-old bracket."

"Hey, hey!" Kit cheered from his spot at the finish line. "We've got a winner with us. I'll take all the winners I can get. See, I knew it was a good idea to bring Uehara along."

Tessa, however, could only gape. No wonder the kids in the alleyway had looked so salty as they'd sprinted away. They knew they didn't stand a chance against Jin.

She couldn't imagine winning anything. The most she'd gotten recently was a participation ribbon for her school's spring reading contest. At least it'd come with a free pizza voucher. It'd given her an excuse to finally order her favorite pineapple and olive pizza (the perfect mix of sweet and salty) that her sisters always said was too gross to even consider. After they'd shared it, Peyton even admitted that it wasn't *too* bad, either.

"That's amazing," Tessa said. "Your parents must be so proud of you."

"It's just my dad. And he's not proud of me, not

really," Jin said, so quickly that it seemed like a gut reaction. Then his eyes shuttered. "My mom...It was different with my mom, not that you'd understand—"

"My...my parents are gone, actually," Tessa said. "Our grandma in California takes care of us, but it's hard for her."

She glanced at Jin, her eyes set, daring him to pity her.

With a softness to his words, he said, "I'm sorry."

Tessa nodded, the knot in her stomach loosening. That was better than when Allison had asked, *So what happened?* and she'd had to explain that her parents had died in a car crash when she was a baby, and she didn't have any real memories of them, just photos. *That sucks*, Allison had said, and hastily jumped into talking about something else, like Tessa's past was too much for her to deal with.

"It's weird, you know?" Tessa said. "I love Gram to pieces, but I wish she would spend more time with us. We have 'family' dinners, but it always ends up being me and my siblings, with the three of us eating rice and natto because Gram has to work another shift or whatever. And we all have to pretend it's no big deal that she's working so much just to keep a roof over our heads, so we won't get put into foster care. My sisters really try hard to raise me right, too. Even if they have their own stuff sometimes, they're always the ones who bandaged up my knees when I was really little and learning how to ride a bike, or even now, trying to take care of me as best as they can."

Tessa had so much she owed her sisters; she wanted to earn enough money someday to pay Cecilia back for that boy's broken phone at the museum. Her sister had depleted her hard-earned cash just for Tessa, so that she wouldn't get in trouble. She wanted to be able to help Gram so that she wouldn't have to work at the grocery store anymore. She wanted her family to no longer feel so many everyday burdens because of her. But she wasn't a hero; she had no way to sweep in and save her family.

"I used to have that. My mom. She was always there for me. We'd spend every Saturday at an art museum or a bookstore in Tokyo, together," Jin said softly. He turned his head away, as if staring at something might prevent the wounds of the past from opening up again. "Those were the best days. Until she left us, when I was eight. That was when I learned: People who leave never come back."

"I'm really sorry, Uehara-kun."

He nodded and swallowed, like he was trying to get rid of a bitter taste. "Now, though, I *wish* my dad didn't notice me. He's the second oldest in a family of five boys, and he beat all of them for the opportunity to take over his dad's dojo. Now he thinks I'm going to follow in his footsteps, even though it's the last thing I want to do."

"Does he know it's not what you want to do?"

His eyes dropped down. "I've told him, once. He pretended like he didn't hear me and started talking about my tournament instead."

"What *do* you want to do?" Tessa asked. She wished she had parents that wanted *something* for her future—other than not getting in trouble, which was clearly what she was best at these days.

Jin looked down. "It's nothing—"

"It's *something*," Tessa said vehemently. "If it matters to you, if your dad truly cares about you, it should matter to him, too. What is it?"

He sighed, shaking his head.

"Some things can change for the better," Tessa said quietly. "If you talk with your father more and explain *why* you're wanting what you want, or thinking a certain way, it might help him understand the things that matter the most to you. Or, at least, that's what Cecilia tells me."

"Doesn't that only work out in anime or movies?"

"I think if it's something that gets shown in an anime, then maybe it's worth trying, right?" Tessa said, and Jin let out a short, small laugh.

"That's—that's actually what I want to do," Jin blurted out, his ears turning a little red. "Well, not an anime, really. But I've been drawing out a historical manga....I love history and art." He peeked at Tessa, as if nervous about her response.

"Wow. Can I read it?" Tessa asked, eyes wide. "I mean, I'm way better at talking in Japanese than reading it, but for something you've written, I'll become fluent."

Jin burst out into laughter. "Wait, really?"

"Really."

He dug through his pocket and drew out a thin paper bag, no bigger than his palm. "This was from the store in the alleyway. So, it's actually kind of my fault that we ended up here."

Jin opened the crinkling paper to reveal a case of shiny gold pieces.

"Are those darts?"

He laughed again. Tessa wanted to capture that sound in a glass bottle and keep it forever. "Close-ish. Titanium-coated steel pen nibs. I use these for drawing characters, and they're flexible but—I'm boring you."

"No. I love hearing about this." This was the *real* Jin: lighting up with energy, yet still thoughtful and surprisingly considerate and loyal and wise. "You *should* tell your dad about what you're interested in. It's amazing. Can I see your art after all of this?"

Jin shuttered, closing off like she'd crushed the nibs under her heel.

"That's the problem," he said hollowly. "My dad won't even let me keep a single manga volume in our house. 'It's a waste of money and time.' Or, 'Only people who end up doing nothing read "for-fun books" like that.' Why would I need manga if I'm going to take over the dojo? I just draw things on the train ride to school and sneak them into the recycling in front of the convenience store."

"Gram always tells me, 'Books that give us joy give us the will to live. They're just as important as any other book.' And I think that's pretty true." Tessa remembered her school year of hiding in the library, with only musty pages to keep her company. She cleared her throat, blinking quickly, and stood up to stretch. "One more time. I can do this. Maybe I can inspire something for your manga. Draw me looking cool, okay? None of that falling-on-my-face stuff."

Jin snorted, but he sobered, looking at the wall clock. "You've got just under ten minutes before the torii opens up again for you."

"Yep, yep, ganbatte," Kit mumbled from underneath his tail. Moments later, the fox let out a snore.

Tessa felt a stinging pain, but then Jin said, "Hey, what do you say in English for 'ganbatte'? Just, you know, as practice. Like what my dad wanted."

"Oh. It kind of translates to 'do your best' or 'you can do it.'"

Jin nodded, repeating the words once. Then he said, "Kit's right. Even when he's asleep, Kit knows the truth.

He and I wouldn't be here if it weren't so, if we didn't believe in you. Ganbatte, ne."

She breathed in deep. Tessa wiped the sweat off her brow and visualized, just like he had taught her, how she'd conquer each of the four obstacles.

Her heart pounded as she stepped up to the starting line. Then she glanced at the Tree of Time. A full day had passed; they were almost through day two. "Um, do you have to head to the second torii?"

"I'm going to see this through," Jin said, and Tessa's heart swelled with joy. He cupped his hands around his mouth and hollered in English, "YOU CAN DO IT!"

Tessa gave him a big grin, even though she felt kind of wobbly. "Thanks, Uehara-kun."

She set her eyes on the concrete blocks. Tessa had to beat the obstacle course; she couldn't let him down.

21

Tessa flew forward, all her hopes and worries channeled into getting to the finish line. She took all of the lessons she'd received from Kit and Jin, and applied them as best as she could.

Endurance. Tessa gathered ku; her feet flew over the concrete blocks. Thank goodness for Lessons #1 through who-knew-how-many from Jin.

Agility. Tessa spun between the shadow warriors, her Miyata-sister braid flying from side to side. She felt like a marionette, pulled by strings, watchful for the next punch that might bring her demise. Kit shook himself out and sat up, his nine tails flicking with interest.

One shadow warrior came flying out at the end, right when she thought she was safe—somehow, the course had magically added another one—and she pulled a strand of ku in and pushed it toward her feet, shooting forward and into safety. She wasn't the marionette; she *could* control how this all ended.

From the sidelines, Jin and Kit cheered; she wanted to smile, too, but she wasn't done yet.

Strength. Tessa faced down the wall. Before, it'd been wood, but now it was solid *brick*. How was this fair?

Nothing is fair. Tessa knew that too well. She just had to fight the best she could.

"You can do this!" Jin roared, and her heart skipped. She wasn't alone. Tessa couldn't let him down.

She bounded backward and eyed the wall for a split second, checking her surroundings to make sure the obstacle hadn't summoned up another shadow warrior. Then, with a cry, she raced forward and flew at the wall with a flying kick.

Boom. The wall cracked from her force, and she went soaring through as it burst into pieces.

She'd made it through.

Mobility. Her fingers ached from countless times climbing the wall of the shrine, but she had to make it up *one* more time. The rough wood threatened to splinter and cut her skin, but she gripped the first ledge and clambered on. Her heart dropped as it let out an awful, ear-piercing crack.

"GO!" Kit roared. "You have to get to the top!"

Tessa didn't waste another second. She pulled herself up, centimeter by centimeter, her muscles straining, but her eyes set on the goal above. Finally, sweat sticking her shirt to her skin, she swung her legs onto the top platform.

Up close, the ring was a shimmery neon, like godfire. It tickled her fingers as she looked down the side of the shrine.

How in the spirits was she supposed to get down to the finish line?

From below, Jin and Kit were shouting, but a wind roared in her ears; she couldn't hear their words no matter how much she tried to focus....

Focus.

Kit had been surprised at how well Tessa had been able to collect ku from the beginning. It was the one thing she hadn't needed a million lessons on, unlike everything from Jin.

Focus. Tessa slid the ring onto her wrist and breathed in deep—using the training she'd gotten from Jin. Maybe something from both of her teachers would work out.

She reached out, hoping desperately to find ku.

Her fingers met empty air.

No. Fight for your family. Focus.

There—a shimmer of light. Tessa felt the silk-smooth threads collect in her palm, and she pulled them toward her. And with her heart in her throat, she rappelled down, using the threads as a rope, her feet bouncing along the side of the shrine.

Jin and Kit roared, cheering as she hoisted the ring into the air. The obstacle course melted into the straw floor, as if it had never been there, and she allowed herself a victorious grin as the ring shimmered out of sight.

She, Tessa Miyata, was no hero. But she wasn't going to stop trying to save her family, either, no matter what obstacles got thrown in her way.

But she was not done yet.

Wordlessly, Tessa marched out of the Dojo to the three torii. She looked between Kit and Jin, who had walked close behind her. "I'm ready to challenge the first torii."

"I agree," Jin said.

Her heart swelled with pride.

"Except for one thing."

She froze in confusion; Kit turned his head sideways.

"I'm going in with you," Jin said. "Let's do this, Te... er, Miyata."

"Wait," Tessa spluttered. "But I told you, I'm going to try to remove that curse from the rock monster, and— wait—seriously? You're in?"

"You... you made me realize something." Jin gave her a long look. "Being here, it's not about helping myself. It's about doing something more for the people around me. I think... I think my mom would be happy to see me help out others. But there's one condition."

Tessa gulped. "What is it?"

"Let's make a plan." Jin's eyebrows furrowed. "We've only got time to go through this torii once, so we need to win. And, of course, break the ofuda."

Tessa and Jin put their heads together as they sat on the dirt clearing in front of the three torii. A few minutes later, they'd landed on a solid plan.

"I think that's it, right?" Tessa said.

"Sounds good to me." Jin nodded, standing up to dust off his hands. Tessa scrambled to her feet; she wanted to throw her arms around Jin in a hug. But on second thought, she kept her hands to herself. She didn't want to get side kicked into oblivion. "Thanks, Uehara-kun."

"Don't forget about me," Kit volunteered. "Best tactical captain right here, you know."

Tessa stuck her tongue out at the fox, who stuck his long tongue back at her.

"Time to go." To her surprise, Jin cracked a sliver of a smile before they stepped into the torii.

22

THE WAY THAT THE TORII OF THE FOREST HAD LOOKED shimmery and pretty from outside was completely deceiving.

This forest was *dangerous*. The trees were tall, casting ample shadows dark enough for creatures to lurk. Thick brambles wove treacherous traps between trees; one misstep would mean that Tessa would be stuck in their grips.

Tessa and Jin strode along the path, keeping a close lookout. Kit was right behind them, his paws padding softly on the dirt path. They'd only been inside for a few minutes, but it felt like years already.

"That creature has to be here, somewhere," Tessa muttered. "Kit, Uehara-kun, you remember the plan?"

"I'll tear off the ofuda," Jin said with a nod. Earlier, he'd told Tessa about a tournament he'd fought, where it'd been similar to pulling a flag off his opponent's gi, the karate uniform. And, to her surprise, he'd volunteered to go for the ofuda.

"And Kit and I will distract the creature," Tessa said, confirming their plan. They walked forward through the trees quietly, eyes scanning the periphery for any sign of the monster.

"You're right, Miyata. If we break the curse, that should be enough to get you through the torii," Kit added from behind them. "Solid enough plan, and good thinking."

Tessa and Jin jumped over a leaf pile, but Kit was too small; he plunged through with a loud crunch. "I always forget I'm so tiny. But I see why animals like doing this. It's fun!"

Tessa called over her shoulder, "*Shh*. You're going to get his attention—"

Jin tugged at her sleeve, his voice dry and scratchy. "Miyata..."

She turned around.

Kit was gone.

Instead, the massive rock creature stretched above them.

Fear glued Tessa's feet to the ground. She stared up at the monster that was more than two stories tall, with rock fists that could pulverize into her pieces.

Jin yanked her to the side. "Get *away*! Follow the plan!"

That finally shoved Tessa into action.

"But—where's Kit?" Tessa cried. The fox was nowhere to be seen; the light connecting them was thin and weak even in the thickening darkness.

"We have to survive first." Jin was in Teacher Uehara mode all over again. He was right, though. There was *only* time to try to survive.

The rock fists rained down like a storm, but Tessa danced backward and shouted, "Too slow!" The beast let out an infuriated roar, following her as she raced through the forest. She didn't have any leeway to look behind her; she could only focus on the fallen logs in her way. Still, she could hear that the monster was close behind.

Then she saw what was up ahead. Her heart ricocheted in her chest. A seven-foot tree trunk splayed out in her path, and she was closed in on both sides by thick bushes and trees.

She was closed in—if not for ku.

With a quick, sharp breath, she gathered in the spirit energy and sent it toward her feet, helping her leap cleanly over.

The monster screeched, crashing its way through the trunk, but it slowed; its feet were tangled in vines. Tessa's bracelet tugged her backward, toward the monster, with a sharp *buzz!* She was getting too far from Kit, wherever he was.

Tessa swung in a wide turn, shouting, "You're slow, monster!"

Come on, Jin. She looked around, but he was twenty feet behind—there was no way he'd be able to grab the ofuda from there.

He was missing the perfect chance. But, to her relief, she saw Kit racing alongside Jin. The fox was safe, though a little muddy. His body shimmered; he was slowly being drained of his ku.

"The monster flung me into a pit!" Kit yapped, annoyed. "Me! A god! Covered in mud!"

The beast froze, hearing Kit. Tessa gasped as it began slowly, but surely, heading toward the fox.

Kit yowled, sprinting the other way, and Tessa had to race behind the monster, the bracelet pulling them together.

"Wait!" she cried out. "Kit, you're bringing me straight toward the beast!"

Their plan was falling apart. The fox was having trouble keeping up; he was too small to outrun a creature nearly fifty feet tall. His form flickered, and Tessa's bracelet tugged her toward him with a burning pain.

"Kit!" Tessa shouted. "Come this way!"

The kitsune let out another screech, darting around the trees as the creature plowed through the forest after him.

"Let me carry you!" Jin shouted, too.

"He needs to be by me so I can move! You get the curse!" Tessa yelled. "Come here, Kit!"

The fox glanced over his shoulder. "I'm not going near—"

"Trust me!"

No one ever did. Tessa began running faster.

But to her surprise, the fox turned toward her, sprinting past the creature, and then diving into the thick shrubs to Tessa's left. "Hey, rock-head! She's all yours!"

Typical Kit. Of course the fox was going to use her as a sacrifice.

The creature cranked his body toward Tessa. There was a sense of torment to the way the creature had belligerently stomped through the forest, and Tessa *understood*. She had spent days hearing the shouts and laughter of her tormentors, and not knowing where to go or how to make it stop.

"Hey! Over here!" Jin roared from the monster's other side. It looked between Tessa and Jin, momentarily confused—but giving Tessa just enough time for an idea to spark in her mind.

The boulder-creature's feet pounded down, slamming through another tree. It toppled over, with a thud that echoed through the forest.

"Kit! Jin!" Tessa cried. She clambered up a slightly slanted pine tree, an older one that had fallen onto another. "Plan C: Lead it over here and run up this tree!"

"Do I *look* like a monkey?" the fox shouted, poking his head out of the bushes, but he dashed her way. The boulder-creature pounded behind the tired, weary kitsune, but he raced up the slightly slanted trunk, as far as he could, and then he jumped—

At the same time, Jin raced toward her, shouting and yelling at the monster, distracting the beast just enough for Tessa to sprint forward.

When the boulder-creature threw out a punch, Tessa leaped with all her might and jumped onto its left rock-arm, dashing up its shoulder. Running from the camera lenses and the bullies had trained her—and she'd always been able to get out of sight pretty fast—but she'd never sprinted like this. She grabbed at the paper, but it was too far out of reach.

From the corner of her eye, she could see the monster's right hand swing toward her, and everything seemed to freeze.

She wasn't going to make it home, after all.

"Rah!"

Kit. The fox had run up the tree. A boom reverberated in the air, and for a split second, Tessa caught the glimpse of a glowing outline expanding from Kit's body—but he wasn't a fox. It was a young man, a samurai in armor with a glittering sword in his hand—and he slammed the blade against the rock creature's fist. Then she blinked, and it was Jin *and* the fox, who had both collided into the rocky fist in midair, stopping it from hitting her.

"Get the ofuda!" the fox shouted from where he'd fallen.

Jin shouted, "Now, Miyata!"

The monster's other arm reared back, to smash the limping kitsune straight into the ground—

Jin dove for the fox, to pull him out of the way, but he wasn't fast enough—

Tessa scraped at the curse paper, her nails chipping. There was a burning sensation at her fingertips, but she pushed through as the beast's fist drove down toward the ground...

...and tore it off.

The rock creature froze, its hand an inch from Kit's muzzle. In the next second, the curse paper burst into flames and crumbled into ashes that blew away with the breeze.

Before their eyes, the rock monster shrunk and shrunk, disappearing into a pile of leaves. It was no longer powered by the curse.

The ōkami charm on her bracelet tinkled; Tessa could've sworn it'd let out a faint howl. She gave it a shake, but all she could hear was a brush of wind running against leaves.

Wait—a breeze? Air was finally flowing through the forest. Tessa's jaw dropped. The thick vines were disappearing from where they were wrapped tightly around the trunks. The trees that had fallen over in the monster's stampede went upright, melding into place like they'd never been broken. A trilling bird's cry echoed through the trees, soon answered by another chirp.

Jin, Kit, and Tessa stared at each other in disbelief. They'd survived the first torii—together. *And* released the curse.

Then a small voice squeaked, "Why, hello there!"

23

A *ROCK* WAS TALKING TO THEM.

It was a small oval rock that barely reached up to Tessa's knees. He had a bright red bib tied around his neck with carved eyes crinkled into little half-moons. His small legs and arms kind of reminded Tessa of turtle flippers; he was using these to dip into a little bow.

"Thank you for saving me," the figure said cheerily. "I am Jizo, and I am quite grateful to be released from the curse."

"The God of Lost Children and Travelers?" Jin looked gobsmacked. "Jizo-sama...you...you *talk*? I've visited one of your temples where there's tons of little statues of you. My...my mom used to tell me that you watch over me. Wait, no, this can't be real."

"I am very real!" little Jizo said. "Someone stuck that curse on me to make me that angry boulder, and I haven't been myself for *decades*! Or has it been minutes? I'm not sure...time passes strangely here."

"Do you have that curse paper?" Kit asked Tessa.

She shook her head. "It burned up."

"Darn," Kit grumbled, scratching his notched ear. "It probably showed who made it. I'd have a word or two for whoever did this to Jizo."

The little god turned to look at them each in turn. "Please do tell, what are your names?"

The fox puffed up his chest. "I'm going by Kit now, but that's not my real name. Do you—maybe we knew each other before—?" Jizo turned his head to the side, and the kitsune deflated. "You don't recognize me either, huh."

"I'm Jin Uehara," Jin said reverently, and Jizo nodded, writing in a little book that had appeared out of thin air, with a pen that looked like it was made of pure rock. The boy sat down, his legs tucked neatly under him, and folded into a deep bow, not even noticing how his shorts were getting dusty from the dirt. "It's an honor to meet you."

"They never bowed for me," Kit muttered sulkily. "Ungrateful urchins."

"Tessa Miyata. Nice to meet you, Jizo-sama," she said, ignoring the fox, and also dipping into a bow.

The little guardian's eyes crinkled into a smile as he jotted down her name. "Thank you, thank you all for saving me! Ready to go to the next torii, so you can try your hand at attending the Academy of Gods?"

"We're going to the next torii, but not for the Academy. We need return to Tokyo," Tessa said.

"Whatever for?" Jizo asked.

Jin cleared his throat, quickly explaining what had happened with Lord Taira.

The rock god gasped. "Lord Taira. *The* Lord Taira! Why, in my time, he was a good soul that always used his strength for the betterment of mortals, spirits, or anyone in need."

"That's what I said!" Kit chimed in.

"Though, of course, he was a little bit of a troublemaker," Jizo added.

"Well, in the current timeline, he's a *big* troublemaker," Tessa said. "He thinks Kit tried to kill him, so he's trying to get revenge, and he's also trying to collect *all* the power in Tokyo for himself."

The rock god turned a whiteish stone hue. "That *is* a lot of trouble. Though perhaps I can help. I am one of the Protectors of the Academy Entrance Exam; I review potential initiates who challenge this torii for their worthiness to go to the school of future gods. Though, obviously, I am usually *not* in a cursed form."

"May we go on to the next torii, then? We can't really linger." Jin glanced over at Tessa and Kit; she nodded.

"Oh, oh." Jizo eyed Jin's fading fingertips and Tessa's

disappearing arm. "I see the City is trying to take its dues. Well, as a thank you for your help, I'll get your results quickly tallied so you can get on your way in no time! Just shake this."

His notebook vanished and turned into a small rock that hovered in the air.

"Um, you want us to shake a rock?" Jin asked. "I didn't have to do this before."

Jizo was already bouncing at their feet, nudging them forward. "Go on! Consider this a little bonus. Give it a whirl."

There was something so sweet about him—at least, when he wasn't cursed.

Jin blinked. "What exactly does shaking this rock do?"

"This is an omikuji. You know, to tell your fortune." Jizo turned toward the boulder, bobbing his head side to side. "Let's see...."

"Can't you just look and figure out what'll happen to me?" Tessa asked.

"Ah, but there is much that is yet to be decided," Jizo replied. "Besides, I store all my ku in this Omikuji, so it's far better at foretelling the future than me. Last time I tried guessing someone's future, I decided they were going to have rice balls for lunch, and they ended up in a tsunami instead. Rather poor foresight on my part."

Jizo paused, glancing between Jin, Tessa, and Kit in turn. "After all, sometimes the smallest of things hides the most extraordinary power.... You never know what you may be capable of. My Omikuji of Stone is just one way to get a glimpse at your potential. Now, dear Omikuji, can you please start up?"

The trees shifted, branches weaving together, and formed a wood board. Leafy vines wriggled onto the front, forming letters.

The Fortunes of Omikuji

Great Fortune

Good Fortune

Regular Fortune

Poor Fortune

Worst Fortune

"And the ranks, as you know," Jizo said with a nod. The vines wiggled and formed into another sign:

The Official Ranks

Ruling God

Major God

Minor God

Guardian Spirit

Minor Spirit

God-Blessed Mortal

Mortal

Kit leaped in front of them. "Me, first! I'll show you how powerful I am—"

The instant that his paws touched the Omikuji, a small pebble rolled out, imprinted with black letters: *Worst Fortune.* On the other side, it revealed *Minor Spirit.*

He howled. "I am *not a minor spirit*! And *worst* fortune? I am great, I am renowned, I—"

"Don't even know who you are?" Jin said, striding past Jizo, who was scribbling in his little book.

The fox protested. "I swear, I used to *teach* minor spirits! Not *be* one! I bet I'm a god of scholars—"

"Recorded!" Jizo said brightly. "Kit, minor spirit. Next?"

When Jin shook the rock, it didn't spit out a fortune immediately; rather, the pebbles inside tumbled and tumbled, as if considering what he might be. Finally, a slightly larger rock plopped out, and Jin caught it quickly: *God-Blessed Mortal, Good Fortune.*

"Why, a mortal!" Jizo exclaimed cheerily. "I didn't

realize—I just thought you were one of the modest gods who hide their powers—"

"That's me, that's totally me!" Kit interjected demurely.

"—but if you're a human...Does that mean you've received the Blessing of one of the Seven Lucky Gods? Or perhaps you've already been Chosen?"

Blessing? Chosen? "We're here to train and get a strong enough weapon to fight Lord Taira," Tessa reminded him. "Kit is here so that he'll have enough time to gather ku and fight, too."

"That's right, that's right. Such a pity, when the Academy could use your talents. Well, come on up!" Jizo bounced at her feet. "Another god-blessed mortal, I presume? This is an exciting day for the City! Times are changing!"

As Tessa walked toward the Omikuji, the pine needles shook from a breeze; the wind nipped with a spine-tingling chill. She tried to shake off her worries. *What if I'm nothing?*

When she cupped her hands around the rock, she was hit with a blast of cedar-scented air, just like she'd stepped through the front door of her grandparents' house. Her heart ached even more with the wish to see Ojiichan and make sure he was okay, or to get wrapped up in her sisters' warm hugs.

Tessa gave the Omikuji a firm shake, and the pebbles inside began tumbling around.

"Whoa, what's going on?" Jin gaped.

She blinked; the Omikuji of Stone—once a solid gray—was *glowing*, flickering with a rainbow of colors.

"Um, is this normal?" she squeaked.

Jizo looked like, well, his jaw-dropped expression had frozen into solid rock. "My Omikuji is having trouble deciding. I haven't seen that in a long time."

The faint sound of laughter echoed through the trees. Tessa glanced around, but only the curious faces of Jin, Kit, and little Jizo looked back at her. "Do you guys hear that?"

Then came the faint clatter of two voices that were joyful as birds soaring in the sky; her bracelet burned at her wrist. Emotions washed over her in waves; the sensation of being small yet held so, so close.

"*I will always fight for you, but I cannot fight anymore*," a voice whispered, heartbreakingly sad. She heard the clashing of blades, then a wailing cry.

Pain swelled in her chest and down her body, sudden and engulfing, and Tessa let out a scream. A sharp *crack!* shook her down to her bones.

Someone shouted, "Stop!"

But it was too late; the agony burned through her. Tessa fell backward, slamming into the forest floor.

24

TESSA BLINKED, THE PINE TREES OVERHEAD COMING into focus. A few cherry blossom petals floated through the branches. She shifted—or tried to—and looked down at the weight on her chest.

Kit stood there on all fours, his fur standing up on its ends; his samurai shadow looked like it was straining to give the rock a piece of its mind. "Jizo! What'd you do?"

"I didn't do a thing." The little god shuffled over, eyes wide. "The Omikuji couldn't finish calculating, and now..."

Tessa and Kit followed his gaze down to the stone that Tessa had been holding. It had shattered into dull shards, the strange glow already faded away.

"I'm sorry." Tessa groaned. "I *knew* I was cursed."

"Oh, no, no! Don't feel bad! After how you all saved

me? This is nothing," the little god insisted. "There must be some sort of calibration issue after all these years of no use! Or has it been only days? I'm not sure....Long days, short years, you know? Or was it short days and long years...."

From Tessa's left, Jin held his arm out to her. "You okay?"

She waved aside his hand and sat up, looking around. The sign that had shown the ranks and levels of fortune had shriveled into brittle sticks; the vines were limp and dried.

"You have another omikuji, right?" Tessa asked.

"I'll build another one—"

"That's great!" Tessa was relieved.

"—it'll only take a year or so."

"Oh."

The small book appeared in front of Jizo again, and the little god scribbled in it. "Tessa Miyata, *postponed*."

"I'm so sorry. I really don't know how this happened—"

"You released me from that curse. That's enough payment for me." Jizo winked. "Besides, those whose strength cannot be so quickly measured may seem unassuming; a blessing and a curse. However, because their potential is not yet defined, it means their potential is also *limitless*."

She didn't understand what the little god was saying. Her? Limitless? One run around the obstacle course had shown how limited her strength was. Still, he had already started collecting rocks for a new omikuji, lining them up one by one.

Tessa looked around for more. "Oh! We can help—"

"No, no! Go on, your fate awaits," Jizo said. With another nod of his head, a shimmering gate appeared, with the dry dirt clearing of the Dojo on the other side. "As long as you promise to return for your fortune, someday."

"But..."

Jin murmured, "We need to get going."

"Lord Taira isn't going to wait for anyone," Kit reminded her.

Tessa grimaced but slowly nodded. "Thank you for your help, Jizo-sama. And I really am sorry about the Omikuji." Maybe, if not now, there would be some way to repay him in the future.

Jizo waved them off cheerily. "Just return here another day...or another year...I'll build a new omikuji by then! That will keep me busy, even if no one else visits. Come back soon! And thank you, too!"

The lonely God of Lost Children and Travelers worked intently on his task. To build a new fortune-telling vessel would require much ku, more than his curse-weakened body could generate for now. Though he was a well-known god, with many shrines in his name, the shimenawa circling the City dampened the strength of the prayers coming in to him substantially; no wonder he hadn't been able to break out of that strange curse.

Surely, though, within a year's time or less—if those travelers he had just met could break the shimenawa, like he hoped—he would be able to gather enough energy to create a new, stronger omikuji.

"Ah!" Jizo said, to nobody in particular. The forest was long since empty; only faint bird calls responded to his voice. "There's a perfect rock."

It had a strange pulse of ku. In fact, it was *his* ku, if he wasn't mistaken.

He dug out the pebble embedded in the dirt, a stone's throw from the area where he had met young Miyata and her friends. Then he paused.

It was a stone from his broken Omikuji. The only one that had survived.

Jizo read the fortune, turning it from side to side.

"Well, well," the god murmured. "This will be rather interesting."

25

WHEN THEY STEPPED OUT OF THE FIRST TORII, JIN paused. "What is that?"

Tessa almost slammed straight into him. "The back of your head?"

"No, that." He pointed at something beyond the mist. At first, Tessa thought it was more clouds. But the winds blew toward her face, and the heavy scent of smoke unfurled around her.

She gasped. "Kit, did you see—look—"

The fox sat on his haunches, staring at the plumes of smoke.

"Is that *godfire*?" Kit gasped. "Remember what I told you about sacred places having more doorways into the City of Legends? Well, one of the most sacred places in all of Tokyo is Meiji Jingu. Taira may very well break through the shimenawa."

Tessa pressed her hand to her mouth, fear lancing through her. "Isn't there some way to go there, now—"

"You must pass the second trial to get out. Worse, it would be a death wish if you two tried fighting without a sacred weapon, and me with my drained ku." Kit slowed in front of the torii. "Let's go inside."

Tessa wiped the sweat off her face with the outline of her barely visible hand, and exchanged a glance with Jin, who nodded. "We have to create our weapons, Miyata. We can't fight a god barehanded."

She gazed up at the second torii; it sparkled invitingly, like a welcome from an old friend. Hopefully, it would have a solution for them, too.

The moment they strode through, her jaw dropped. They stood on the banks of a river, the soft, cool breeze swirling along the narrow waterway and over their skin.

"*This* is the second torii?" Tessa asked in awe. Where the first torii's forest had been thick and dark, here the waters danced with the reflection of a crescent moon. Trees arched over the river, branches heavy with white-pink cherry blossoms. On the top of the grassy slope where they were standing, there was a small hut about ten feet away; from its front step, a curving rock path led down the gentle incline and to a dock.

"What do we do here?" Tessa asked, following Jin to the hut. A draft shifted the trees, and petals swirled through the air like snow.

"You're going to make your weapons," Kit said. With a paw, he gestured at a pile of wood within the sloped hut. "For this first step, you're going to train those god-blessed senses of yours to pick out a plank for a weapon. Then use ku to whittle the wood down and make it into a weapon. Transfer your power to it, so it is as strong, no, *stronger* than you."

Jin sat down in front of a low worktable that Tessa hadn't noticed earlier. But he did take a look at Tessa's shocked face as he carefully placed his hands on a cut-up piece of wood.

"Whittle. He said 'whittle,' and he *meant* it," Jin said forlornly to Tessa. She bit down the urge to laugh. Despite her initial hesitations, Jin was growing on her.

"This may seem simple, but you've got to beat a god that's destroying Tokyo with an ancient, legendary sword." Kit stared her down. "You need the best weapon you can create."

"But what kind of weapon is made out of *wood*?" Tessa questioned. "Do we cast it into steel after this?"

"It's no ordinary wood. These are fallen branches from the enchanted Tree of Hope, similar to its cousin, the Tree of Time. Hinoki is a type of cypress known for its signature lemon-like scent and its usage in creations from things as varied as temples to palaces to magical torii," Kit said.

"But, again, *wood* against steel?" Tessa asked.

"Hinoki is pure, and by nature collects ku. It is one of the most powerful weapons a human can wield in the face of evil. *This* is what will give us the advantage over Lord Taira. That is, if you fight with every drop of sweat, with every bone in your body, even if it burns or even if you bleed." Kit padded closer. "Ame futte, ji kata-maru. *After the rain, the earth hardens.* The two of you have gone through a *lot* of rain, a lot of training, and the final thing you need is a weapon all your own. Without a hinoki weapon, even *thinking* of beating Lord Taira with your wimpy mortal strength is impossible."

"Seeing as we're hanging out with a nine-tailed fox who talks, maybe things aren't so impossible after all," Tessa muttered.

Kit winked. "I'll take the credit, thank you. Now, go. Look at the wall of weapons on the hut. Determine which is the right one for you, plan it out, find the right piece of wood." He gave them a toothy grin. "No more time to dawdle. Or I'll show you just how sharp hinoki is."

"Okay, okay," Tessa mumbled. "I'm moving!"

She spun around. There was a rack of wood weapons displayed on pegs, from a katana just about the same length as the Sword of a Thousand Souls to a battle-ax and a sharp, pointed naginata, all the way down to a kunai dagger.

"What are you making?" Tessa asked Jin.

"A bō." Jin tapped his hunk of wood. "It's reliable,

straightforward. Good for longer-distance fighting and a solid defense."

Tessa hovered in front of the katana. Was *this* going to be her weapon? Could she fight using something like this that was almost as tall as her?

"Make your choice." Kit paced behind her, faster than ever. "You must create your weapon, quickly. We don't have a minute to waste."

Tessa didn't need to summon the Tree of Time to know they were almost already through their third day. Then she noticed something small hung on a peg beyond the katana, with four points and a little circle in the middle. When she picked it up, her hands filled with warmth, like there was something familiar about it, even though she'd never held anything like this before. The wood was intricately whittled, with sharp edges zipping along the sides and a circle in the middle in the shape of a ring.

"A shuriken?" Kit asked. "I thought you were going for the katana."

There was no time to waver. "I'll make this."

"Good," Kit said. "Now, I have to rest and try to gather more ku."

Tessa's shoulders weighed down with guilt. The fox had lost a lot of his strength because of her.

Kit gave her a knowing look. "We have to do whatever it takes to win. That Lord Taira has done plenty of

destruction in three minutes. But we're spending those few minutes away from the real world to get stronger, so that we *do* survive when we see him again."

Tessa and Jin exchanged glances. Jin, who'd had access to the second torii before her, didn't seem any more confident.

Kit's nine tails flicked. "It's not going to be easy, but you *have* to get through."

Tessa looked up at the moon low in the night sky, and swallowed. Then she took a seat at another table that had appeared in front of Jin, so that she faced him. With a deep breath and a singular focus, she began to draw ku out of the air and into the wood. The plank shimmered with a gleam of white, as the outline of a throwing star began to form.

But—Tessa faltered, thinking of Lord Taira, rampaging through the buildings of Tokyo—and the wood cracked. She groaned. The fox eyed it, curled up, and went straight to sleep.

"That's what happens to me, too." Jin gestured at the pile of broken pieces next to him; he hadn't been able to get very far on his bō. "It's impossible to keep gathering ku for a whole weapon; it breaks the moment I stop to take a breath or anything."

"What do we do with these weapons, anyway, to prove that we've beat this challenge?" Tessa asked. "Do we have to fight each other and show how worthy we are or something?"

"Look," Jin said, his voice hushed, nodding toward the river.

She followed his gaze to the dock. Where there had been simply empty water before, a small boat floated with a ghostly figure standing inside, holding a pole to guide the boat.

"That woman comes by every once in a while. Kit says that's how you get out of this torii." Jin grabbed a piece of wood off the ground. "Follow me."

They walked down the weathered, mossy stones to the water's edge and stepped onto the wood dock. The woman was dressed in beautiful robes, with a sword at her waist, and she watched them with misty eyes.

Jin bowed and handed over the piece of wood with

outstretched hands. The woman plucked it up, turning the piece of wood over—

And it burst into neon flames.

The woman shook her head, grabbed the long pole for the boat, and pushed off.

Jin sighed. "If she accepts it, Kit says you're allowed onto the boat and get to take it down the river and into that torii."

A red-orange gate was visible on the far right, shimmering through the mists that covered everything else from view.

"That's the way out?"

Jin nodded. "Kit said that'll take us to Lord Taira."

Tessa trained her eyes on it, searing that image into her mind: the long pillars, the stretch of painted wood connecting the two pillars on top, but most of all, the ku in between the posts, murmuring of the future.

She felt the imprint of each passing second, like rope winding around her lungs, making it difficult to breathe. Tessa had to clear this challenge.

Her sneakers squeaked as she turned and ran up the riverbank. Her footsteps were light on the stone, but her heartbeat pounded as she raced to the pile of wood.

No matter what it would take, Tessa *was* going to make it home to her family.

26

NEARLY A FULL DAY LATER, TESSA SWEPT A PILE OF splintered wood to the side, the faint earthy scent coating her every pore.

She could barely see the outline of her lower body anymore. She was becoming part of the City, but she wasn't ready to disappear yet; she knew that much. Tessa hadn't even wanted to sleep, but Kit and Jin had nudged her out of the second torii and into the Dojo. Seeing the Tree of Time—its beautiful, fragrant blossoms fading away—had made it difficult to fall asleep, but exhaustion had taken her into a dreamless slumber. Still, resting hadn't been enough to help her.

She was missing something. These tests weren't about dumb luck or brute force. Each obstacle led one step closer—for any normal test taker—to that Academy of Gods. If trials were all about collecting the brightest and best in Japan, for the potential of serving or even becoming a god, its standards were obviously high.

Just whittling the wood with spirit energy didn't seem like the right answer.

"The first torii was about survival," Tessa murmured out loud. Jin looked up, and she continued, "At least, that's what I thought it was about, with the one-hour countdown and all. But it wasn't really, was it? I wouldn't have been able to survive alone; I think it was about teamwork."

Jin bowed his head. "I passed the first time because I dodged and outmaneuvered that cursed version of Jizo-sama, so I guess I got through only because of my karate experience. Or maybe it's about being valiant, because you can't face a creature like that and not be brave."

Kit's tail twitched, but it looked like the fox was still sound asleep. He wasn't going to be sharing answers anytime soon.

Then Jin turned his head to the side. "What if it's both? Maybe the Dojo expects everyone to be valiant and have some sense of teamwork to get into the Academy."

She nodded. That did sound reasonable; the torii wouldn't necessarily test just one thing.

"So then what's this one about?" Tessa asked, looking around.

"I think it's about focusing on ku. Understanding ku."

"That makes sense, I guess." Tessa tapped her fingers

against the wood plank. Somehow, though, she wondered if it was about more than just that.

"Or maybe it's about getting rides from strange people on boats," Jin said.

"Good point. I hope you finish your weapon first so you can test that theory out."

With a snort, he tucked his head down to work on his weapon.

Tessa studied the plank in front of her. Then she stood up to pace in front of the pile. All the pieces were different sizes and shapes, half hidden in the shadows of the hut.

She had to use ku to whittle it. . . .

There was a sudden growl, a flash of heat on her wrist. The ōkami charm. Tessa needed to think this through better. There was something she was missing . . . the key to *why* this torii was so important to beating Taira Masakado. . . .

What if she also had to use *ku* to find the right piece of wood?

Tessa reached out for the strands of energy—just out of sight, though she swore she caught a glimpse of glowing white strands in the corner of her eye—and tugged, pulling it around her right hand.

Her fingers prickled with energy, filled with a warmth that was like grabbing one of Cecilia's special oatmeal raisin cookies, straight off the tray. But getting through the second torii would be sweeter than even the piles of snowdrops and gingerbread that she and her sisters baked during the holidays for her sisters' cookie exchanges with their friends.

She stretched her right hand toward the wood, but she didn't feel anything.

Yikes and Yakult. She'd been hoping for some sort of divine guidance that would tell her which piece to pick.

Tessa paused. What if she needed to *see* the hinoki?

Another handful of ku, warm and soft as yarn. This time, she guided it up, like the way she washed her face in the morning with a splash of water.

The ku covered her skin in a strange, warm layer, almost like a hoodie. She blinked, the world around her shimmering with ku strands, but she didn't have time to gape in awe. Instead, she focused on the pile of wood.

This time, she could *see* the hinoki for what it truly was. Some blocks were filled with light; others were dim, like a bulb that was just about to burn out.

She dug around. At the bottom, she found a wide, flat piece that she swore had faint outlines of not just one, but multiple shuriken.

Perfect.

Tessa was about to return to her table when she noticed another slab of hinoki. Long like a staff, it glowed with warmth, though there were hints of darkness at its edges.

She hefted it over to Jin. The piece was almost as tall

as her, and Jin looked up in surprise, his concentration breaking. The block he was working on shattered, and he groaned. "I was just about—"

"I used ku to choose this hinoki," Tessa said. "This one might be good for a bō...if you want it, of course."

His eyes widened. "Thanks, Miyata."

She nodded, grabbed her block, and quickly hurried to her table. But when she peeked up, Jin was looking at the wood thoughtfully, like he was seeing something he'd never noticed before.

He glanced up, and their gazes connected, fast as a spark of ku. Tessa gave him a tiny, hopeful smile—*I hope you're not mad; I didn't mean for that piece you were working on to break*—and her pounding heart settled when he gave her a quick nod.

With that, Tessa was ready to focus on making the best shuriken that she'd ever wield. Strong enough to fight a god and save everyone she cared about, too.

Which, to her surprise, was beginning to include Jin.

27

THEY WERE DOWN TO THEIR LAST HOURS. KIT SUM-moned the Tree of Time and used some ku to make it stay; an ominous presence, despite its beauty. Only three cherry blossoms remained on the fifth and final branch.

Tessa sat cross-legged in front of the low table, the gentle air currents filled with the prayers swirling around her as she glared at the hinoki block that she'd picked out. Her fingers hesitated whenever she inched them forward.

Her body still ached from the fight to free Jizo. Her soul was weary from trying and trying to form the other pieces of hinoki into *something*, and from coming up with no more than ashes. Her bones and muscles ached with tiredness, and she knew it'd be better if she slept. But she couldn't stop thinking about that vision of Lord Taira rampaging through Tokyo, and worrying about where her sisters were.

Jin sat in front of his table, his shoulders sloped with weariness. They hadn't broken these blocks that Tessa had picked up—but that was only because they hadn't attempted to try whittling them yet.

It felt like there was something too real about using ku on it. Like, if the hinoki did break, then it meant they'd *never* be able to save Tokyo.

Jin looked up at the moonlight filtering through the trees. Half of his body was an ethereal shimmer; it was strangely split sideways, turning invisible from his chest down. "We'll be stuck here if we don't try."

She sighed. Jin was right.

Tessa glared at the wood, wishing it was Lord Taira; at least if he was a piece of hinoki, she'd be able to crack his armor easily. "After the rain, the earth hardens. There is no way I'll let all of Meiji Jingu burn up before we fight Lord Taira. And I've had *plenty* of rain—"

The hinoki glowed.

Tessa scrambled backward. "Did you see that? No. Way. I need to sleep."

But the hinoki was *still* glowing, and Jin's wide eyes were glued to it, too. "You did it."

Kit poked his head up, his tail uncurling. "Keep working, Miyata."

Jin hurriedly put his hands over his wood piece. But Tessa couldn't focus on him. Her fingers felt like they were burning with a lightless flame, with energy itching to go somewhere, or she'd combust. She guided the ku out through her fingertips, into the wood, and felt it jump back to her.

"It's like a circuit," she whispered. "A continual system."

Kit nodded. "That's right. Your ku goes into the purified hinoki, which reflects it back."

"Like the Yamanote train line?" Jin asked. "A perpetual circle."

"Exactly." Kit grinned, his sharp teeth peeking out. "But with the power of a god-blessed, so it's a ton stronger. Think of a windstorm, with speeds picking up and up."

"As an idea, that makes sense." Jin shot a look at the glowing light flowing from Tessa's fingers to the wood. "But seeing this? It's hard to understand."

"What I understand is that we're getting what we need to fight Lord Taira," Tessa said, grinning. Euphoria filled her veins, bright and happy as listening to her favorite song on repeat, at just the right time. It was almost *like* that—having her earbuds plugged in, and in that moment, it wasn't the teasing or the videos from her classmates bothering her; it was just her and her favorite playlist.

Tessa closed her eyes as she gathered a breath and pulled in more energy from the air—feeling that peculiar *tug* in her heart as she gathered in the prayers and pushed them out her fingertips.

Jin gasped. Kit cleared his throat. "You've got a lot to catch up on, Uehara."

Tessa's eyes flew open, and she stared at the wood; the swirling light had carved it out like a laser, into the shape of a star. No...it wasn't any star....

"Nice shuriken," the fox said. Tessa might've been hearing things, but she could've sworn that there was a trace of pride in his voice. "Time for you to make another. It'll be better to have more than one." His eyes cut to Jin. "And you need to catch up."

Jin glared at his lump of hinoki, still a solid slab.

Her body felt like it had been opened up to sensations. She could hear his frustrated sigh, even though it was impossibly soft.

"How do you get ku so easily?" Jin asked.

Tessa paused. She hadn't thought of it before, but it had seemed simple, oddly enough, though Kit made it out to be mystical.

"I focused on memories where I was trying to help others, because I figure that ku is prayers, right? So I just thought that the spirit energy is looking for someone who wants to do something with that energy, something to help out." Then she paused. "This torii...this challenge...maybe it's about resilience. About not giving up. And a part of that is *focus*. Which is why we have to use our ku on the wood."

Jin nodded slowly, his eyes lighting up. "You're right, Tess—er, Miyata."

She grinned back. They were in this together. They would fight against a god, side by side. He wasn't like her classmates, not after all they'd been through together.

Again, she bent her head over the hinoki, her heart burning with prayers.

Sweat dripped from Tessa's forehead, curving down her nearly invisible cheeks. It had been almost five full days since they had first entered the Dojo. It had been two full tries to free Jizo. It had been countless attempts to build a weapon worthy of fighting Lord Taira. And with every day, another minute passed in the world outside.

The Tree of Time was all but a stump. The last petal clung to its stem. But, this time, Tessa was ready for it to fall.

Now, six shuriken, carved out of hinoki, hung from a red string on her waist. Kit had given her the magical scarlet cord; it released a throwing star into her hand whenever she brushed her fingers against the string. She held the seventh shuriken in her right hand as she spun and ducked under Jin's incoming attack with his hinoki bō—the long staff gleamed with god-blessed light—and threw the throwing star, pushing it forward with her energy.

It landed straight and proud on the wall of the hut, a more intricately designed version of the sample. It was, to Tessa, absolutely perfect.

She was almost pure ether; her body ready to stay as part of the City forever.

But she couldn't stay. She *refused* to stay.

Jin slipped to the ground, his cheer another sad sigh of relief. He was almost no more than an outline, his life-force almost completely tied to the City, too.

This was no celebration.

Tokyo was getting destroyed by Lord Taira. They could wait no longer.

Side by side, they walked down the riverbank and onto the dock, with Kit close at their heels. Tessa held out a shuriken; Jin held his bō. The citrusy scent of hinoki flowed all around them, like the air itself was filled with promise.

The woman standing in the boat looked them over and held her hand above Jin's bō. Tessa gasped as it burst into neon flames—

But the bō stayed intact, burning within the bright glow.

"That's the power of purified hinoki." Kit nodded in approval.

The woman gestured for Jin to step into the boat. When he was seated at the front, the woman turned to Tessa.

Her heartbeat pounded like a drum. Wisps of hair stuck to her forehead with sweat, but she didn't dare wipe her face.

Instead, she held the seven shuriken out.

The woman paused, her fingers running over them, then *whoosh!*

Neon flames blazed...yet Tessa's shuriken stayed whole.

She wanted to melt to the dock with relief, but the woman was already motioning her onboard and picking up her long pole to push off.

When she slid onto the bench next to Jin, she felt like she was as fluid as the water flowing around the boat.

"You did it," Kit said proudly from his spot in between them.

Jin nodded. "We did it, together."

Tessa's heart brimmed with hope. "We can save Tokyo."

The ghostly woman began rowing, her pole sluicing through water, and the boat picked up with a magical speed. A soft, gentle music flowed from the torii, beckoning them out of the second challenge. The mist cooled Tessa's body, helping her focus on what lay ahead.

They were as ready as they would ever be to return to Tokyo...to face Lord Taira.

As they glided through the gate, the last petal from the Tree of Time tumbled down, fluttering a quiet farewell.

III

A Dull Blade

28

Lightning flashed, burning everything to white. Creaking gears screeched, like time was changing around them, then—silence.

Tall grasses rippled at their feet, as they stood behind the main shrine of Meiji Jingu, without a dojo anywhere to be seen.

Jin breathed out with relief. "We're back. Our bodies are whole."

Tessa and Jin were full flesh, no longer shimmering mirages with each passing hour counted by another inch of disappearing skin.

But not Kit.

The fox looked down at his body, nearly fully transparent, with the lightest of outlines. All of his nine tails were like curls of mist, faint and barely there. If not for the bracelet connecting the two of them, Tessa might've not seen him at first.

She stared. "I thought we were disappearing because we were in the Dojo. What's going on?"

"I'm a little low on ku. But I'll be okay once the Seven Gods reinstate my memories, because I can figure out my identity and claim the ku that goes to my shrine." Kit's tails unfurled. "It's fine. We just have to beat Lord Taira, okay? Meiji, first."

Guilt filled her stomach. It was because of her that Kit was out of ku: first to get away from Lord Taira, and then to survive the Armory.

But she couldn't go back in time; Tessa could only fight the next challenge—and hopefully survive. They turned to face the shrine, but Meiji Jingu was almost unrecognizable.

It burned. The stately wood building was consumed by flames that almost looked like water, stretching over the planks with a glossy neon sheen. The blaze tore at the wood foundation and fire plumed from the seafoam-green rooftops; Meiji, one of Tokyo's most famous shrines, was burning away into ether as the fire spread, inch by inch. The breeze carried a smoky, slightly bitter scent.

Kit gritted his teeth. "With that godfire, I wonder... yes...he might be very well trying to destroy the City, too."

Tessa gasped, remembering the shrine she'd seen

when they'd first entered the magical City. The neon flames had looked beautiful—until Kit had told her how they could destroy a god.

"How can we put it out?" Jin asked, his face pale. "Is there water around here?"

A group of coughing shrine workers stumbled out a side exit. They were dressed in white shirts and flowing red traditional pants.

"Is everyone safe?" Jin leaped forward. Tessa and Kit ran close behind.

A woman with a thin face looked around. "There are still a few people missing.... My younger brother should be out here. I told Manjirō to leave first. Have you seen him?"

The others shook their heads.

A man, maybe a few years older, glanced worriedly over his shoulder. "I ran.... We all had to run. We'll do a count. We can't do much with this strange fire, so we all had to get out. I'm sure Manjirō's around, up to no good as usual."

Tessa swallowed. "We have to do something about the fire—"

"Over there!" Kit led the way as they raced along the walls of the shrine, rippling in that deadly fire. The shrine was as wide as a football field, and Tessa finally thanked Jin for their seemingly endless rounds of running around the Dojo.

There were a few hinoki buckets next to the fountain that shrinegoers used to cleanse their hands before entering. Holy water had to fix things. Seconds later, Tessa and Jin stumbled toward the fire with sloshing buckets. The crackling flames tickled her cheeks, but her skin didn't burn from the heat.

Bucket by bucket, they put out about six feet of the fire that had been devouring the building.

It wasn't enough. The godfire spread elsewhere along the walls.

A shriek came from the side of the shrine, where workers had gathered.

"Manjirō!" the woman from earlier cried. "He's missing. He's still inside!"

"There're others missing, too," gasped another of the shrine workers. "All the ones that work in the innermost area. If they're not here, that means none of the tourists made it out, either."

Her sisters.

No. Surely Peyton had convinced Cecilia to go look for some ramen, or Cecilia had seen a stationery store and gotten lost in its aisles.

Tessa's heart thudded in her chest. She looked down at her nearly empty bucket. The fire wouldn't get quenched in time, no matter how many buckets she poured. Not enough for her to save anyone. But she couldn't let Meiji Jingu be razed into flames.

"Wait—" Tessa waved her hand close to the fire. Oddly, she didn't feel a prickle of heat. "Is this—"

"Mortals can bypass godfire," Kit explained. "It doesn't hurt if you're still a human. However, you see it since you're god-blessed. Since Meiji is so sacred, it's unsurprising that those working here were able to sense the malaise of the godfire and see it as some sort of fire, too. But if you stay too long, it'll start melting your life-force again, like the Dojo of Many Doors."

"Where are the Seven Gods during a time like this? Are they still stuck in their shrines, refusing to help? Then there's nothing that'll save Manjirō and the others in time." Tessa studied the side entrance, flickering with godfire. "My sisters could be in there."

Jin shook his head. "No. No, Tessa. Don't get any ideas."

"Manjirō is her brother," Tessa said firmly. "And there are others who are someone's brother, someone's friend...someone's somebody."

And that was reason enough.

"Stay back, Kit!" Tessa called over her shoulder. "I'll find them!"

With that, she plunged into the fiery shrine, the flames dancing along her skin, and a fire of her own burning inside her heart.

29

THE SHRINE WAS BEAUTIFUL EVEN AS IT BURNED INTO flames and ether. It reminded Tessa of an ant she'd studied in sixth grade science, encased in amber. Its legs were set at a funny angle, as if it'd been just on a casual walk, not realizing it was about to be stuck forever. Not realizing it was dying until it was far too late.

Tessa ran to the small counter that sold omamori. On the shelves, the beautiful cloth protection charms were unraveling in the flames. She rose on her toes to look beyond the counter, but no one was around.

"Manjirō!" she shouted. Flames filled her, drying out her mouth, but she didn't burn even as she sweated from the strange feeling of standing in fire.

"You're not doing this alone," said a voice behind her.

The string on her wrist hummed with energy, the

line leading straight to Kit. Jin was holding the fox in his arms. The kitsune's eyes flashed with fury.

Tessa protested. "But—"

"I said I'd protect you. And tell me how I'm supposed to do that if you run off without me? We're connected, remember?"

"Our connection is getting weaker," Tessa snapped. "You could've stayed outside."

"Just because I could've, doesn't mean I should've," Kit replied snarkily. Deep down, Tessa felt a flicker of warmth. Still, that didn't mean he *should* be in danger.

She switched her glare to Jin.

"I'm just here to make sure no one gets hurt," Jin offered. "What? I mean, it wasn't like Kit could cross over the godfire alone."

Tessa rolled her eyes, even though she was secretly glad to have them with her.

"Where are you, Manjirō?" Jin called. "Hello? Can anyone hear us?"

An answering shriek came from deeper in the shrine, and Tessa's stomach curdled.

"Duck!" Jin cried out.

Tessa flattened herself against the dirt; something swooshed overhead.

An arrow made of shadows embedded itself in the wall behind where she had just been standing, before dissolving in godfire.

"I'm guessing these visitors aren't here to pray," Kit growled.

Warriors flew toward them, formed from an inky bleakness.

"Shadow warriors," the fox snarled. "These are the real deal, more dangerous than the ones from the obstacle course. Their blades may look like smoke, but they *will* harm you."

Seven warriors fanned out to surround them, with sharp katanas pointed out.

Tessa held a hinoki throwing star in each hand. She breathed in a deep breath, filling her lungs with prayers and hopes, and threw them at the nearest one, to her right.

Her first shuriken flew straight past the warrior's head, and he let out an inhuman shriek of glee as he darted forward. But the second embedded itself into the warrior's outstretched arm. The warrior let out a garbled cry and then faded in swirls of mist, leaving the hinoki to drop onto the empty ground.

Jin darted forward with a yell, sliding into the form of the first kata, a basic but reliable fighting pattern. His bō slammed down, but the shadow warrior deflected it with a sideways swipe of a katana, and Jin stumbled backward. He parried quickly, protecting his side from another attack.

On Jin's other side, Kit was snapping at two of the shadow warriors, using his smaller size to his advantage and zipping around them, his nine tails whirling and his teeth flashing.

But if they were fighting four shadow warriors, where were the others—

Kit let out a piercing yelp as the remaining two shadow warriors leapt toward him, and Tessa flung her arm out, but the shuriken couldn't fly fast enough as one of the shadow warriors' katanas sliced at Kit.

She screamed, fumbling with her string of shuriken to grab another, and shot the hinoki star toward the attacker. The shadow warrior vanished in a swirl of smoke, but Kit limped as he tore off another warrior from his shoulders.

Sweat beaded their foreheads when Jin battled the last warrior and sent it away with a succession of raps on its body.

"Kit, are you okay?" Tessa said, dropping to her knees. "Your leg—"

The fox shook his head. "We don't have time to waste. The godfire is burning stronger."

Above Kit, Tessa and Jin's eyes met, both filled with worry.

"I'm fine," Kit said quickly. "Every moment we stand around is a moment wasted to help anyone trapped. I'll visit the healers in the City after this, and they'll fix me up good as new."

Tessa nodded. She'd make sure the fox got the best of care. "Let's go!"

She jumped over the godfire—still low, thankfully—in the next doorway that led deeper into the shrine. Jin held Kit, following close behind.

But when they entered the next section, she stumbled in shock.

The main area of the shrine was a square, with the prayer boxes on the far side. For one impossible moment, she hoped to see the shrine workers walk out, unharmed but eager to get out of the fire.

"No..." Kit growled from her side.

In the center, a samurai in dark armor stood, his sword flashing from the light of the flames, and a dozen shrine workers were crumpled before him, dazed and confused. A teenage boy was curled up, tear tracks staining his cheeks. "I want to return to my sister!"

Those words stabbed Tessa's heart. These were the people of Tokyo she'd been fighting through the Dojo to save.

But when the boy tried to move toward the doorway, Lord Taira flicked his hand, and shadow warriors chased him back.

Manjirō.

The boy jolted as the roof crashed into the prayer boxes. The other shrine workers gathered him into the protection of their circle. But Lord Taira didn't flinch; he merely tapped his fingers on his other arm, the black armor gleaming with the reflection of the neon light.

"That armor," Kit gasped. "It repels godfire. Now

I'm wondering if Lord Taira sold his soul to Kagutsuchi. No one but the God of Fire knows the secret of how to make that."

Lord Taira looked up, his dark, cold eyes meeting Tessa's and then sliding over to Jin.

Then, finally, Lord Taira looked down at Kit, and his lips twisted into a sneer. "Ah, I sensed that you were close by. Of course, I was right. And I am *so* happy to have you join us."

Tessa felt sick. They were the reason why Lord Taira had rampaged all the way from Asakusa to Meiji Jingu. They were why so many had gotten hurt.

From where they'd entered, godfire roared up, beyond a height that Tessa or Jin could jump with Kit in their arms.

They were trapped.

Worse, there were a handful of tourists—Tessa could tell by their casual clothes—looking around in confusion, and she wondered what it would be like to not be god-blessed, and to not see the shadow warriors or Lord Taira, or even Kit, yet feel the imminent danger. But she was distracted, looking at two tourists who were huddled against each other.

Two very familiar figures. One in all black, the other with flowing hair and a floral dress.

Tessa gasped. "Peyton. Cecilia."

Her sisters were here.

30

Kit flicked his nine tails, and Tessa felt something cover her face. A mask. She pulled it off to see that the thin wood was carved into the sharp face of a tiger, matching her coat, with the citrusy-sharp scent of hinoki.

"Why—"

"You *must* hide your identity," Kit said. "Use this mask. It's like the ku-shield I used on you to hide your life-force from the Gods, but this one is used against mortals."

"But—"

"You'll try to get your sisters to escape, but once they see who you are, won't they want to stay and help you?"

They would refuse to leave.

Kit continued, "Those who aren't god-blessed will see a mortal, moving around, but with this, your sisters won't be able to tell who you are. Further, when they see you doing things that only a god-blessed can do, the mask helps them forget it."

He was right. Her sisters would do anything to make sure she was safe. She slid on the mask. The fox had created one for Jin, too; his matched the dragons swirling through the deep blue fabric of his haori.

But Jin wasn't looking at his mask. "Kit! Behind you!"

Lord Taira shot forward, and they barely jumped back in time. Kit yelped, a few of his tail hairs sheared off by the speed of the god's blade. His body shimmered, more transparent than ever.

The god and the fox danced, like a hunter and its prey, throughout the inner confines of the shrine. But Tessa had no time to watch. She was trying to survive.

More than anything, she had to save her sisters.

The god pressed his hands together, and figures rose out of the darkness. Her stomach plummeted. More shadow warriors.

Six warriors descended on her, blades flashing, and she shot out her shuriken, one by one. On the other side of the square, Jin's wood staff flashed left and right, whirling like the blades of a helicopter, but more shadow warriors edged him in, too.

"Get your sisters and the others out of here," Kit shouted to her and Jin. Tessa could feel the air around her spin, as if Kit was pulling all the ku straight into his small body. "I'll fend off the shadow warriors and Lord Taira."

She didn't need to be told twice. Tessa darted around a shadow warrior and headed straight to her sisters.

Peyton, Cecilia, and their five friends clung together, their faces scared and nervous. Dust coated their hair; their eyes were wide with shock.

Tessa wanted to cry with relief to see them, but she had to keep herself together. She needed them to get to safety.

"All of you, follow me!" Then, to Jin, she shouted, "Behind you!"

Jin's staff sparked against one of the shadow warriors' katanas. Some of the tourists stood up, but Peyton shook her head, staring up at Tessa. "We shouldn't leave this place. Nothing's safe! People are disappearing into cracks in the *ground*!"

Tessa's heart dropped. That's what her non-god-blessed saw Lord Taira as: an earthquake.

"It's safer outside of this shrine, I promise," she said, her heart racing.

"I don't know...." Cecilia looked around. She definitely didn't see the shadow warriors, and only frowned, puzzled, when Jin spun around to reflect another sharp blade; her eyes dazed from the magic of the mask.

"Go home!" Jin shouted over his shoulder. "Just get anywhere outside of Tokyo, and you'll be safe."

"We have to stay." Peyton shook her head. "My grandma messaged us. She says our little sister went to Asakusa. If anything we have to head there. I can't leave Tessa behind."

Her chest lurched. They wanted to search for *her*.

"I'm sure she's fine." Jin cleared his throat. "The best thing you can do is to get to safety yourself. I bet if you go home, Te—ah, your sister will be waiting there for you, worrying about you."

Part of the shrine nearest them collapsed; the sacred building was disintegrating in the godfire. Cecilia shrieked as the earth rippled. "We're not going to get out of this alive!"

And behind them, Lord Taira and his shadow warriors were fighting Kit, who raced and bit and growled, controlling the ku as a shimmering outline of a sword. But he was slowing, and his leg wasn't helping him keep up.

"We're out of time!" Jin shouted over to Tessa.

She turned to her sisters and took a deep breath.

"Do this for those you love," Tessa begged. After everything they'd done for her, if she could get them out, this would be the one thing she could finally do right.

"Who are you?" Peyton asked.

"Just a passerby." Sweat pricked Tessa's skin; the flapping edges of the loose haori stuck to her thighs. "But I know there are people who care about you, so won't you please get to safety?"

Cecilia and Peyton looked at each other and finally nodded. Tessa didn't waste a moment; she helped her sisters and their friends stand up. She recognized them from pictures of her sisters' previous trip, and she wished she could take purikura, go eat out, and play arcade games together. This wasn't how she'd wanted to meet them.

But these were her sisters' friends, not hers. And, Tessa's world was completely different now.

"Let's head to that doorway!" Tessa said.

The earth shook beneath them.

Lord Taira and Kit circled each other in the center of the square. Dirt spun through the sky, carried by fast winds, scratching at her skin.

"Run!" Tessa shouted. "Now!"

She led the way, waving her sisters' friends out the door. One, two, three, four, five... All of them, but—

Where were her sisters?

The wind suddenly died out, and a strange feeling tugged at Tessa. A faint howl echoed in her ears; the sound of the lone wolf charm chilled her blood.

She slowly turned around.

Lord Taira stood between Tessa's sisters and the exit.

They were too far away; only twenty feet, but it felt like they were worlds apart.

Kit—blessed, wonderful Kit was in front of them, protecting them from Lord Taira.... But the fox was limping. His shadow—normally a strong samurai, taller than Tessa and Jin combined—was nothing more than a fox, meek and tiny, and his head was bowed.

No. Something was wrong. Terribly wrong.

Could...it couldn't be...

Was...Kit out of ku? Had he used all the prayers and energy he could find...and been left with nothing?

Tessa searched through the air, feeling for the ku that had always seemed to be right there. The air was dead and still, like a stagnant pond, immovably thick. Godfire. It'd stopped all the ku from coming close.

"Kit!" she cried.

Jin echoed her: "Kit? What's going on?"

The fox looked at them. "Change of plans. Get out!"

Her mind flashed back to the alleyway, when he'd used his energy to create a door.

Then, in the Armory, when Kit had used his powers to save her from the blade.

No. No way, no matter if this was Kit's Plan Q or R or S, no matter *what*. There was no way she would leave him.

Tessa kept trying to battle through the warriors, to get back to the fox. But another shadow warrior came from the left, and she had to spin down, pick up a shuriken she'd lost, and fling it up, to make the shadow warrior jump away.

A sharp cry pierced the air; she spun around. Kit crumpled to the ground, huddling around his front right leg, the one that he'd wounded, but he was still fiercely in front of Tessa's sisters. Peyton and Cecilia couldn't see him, judging by the way they shivered, eyes roving around, but they could sense the fear that spiked through the air. Lord Taira victoriously held his sword above Kit's wounded leg.

"See how far this has come," Lord Taira sneered. "There is no way out, other than the way I choose for you. It is finally time for me to get my revenge, murderer."

Tessa ground her teeth. They were stuck. From every angle, Lord Taira's shadow warriors had caught her, Jin, and Kit in guarded, close circles. There was no way to get out.

Even the way that Jin held his wood staff—close, defensively, without much room to spare—told Tessa that he was struggling, too.

"What's the next plan? C'mon, there's a Plan V, right?" Tessa called. Even for the two torii, the kitsune had been able to help her get through them, one by one. It hadn't been easy, but they'd made it through.

Yet there was something strange about the way that Kit slowly straightened, standing up, with his eyes beginning to burn with some sort of fire. Like he had a plan, finally, and no matter if Jin or Tessa tried to dissuade him, his mind was set.

"Let me talk with the children," Kit said to Lord

Taira. "If I do not speak with them, they will continue to fight."

The god sniffed. "Only a minute, then. A second more, and my warriors will take care of them so that there is nothing *to* talk to."

Kit's eyes looked faintly misty as he gazed at Tessa and Jin, and the nervous panic in Tessa's chest was quickly siphoning away, replaced by fear.

"I think I was put in that charm for a reason," Kit started softly.

Tessa's worries compounded. "Wait, no, you're not seriously thinking of agreeing—"

"I...think I remember enough of the past. I was betrayed by those I had once trusted," Kit said. "But I fought to live on, to find people who would treat me well. I fought to find ways to make my family—the family that I deserve—whole again."

"What are you trying to say?" Tessa whispered, her throat tight. This wasn't part of their plan.

"You both still have families who care about you. Friends who want to see you again." Kit laughed sadly. "Without my identity, I've got neither. I thought I'd be able to help Tokyo, but it doesn't seem like it, really. Time's up."

Jin let out a gasp. Tessa tried to push toward the fox as the sharp, frightening words of his confession sunk in, but the shadow warriors locked their blades. "There're other options, Kit!"

"We can figure something out," Jin added.

The fox shook his head. "I've been toying with destiny too long. This time, we're not all going to make it out. I think my fate ends here. I can feel my ku giving out."

Tessa's lungs had lost all air. She tried to speak, but nothing was coming out. *This is all my fault.*

He grinned at them bravely. "Don't worry about me. When I give you this chance, run, kids. This is all I can do. The best thing about being a nobody is that you can do anything, and it's only upward from here."

Tessa shook her head wildly. She knew what it felt to be exactly like that, but... "Not like this. I know you. I care that you exist. I'll give you my ku, everything I have. I want you to stay alive—"

"If you two remember me, then I'll say this is worth it. And it's the most I can do for you both for getting you into this mess. Promise?"

Jin spluttered. "No, Kit, don't. Tessa, don't you agree? This is a horrible idea!"

And Tessa couldn't let him do...what she was thinking of. "Please—"

Kit's face was firm. "You two...there's no other way to get out, not all three of us. Do you want Lord Taira to take your god-blessed powers for his? To go down with the last magical city? Tessa, don't you want to save your sisters?"

But Tessa and Jin couldn't speak.

Kit looked at each of them, with warmth filling his eyes. "Tessa-chan, Jin-kun, you won't have a chance to get home any other way. Are you going to take this gift or not?"

Tessa met Jin's dark, solemn gaze as he said, over the crackle of the fire, "If we don't have any other options..."

She sniffled, rubbing her nose on her sleeve. "There's gotta be something—"

Kit grinned a heroic, brave smile. "When Lord Taira lets your sisters go, you go with them."

"Yes, yes, little ones, leave us to be." Lord Taira flicked his hands, and the shadows receded. Tessa ran to her sisters, pulling them away, but she stopped.

"Peyton, Cecilia—"

"How do you know our names?" Peyton asked.

"I, um, heard you two talking to each other," Tessa said, tears stinging her eyes. "Run, okay? Leave this place, fast."

The samurai let out a satisfied laugh. "Hurry along, little mortals."

Moments later, fire receded from a doorway, and Tessa pushed them forward. "Go, while you can!"

"C'mon, we have to leave," Peyton said, tugging at Cecilia.

"But what about you?" Tessa's oldest sister turned to look at her, her eyebrows scrunched. "There's no reason to stay here—"

Tessa shook her head. "Go without me. Your family... they want more than anything for you to be safe."

Peyton and Cecilia looked at her in confusion, but they didn't argue. Instead, they murmured, "Thank you. You've saved our lives."

And with that, they turned, fleeing into the darkening evening, Tessa's heart aching and aching.

"Go with them!" Kit shouted, but she shook her head. She couldn't leave the one god who had been at her side from the first moment she'd stepped into the City and taken care of her, a nobody.

"Miyata..." Jin said hoarsely. "It's time."

"Or you can stay here, too," Lord Taira said, pointing his sword at Tessa and Jin. "I wouldn't mind more power."

"Don't let my sacrifice be in vain," Kit whispered. "This is Plan Z. I always knew it might come down to this."

"This was never in our plans," Tessa cried.

"Come here, now, little fox," Lord Taira said. "Or I won't let your two friends out."

"Kit is doing this for us," Jin said. "We have to respect his wishes."

"But...but..." Her heart was hollowed out. She could protest, but she wasn't strong enough to save Kit.

Jin pulled at Tessa to follow him, and she stumbled out of the shrine in a horror-filled haze.

Beyond the doorway, she turned.

The flames blazed up; through the neon flickers, she could barely see the silhouette of the fox, standing up against the gigantic samurai.

Kit was only an eighth of his size. His power was waning.

He didn't stand a chance.

Lord Taira lifted his blade.

The Sword of a Thousand Souls.

"We've got to go." Jin pulled at her hand.

He was right, he was right...but she couldn't take her eyes away from the way the figure raised the sword high above Kit's neck, high in the air....

And the whistle of air as it sliced down.

Kit crumpled to the ground, his sharp cry fading into nothing, as if he was already becoming ether.

The glimmering light from her bracelet, connecting her and Kit, faded out. The red string was still wrapped around her wrist, but now only the wolf charm remained, and the band looked dull and worn out. She let out a cry. In all her twelve years, she'd always seen that nagging little fox charm.

The mask on her face disappeared into thin air. Even that magic was gone.

"Tessa, we have to escape!" Jin cried.

Shadows slithered out from under the godfire, swarming toward her and Jin. One of the warriors grabbed at her, yanking at her braid.

With a scream, she pulled out a throwing star and sliced down, hard. The fighter slid its hand away, and the sharp edges of the throwing star sheared through her hair instead, her braid unraveling—her connection to her sisters—cold air pricking her scalp.

"Run, run!" Jin pulled at her hand, the only warmth she felt in this awful place.

They were helpless. Outnumbered.

It was far too late to help Kit. So they turned and ran and ran.

She didn't want to leave the fox behind....

Even though he was already gone.

31

Surrounding the shrine, mortal firefighters doused the walls; it seemed that the water, drawn partially from a nearby well, had the power to quench godfire, although she overheard some of them murmur in surprise about the strange hue to the flames.

Tessa looked over her shoulder, in time to see Lord Taira and his shadow warriors bounded up, jumping over the rooftops and into the dark forests surrounding Meiji Jingu. She shifted toward them, but Jin shook his head. "Don't ruin Kit's sacrifice."

So Tessa followed Jin, her head tucked down, her eyes burning with unshed tears, her hair sticking to her sweaty face.

"All clear inside! Empty here!" one of the firefighters called, stepping out from the ashes. Tessa's heart strained from the weight of her pain. The scent of hinoki wafted, strong and deep from the trees surrounding them, but there was no protecting Kit, not when he was gone.

"Let's head home," Jin said, tugging at her wrist. "The train is this way."

"*Home*?" Tessa whispered. "You're going to leave Kit behind? All of Tokyo?"

"He's gone, Miyata," Jin whispered. "We're *kids*. We're not strong enough to fight Lord Taira."

"We can still do something—"

"We can't." Jin was soft and sad, and it would've hurt more if he had shouted. "Let's return to Kisarazu. You want to make sure your sisters will get back home safe, right? And you need to check on your grandpa, don't you?"

"But—Kit—"

"When people leave you like that, it's final." Jin's voice was flat and bleak. Tessa remembered, then, what little he'd said of his mother: *People who leave never come back.*

She wanted to believe that they *did*. That there were chances to fix things and change things for the better.

"Do you ever wonder why I like history so much?" Jin asked suddenly. "It's not because I'm a total nerd— okay, I totally am. But don't tell anyone. I always love history because it's set, and there's nothing you can change about it." Then his voice cracked. "But Kit—he's *history*. He's gone."

"We spent five full days training—"

"We ran around like fools, thinking we could fight

a god!" Jin said sharply. His eyes simmered with anger. "Kit gave us these ridiculous ideas, but don't you see? You're not strong enough! Neither of us is! We should've just gone home from the beginning!"

"Now you're blaming me?" Tessa whispered, horror filling her.

Jin looked away, but she recognized that set to his shoulders, the coldness to his expression, even when she'd never seen it on him before. That was *exactly* how Allison had looked moments after she'd uploaded another video, and each time she'd made fun of Tessa in front of their whole class.

"If you didn't make that deal with the Seven Lucky Gods, then maybe they would've done something," Jin muttered finally.

His words were more piercing than a katana, slicing her to her core. Jin had never believed in her.

"They weren't going to do anything!" Tessa shot back, anger burning her heart.

"Miyata, you can't save a city. One person? You're not strong enough. You're just going to wreck the last magical city *and* all of Tokyo, forever." He spat out those words as if he could truly see her as the curse she was. With that, he spun on his heel and ran toward the train station.

Tessa stood on the path; the darkening night chilling her to the bone.

Kit was gone. Jin had left her.

She was truly alone.

32

Tessa banged her fists on the shiny golden gates of the Seven Lucky Gods. They had gleamed so prettily the last time she was here, but now it all felt like a lie.

They had their doors shut. Of course. She'd sprinted all the way just to find herself at a dead end.

"Please!" she called.

Her tears slid down, hit the golden gates, and then bounced off, as if the Seven Lucky Gods refused to acknowledge her pain.

"You."

Tessa jolted, and hope swelled. "Hachiman. Sir, please!"

The samurai clanked forward. "You know the answer, minor god." Then he squinted. "Are you a mortal? No, you can't be—there haven't been mortals in the City in a decade; I just need a burst of ku and—"

"Kit said this is the last magical city in all of Japan," Tessa said, horrified. "Will you not take care of the City?"

"If Lord Taira comes to these gates and tries to get in? Yes. But until then, this is beyond what the Seven Lucky Gods will touch." Hachiman paused. "I am sorry, you know. But as a god, I want to survive, too."

Tessa's heart seared with pain.

The Seven Lucky Gods had turned their backs on Tokyo.

Jin had left her, too.

She was friendless, as she'd always been. A burden to her grandparents, her sisters, Kit...in a wrecked city that was all her fault.

Tessa slumped down to her knees, eyes burning as she pressed her forehead to the gate.

A breath in, a breath out.

Her hopes broke apart inside her. She could no longer remember the determination that had burned when Kit had taught her and Jin for those five days. Though she had almost died trying, it had ended up being worth nothing.

The prayers gathered in the air, thicker than ever, thrumming and tugging at her, but she wasn't able to answer them. No one would help until it was too late, until mortals were chased out of Tokyo and the gods and spirits were extinguished—all but the Seven Lucky Gods.

And she was to blame.

The wishes in the air tugged at her, *insistently*. She turned her head, pulled by a current of hopes, and then she took a deep, surprised breath.

Down, down the road, a red-orange torii shimmered through the curling smoke. From within, she caught a glimpse of dry lands, with a wicked glint of steel.

Kit's explanation echoed in her mind. *When a torii opens, it means the City has been calling you, asking you to come.*

The Armory of the Fallen Souls.

She had nothing to lose, now, and only everything to gain.

Tessa pushed herself off the ground and ran toward the gateway.

33

THE SKY OF THE ARMORY OF FALLEN SOULS GLIMMERED as if candles floated above, droplets of waxy stars scattered across the deep blue-black. Last time, Tessa had been full of belief that she would get a blade, and she'd ended up with nothing. This time, she believed in nothing, not even that she would end up with a blade, not even that she could walk back out the torii alive.

Jin's honest words were etched into her bones. *You're not strong enough.*

"*You, again. Why?*" the Armory said.

"I am fighting to save all of Tokyo," she declared, her heart clenching.

"*Tessa Miyata is no hero.*"

Tessa took another step forward, her shoe crunching into the cracked dirt.

"None of the gods are here, are they?" she responded.

"I may be the only one fighting for the last magical city of Japan, but I *will* fight for it, with all that I have."

Then the Armory was silent, as if she'd passed an initial test. That only lasted for a minute before a haunting melody swept around her, pulling her forward. It was the same song as last time. This time Tessa could catch hints of what sounded like words, though she couldn't quite grasp the meaning.

Tessa ran past the skeletons, rib cages curving up toward the dark sky. Moments later, she stood in front of the sword that had almost, *almost* swallowed her alive last time.

It sparkled in the moonlight, the edge of the hilt dark as ashes and its blade glittering like ice. This sword was truly a legend, beyond even her shuriken, as much as she had come to appreciate the hinoki weapons.

"What sacrifice will you make to show you are worthy of me?"

The Armory and the sword...it was the same voice, the same buzzing voices, all merged into one.

She sucked a breath in, and it rattled in her lungs like she was already turning to dust. The melody twirled in her ears, pulling her in, and she clasped her hands around the hilt.

A scream.

The scream was hers.

Tessa stood in front of her classmates as they laughed,

fingers outstretched like they were arrows, the strings twanging and their words shooting her down.

Her mind burst with pain.

This time, though, she didn't curl up from their taunts. Tessa raised her eyes to meet theirs.

Hadn't they always been the true shadows of her days? They did not understand her; they never had.

"I am not going to be destroyed by them," Tessa shouted, her eyes burning with glimmers of tears. She forced herself to stare down at the hand guard, mottled with rust.

"But they have already destroyed you. Look at how weak you have become. Look at how your shoulders sink at the thought of them. They do not even burn like a blade, and yet you shy away."

And that was it: Tessa had been broken too many times to be whole.

She was always going to be left behind. First, by her parents. Then, time after time, she'd seen she was a fractured person, turned into pitiful laughter by her classmates. A duty for Gram. A second thought to her sisters, who always had each other. Jin and Kit had left her, too.

The sword rose; a misty figure of pure white held it comfortably, with familiarity. *"I was the first to forge this Blade, and it won over me in the end. This weapon is far more powerful than others. You, weak human, would fall immediately from its strength."*

A slash in the air; Tessa jumped away, throwing up her shuriken. But steel sliced through it like the blessed wood was no more than paper.

"No!" she cried out, reaching for another.

There was a flash of light, a creak of gears.

Another owner stood next to the first, another silhouette of light and mist, but this one was the color of molten gold, of metal jewelry heated by flame until it was burning bright. This one, too, held a matching blade.

"*See how weak you are?*" came a soft, sweet taunt. "*Weapons of gods are not meant to be playthings of humans. Especially a scrap of a mortal like you, Tessa Miyata. You never did have a spine; only those with otherworldly strength can sacrifice enough to harness this Blade. See?*"

With a flash of movement, the fighter danced forward like splashes of melting metal; Tessa's eyes seared from the brightness of each step—

She threw out another shuriken, then another. All too soon, Tessa was empty-handed.

The blade came down, and she screamed, throwing up her arms.

This was no ordinary steel.

The moment it tore through the flesh of her arm, the wound burning with an unmeasurable degree of pain, more memories flashed through her, and she relived her darkest moments all over again.

Her parents' photos, their bright-eyed smiles, and the pain of knowing what had happened to them, in the end.

Allison laughing with her; time flashed and churned, and then the girl stared at her with an emptiness in her eyes and asked, "Who are you, even? Get away from me."

Cecilia and Peyton walking out of Ojiichan and Obaachan's front gate, arm in arm, laughing as Tessa cried by herself.

"This is who you're trying to save." The voice was sharp.

Blades rained down, each with a searingly excruciating memory, the memories that stopped Tessa from sleeping at night, the memories that haunted her waking moments.

Memory after memory, cut after cut.

This was who she really was, after all. No one worthy of anything, as she'd always known.

She stumbled, her arms scored with cuts, her heart aching with pain. "I can't leave Tokyo alone, not like this."

Then a memory flashed before her eyes, sucking her in.

She was in the apartment, standing in the kitchen as Gram, Peyton, and Cecilia mourned for Tessa's parents, their hearts aching.

This time, Tessa could see the ku that untangled from their hearts and words and hopes, breathing out into the world, *We wish they hadn't died. We wish they were here safe, now.*

Tessa let out a sob. "I'm sorry! I'm sorry!"

The world around her flashed.

It was her birthday, still. Lunchtime in the cafeteria, the tray of fries cold in front of her and Allison, Tessa's heart like lead as she whispered to her best friend what she'd overheard.

The other girl was quiet for a long, long time, and the emptiness of words made nervousness slide into her stomach like a pit of snakes.

"I shouldn't say anything, right?" Tessa asked. "I mean, it's—"

Allison stood up, abruptly. "This is too much for me. I can't deal with this."

Tessa gaped as her best friend strode off, with a flip of her hair, to walk out with Jenna and the other popular kids, who were just about to leave, too. One of the girls sent Tessa a pitying look, but they all turned on their heels and sashayed out the cafeteria.

That was truly when Tessa and Allison's friendship had fallen apart. Because Tessa had told the truth, looking for someone who might understand—

Her pain was too heavy for a friend like Allison.

And if it hadn't been for Tessa, her parents may very well have been alive, still.

"I'm sorry!" Tessa cried out, her heart pulling into

pieces. "I wish...I should have..." Words failed her as her eyes burned with tears, pouring down her cheeks.

"But you didn't...you couldn't *do anything,"* the Armory responded.

And it was the truth. She couldn't do any more than what she had.

Was this where it ended? Was this all that Tessa would ever become?

Sobs wracked her body as she crumpled to the ground.

34

THE BLADE SLICED AT HER, TEARING HER APART.

Kit. She grasped at her wrist, in one last futile hope.

The fox charm was no longer there, of course he wasn't; only the white wolf dangled from the red chain, cold and lifeless—

A blast of ku from the air knocked her down, her palms stinging from the grit.

She thought of Kit, who had a past he didn't remember, versus Tessa, with a past she wished she could forget.

She remembered Allison: the sneer of her lips, the sudden silence like a wall she couldn't break through... because Allison had *chosen* to go her own way.

"It isn't my fault!" Tessa shouted, banging her hand against the wall, the realization shocking her like lightning. "I gave her my friendship, and she didn't want to be at my side! But that is *not* my fault!"

Her parents, too. After, after she'd found out about *when* they had passed away, Tessa had looked up the local news on her birthday, eleven years ago....It had been a drunk driver, careening through the streets. An awful accident by someone else who'd made a horrifying decision, by someone else who had the burden of her parents' lives on their soul. That was why, during their family Christmas get-togethers, Gram always pulled Tessa and her sisters close to her and hugged them tightly, murmuring, *I love you. Your parents love and miss you, too. If they could get any gift from you this year, it would be your happiness, my dears.*

The way that Kit had chosen to sacrifice himself for her...

The way her parents had chosen to try to be at her side...

Tessa was worthy of their sacrifices, and she would give all that she could for her family. She could choose still, too.

Her fingers curled in, her nails cutting at her skin, reminding her of the gritty pain she was going through, but also of the reason why she was fighting. Her sisters. If she lost here, if she gave up, it wasn't her who really lost out...it was Cecilia and Peyton, Ojiichan and Obaachan. It was all of Tokyo, all of Japan.

Tessa might not have been much, but she *was* here to fight.

"I'm here for a reason. I'm no hero; I may not be a chosen one that wears a cape or can easily jump in to save the day, but I will do *everything* to protect those I love," Tessa ground out from her gritted teeth.

"*Everything?*" the voice returned. "*And what do you mean by that?*"

"You can have my past!" Tessa cried out, to the Armory. "You can have my future! But I need to stop Lord Taira—that's what matters!"

And it was her promise to do anything she could to take care of those she loved, going forward.

More ku slammed her into the ground, and her eyes stung with fresh tears. But she moved forward, toward the blade.

"I. Will. Fight." Tessa crawled onward. "I will continue to fight, until my last breath."

It was as if those words unlocked something in her. A part of her heart she had never dared to venture into, to settle into. To dream. To believe. To know that she was enough. That the people who came in and out of her life were there for a reason, even if they didn't want to—or couldn't—stay for longer.

"You are not them! They are not here!" Tessa shouted. "*You*, whoever or whatever you are, *you* are trying to test me."

"*Yet, what if I am?*"

"Test me all you want," Tessa declared. "But know this: I will not give up. I will fight and fight to take care of those I love. My once-friend and her group back home, yeah, I don't like them, and my mind still feels that pain, but I'll find better friends, someday. Gram has a ton to worry about, but she loves me with all her heart; it's why she makes the sacrifices that she does. My parents always loved me. My ojiichan and obaachan opened up their house to us in our time of need. And I'll always, *always* have my sisters—they were worried about *me* when I was trying to get them to escape, and this is my chance to protect them just as they protect me. Even now, I will fight to stop those who try to hurt the ones I love, those that try to hurt others the way they hurt me. And I *am* worthy of their love, because I'm enough as I am, and *I* believe in myself, too. Even though I'm nothing much, I *can* be a hero."

"*There are those in Tokyo that want you dead, Miyata. Starting with the one who destroys the city, but he is not alone.*"

Tessa gripped the hilt tighter, refusing to loosen her fingers. "I will fight for us all to survive."

"*But what if we* don't *want your help? Tokyo is not your city to take care of.*"

Indignation burned her blood. "Tokyo *is* my city. I can feel it in my blood, and I will fight for its people. Even if they're all like the Seven Lucky Gods, even if they're like Hachiman, there *are* others! Kit, Uehara—even if he's more worried about his father. My *sisters* are here, too."

"But you could leave."

The world around her flashed. She was in the white chamber, her hands clutched around the sword still stuck in the ground. But it didn't budge a centimeter. Tall, rectangular mirrors filled the room, reflecting the image of a small girl, trembling hands trying to yank at the sword. Images from her past flashed on the glass: Allison and her classmates laughing. Her standing alone at school, forgotten. Jin's back to her as he walked away, leaving… Worst of all, Kit pushing her away, sacrificing himself.

But…*but*, he hadn't left her completely empty-handed.

Tessa reached out for the ku, from where it shimmered in the air, and pulled everything within her grasp— and combined it with everything inside of her.

All the hopes and all the fears, everything that made her soul burn like it was filled with godfire. Every memory she had of being with someone she cared about—and every moment she had stood on her own. All of this, she realized, was ku. She was filled with energy, filled with life, and she'd use it to protect everything and everyone she loved.

Ku swirled around her. She gathered the energy into her hands, re-forming her broken hinoki shuriken whole again.

But a blade came down, out of thin air, and Tessa cried out, stumbling.

This time she was not fast enough—it arced down, straight toward her heart—

Tessa knew how this would end.

Alone, yet again. Lost, forever. No one would know where she was, or how she'd died.

Tessa still had so much to do, and she realized she still had so much that she wanted to become. She didn't want to die.

Even as the blade sliced down, she wanted to scream that out.

This isn't over. This can't be over!

Then—

Her wrist burned with fire. A white wolf leaped out, fur whipping in the wind, as it snarled, meeting the sword head-on and biting it into two, tossing the pieces to the side.

It landed, turning to look over its shoulder.

The wolf had saved her.

A voice reverberated in her mind, soft yet slightly husky. It was the woman in white, from the museum. "You are right, young mortal. You are not alone."

The words resonated in Tessa's blood. It was true, wasn't it? She was never alone, even in all those seemingly endless days at school, even now. She had so many she loved—her sisters, Gram, Ojiichan, Obaachan, even

Kit—to fight for, to fight for the chance to stand at their sides again.

The wolf began to fade.

"Wait!" Tessa cried out, reaching toward it. "Who are you? Why did you come for me? How did you know this would happen?"

"We searched for you for a long time. You were marked from birth, but there was always a question of chance and fate." The wolf's yellow eyes met hers. "However, we knew you were the right person because of your noble acts; it was further confirmed when you saved Jizo-sama from his curse. There are others who are also cursed, Miyata. With your help, you can reunite this sword, the essence of our souls that fight for justice, with its true owner. Answers, should you choose, that you will discover in time."

"Marked from birth? True owner? Who—"

But the wolf had disappeared into thin air, like it had never existed. And now, finally, Tessa's wrist was bare.

The panels of the mirror filled with gloating images of Allison, her sisters, Jin; they laughed at her misery, mocking her words. *Who, who, who.*

But, this time, Tessa knew they were only illusions. She did not shy away.

This can't be over. I still have so much that I want to become.

Steadily, she stepped toward the mirror, her hands armed with her real hinoki shuriken, and she sliced down.

It cracked into a thousand pieces, iridescent like god-fire, as the world flashed around her again.

She was in the Armory, with the ominously sparkling sky above, the dry dirt packed thick below her feet. Her heart thrummed as she spoke. "I will fight for Tokyo. I will fight for the last magical city until my last breath."

A line of people, their faces too shadowy to make out, stood in front of her. Their voices melded together, in a strange harmony that sounded like the music that Tessa had heard from outside of the Armory.

Together, the mysterious figures said, the noise reverberating through Tessa's skull, "*Noble. You are noble, indeed, in a time when many others—even the Seven— refuse to heed our beckoning. You may come to regret these words, perhaps. However, we will not let a wayward god wreck our City. Very well, then, young Miyata. This sword will fight at your side, if only for this time.*"

She had done it.

"*You have grown stronger since we last met. Your training has done you well.*"

One of the figures to the far right looked strangely familiar. Tall and pale...with a wolf's mask. The woman in white took off her mask, her dark lips curving into a smile, and winked.

The sword jumped into Tessa's hand, shiny in the moonlight. The hilt was warm to the touch, yet smooth. At her waist, the hinoki throwing stars clinked softly, greeting it. The katana was much lighter than she'd expected—just about the same weight as Kit. Her heart tore at the thought.

Carefully, she tested it, and the katana swooped through the air like it had wings.

The voices of the sword spoke one last time. *"This City is indeed connected to you in ways you do not yet understand. Let us save the last magical city. Tessa Miyata, lead us to victory."*

Tessa's hopes rekindled, blazing brighter than godfire.

35

IT DID NOT TAKE LONG TO FIND LORD TAIRA.

The moment Tessa stepped out of the Armory's gate, a spirit almost plowed her over; she stepped away just in time, breathing in the smoky scent of incense, edged with bitterness.

Godfire.

Down the main street of the City, neon flames flickered, consuming shrine after shrine. A shadowy figure outfitted in shiny black armor strode down the street, his katana held in one hand. Shadows swirled around him in the form of warriors, prowling forth.

Gods and spirits took one look at the blazing godfire and ran. Frustration battered through Tessa; how could they not fight to save their city?

Still, she strode forward, the sword light in her hand. The katana seemed to be carried by the strength of the prayers thick on the gusts of wind, with the power of all the Souls that were in the blade, like the woman in white, who fought with her.

This was her Plan K, for Kit. And there were no backup plans after this. It was Plan Kit or nothing.

And how could Lord Taira walk onward, as if Kit's death was nothing to him? How could he believe in the destruction he had wreaked upon the last magical city, and all of Tokyo?

Tessa's blood boiled.

"Lord Taira!" she shouted. "I challenge you to a fight."

Her heart thudded with each step. She quickly analyzed the situation, the way she'd studied her classmates' phones and the closest exit, searching for a way out. Lord Taira was not weary like Kit had become; he was solid and real. He'd fed well on the lifeforces of mortals in Tokyo, and was more corporeal than ever before.

"Who dares to challenge me?" He turned away from where he was heading—the sealed-shut gates of the Seven Lucky Gods to their left. The gods' fortresses were still quiet; perhaps they, too, watched in the same way the minor gods and spirits peered out from the shadows on the other side. But for the Seven Lucky Gods, Tessa was no longer holding her breath in anticipation of their help.

"*You?*" Lord Taira scoffed. "You're the one that the fox sacrificed himself for. You'll die if you fight me."

"I will fight you until you stop harming Tokyo and

the hidden City." Tessa raised her sword in her right hand and a shuriken in the left. "I will never stop fighting you, Lord Taira, until you leave us in peace."

"Fine words for a little girl," the god spat, his gaze skimming over her sword. "Such lovely words. It's a pity they'll be your last."

Lord Taira lunged forward, the tip of his blade pointed straight at her neck.

Tessa darted to the side, and Lord Taira Masakado's sword whistled in the air where she'd stood a split second ago.

He raised his left hand up and pointed at Tessa, his voice guttural and low. "Extinguish her."

Tessa jumped away, holding the katana defensively. But she watched in horror as his shadow split out from his body and formed into warriors. This time, they carried two swords, one in each hand.

Her throat went dry.

But she had no regrets, now. She'd fought as best as she could, even if she wasn't going to get out.

Tessa Miyata was a legend all on her own terms. She might be the only human who remembered this—before she probably became the first mortal to die in the last magical city—but she would die knowing she had fought. She held the blade, her heartbeat pounding, and she took her first steps toward her fate.

"I won't let you destroy Tokyo!" she shouted.

When the shadow warriors advanced, she didn't hesitate, and she threw the first of her seven hinoki stars at the shadow to the left. With the katana in her right hand, she made a clean swipe through the closest warrior; it blinked out of existence like she'd popped a balloon.

It wasn't enough. She needed more.

Tessa pushed ku into the blade, and the metal glowed with light. Heat flowed through, burning at the tarnish covering the tsuba. She didn't have time to study the hand guard, but flakes of dirt and rust melted away, showing shimmering gold, carved into the form of flickering flames that matched the fury in her heart.

She would *not* let Lord Taira get past her.

"Let's go, sword," Tessa murmured, pushing ku into the metal, and she let it guide her. The blade moved, Tessa's feet somehow knowing how to follow, as it led her into an intricate sword dance, darting to and fro around the shadow warriors, knocking one down, deflecting the blade of another.

Tessa could do this. Sweat raced down her face as she ducked around another shadow warrior's fist, and her sword sliced through its dark body. It dissolved into thin air, but almost instantly, another warrior took its place.

"You may have survived until now," Lord Taira snarled. "But I don't need you."

With a flick of his hand, the shadow warriors

duplicated. Her heart pounded in her ears; the drain of ku was so much, too much for her to keep going on.

Then the warriors were all on her at once. Tessa cried out as a fist pummeled her in the gut, knocking the air out of her lungs. She spun away from another shadow, letting two slam into each other. With a quick thrust of her katana, she got the one that'd hit her.

A pair of ice-cold hands grabbed her wrist. Another warrior had snuck up on her from behind.

Tessa cried out as she was thrown to the ground, and her sword went clattering out of her hands to land in the dirt, five paces away.

Footsteps crunched along the ground, and her heart thudded in her chest.

Lord Taira's eyes were cold as he raised his sword above her. "It is laughable to think a weakling like you could stop me."

Tessa lifted her head up, sweat burning into her eyes. This was where it ended. To die alone, in the last magical city, in a place where her sisters and grandparents would never be able to find her. Where she would be forgotten, for the rest of time.

Then, in that split second, she looked up at the sword that Lord Taira carried. The tsuba glinted in the lamplight. Flames and dragons raced along the guard. *Flames and dragons—*

She glanced over to her sword, where the tarnish had burned away.

Flames and dragons shone.

It was exactly the same.

The Sword of a Thousand Souls that Lord Taira carried was *identical* to the blade she'd drawn from the ground of the Armory.

How could Lord Taira have the same sword as her? She had walked through the Armory; every blade had a different metallic sheen and varying guards and hilts; there were no two swords that were exactly alike. Yet— yet, these two swords had the same exact design, the same exact angle to their slightly curved blades, *everything.*

She had pulled her sword straight from the dusty grounds of the Armory. Kit had said that no two swords could be alike....

Which had to mean his was a fake.

When Lord Taira sliced his imitation Sword of a Thousand Souls down, she rolled out of the way and felt for the prayers on the breeze. Her fingers snagged and she held on, letting the prayers draw her forward so she could grab the hinoki stars at her side, pulling one off the magical chain. She threw it upward, toward the eye opening in the samurai's armor; Lord Taira roared as he batted away the shuriken, sending it straight into the dirt.

This time, he swiped down toward her, fast, and her

gut clenched, already expecting the pain of the metal sword in her shoulder.

But his blade met a hinoki staff, held by a boy with messy hair and remorse darkening his eyes that met Tessa's.

Then Jin glared up at Lord Taira. "Not on my watch."

36

Lord Taira's sword sparked against Jin's bō, embers smoldering and biting into the hinoki.

"Kit said to make our blades out of wood." Jin gritted his teeth as he darted forward and tried to slam one of the shadow warriors in the side; it deflected his staff with quick blade work. "You're right, Miyata. I don't see how wood beats steel."

Another swing from Lord Taira sent him flying backward. Jin landed on his feet, at her side, sweat beading his brow. In the next moment, Tessa spun her sword up to meet Lord Taira's blade. With a grunt, she pushed the samurai away.

Tessa and Jin stood back to back, as Lord Taira and his shadow warriors circled them.

"It's nice to see you," Tessa said over her shoulder.

"It's too bad we're saying hello again only to say goodbye," Jin said.

Before, Tessa's plan had been to defend against Lord Taira until the Seven Gods stepped in, hopefully drawn out by the commotion in front of their gates. Now, though, she knew the truth.

She wasn't aiming high enough. Waiting for the Seven Gods was like counting on rain that might never come.

That wouldn't save Tokyo.

Tessa had to beat Lord Taira. *She* had to win.

Her fingers wrapped tightly around the hilt. "The only person I'm planning on saying goodbye to is Lord Taira."

Jin did a double take. "You got a sword. From the *Armory*. Are *you* an actual god now?"

"I wish. Just one very lucky, god-blessed mortal. With more allies than I expected," she said with a desperate laugh. She tightened her grip on the sword. Even with Jin, they were outnumbered....

No. They weren't.

"You focus on the shadow warriors," she hissed. "I'll take care of Lord Taira. But first, we need to get him toward the gates."

Jin looked quizzically at the locked golden entrance to Seven Lucky Gods' shrines, about fifteen paces away.

"Trust me?" she whispered.

This time, Jin spoke in English. "You can do it."
Then he flashed her a smile, through his weariness. "*We*
can do it."

Ganbatte.

He strode toward the shadow warriors, his staff
extended. "You lumps of darkness, you want a piece of
me? You'll have to beat me before you get a chance at
attacking Miyata. I'm not leaving her." His voice cracked,
but it was edged with a sense of newfound strength. "I've
been left behind before, and I swore I'd never do that to
someone I care about again. I'm going to protect her with
all that I've got."

Tessa's heart soared as she lunged toward Lord Taira.

She blocked a thrust of a shadow warrior's sword,
spinning around another that Jin extinguished with a
sharp rap of his bō. Then she danced between another
two warriors to face Lord Taira head-on.

"I'm not going to let you beat me," Tessa shot out.

"We'll see about that," Lord Taira snarled, sending his sword down, barely missing Tessa's arm as she
jumped to the right.

As she fought, her heartbeat thrummed like a drum.
The faint, haunting music from the Armory seemed to
sing in her ears as she spun, fought, and deflected. Sweat
drenched her shirt; her legs felt ready to give out, but still,
Tessa fought.

There was a shout—

She looked to her left. Jin was overwhelmed by shadow warriors. He yelped as another one yanked at his staff, pulling it from his grip.

"No!" Tessa cried. She couldn't wait any longer.

But Lord Taira was ready; he sprang forward, the samurai's movement seeming to slow in time.

You can do it.

Tessa raised her arms, holding her katana in front of her. The haunting melody seemed to grow louder. The words were clear, now.

Ame futte, ji katamaru.
After the rain, the earth hardens.

Her eyes stung. She wasn't ku, the void. She wasn't made of godly elegance or inhuman strength. She wasn't fire that burned.

But she was solid; she was earth, real and gritty, and she'd always, always fight, even if the rain pounded down.

Sweat dripped off Tessa's forehead and splashed on the dry ground. The earth seemed to absorb her efforts; it was literally just a drop in the ocean, a lonely, meaningless speck.

After the rain, the earth hardens.

Jin was overwhelmed by shadow warriors; he'd disappeared behind them. Lord Taira was mere feet away, ready to deal a fatal blow, his eyes gleaming in sick anticipation.

It was only here, at the last edges of her life, where Tessa was able to find the core of who she really was. That she *would* fight, even if it burned and made her bleed and break.

She would not stay broken.

Tessa Miyata had to survive.

She had thought she was an outsider. A loner. That she never had a place to belong, that she was always a problem to watch over. But she had Jin and Kit, and her sisters, her grandparents.... *And*, she believed in herself.

The seven shuriken levitated around her, like a floating half ring of glossy, pale wood, like a crown of sunlight. Lord Taira's eyes widened with near-comical surprise.

Tessa threw her katana—the *real* Sword of a Thousand Souls—with her right hand, feeling for the strings of prayers connecting her to its blade, and it flew forward; the god ducked in a fast kneel.

But he was not prepared for Tessa. She flung her left hand forward; seven throwing stars shot toward him, in sync.

Her Sword of a Thousand Souls sliced the gates, right where Lord Taira had been.

The gates that had not let in a single soul in more than a decade crumbled, breaking into a million tiny pieces.

And when the dust faded, Lord Taira lay out on the dirt, struggling like a bug that had been upturned. The hinoki shuriken were embedded in his armor and pinning him into the ground. Impossible for wood to do, if it had not been the magical wood of gods. Impossible, if it were not for Tessa being the wielder of the *real* Sword of a Thousand Souls.

The katana jumped into her hand. She stepped forward and slid the blade smoothly to the gap between Lord Taira's neck armor; the shadow warriors disappeared with the samurai's nervous squeak. From the other side, Jin held his bō against the samurai's neck, too.

Checkmate.

"What's going on here?" Hachiman squawked, gaping at the broken golden gates.

Tessa wiped her forehead with one arm. "Here's the renegade samurai, as requested by the Seven Lucky Gods, delivered right to their doorstep."

Hachiman stared, his jaw so far from the rest of his mouth, he was only able to gargle in shock.

Tessa shot the grumpy guard a brilliant, charming smile. "And you should know…he calls himself Lord Taira Masakado—but he's a fake."

37

HACHIMAN PROTESTED, "HE *IS* THE LORD TAIRA—"

"He's not," Tessa said loudly. To Jin, at her side, she whispered, "He's faker than Hachiman's mustache."

Jin let out a snort. Hachiman grumbled, twisting out the ends of his hairs. The spirit and god onlookers whispered amongst each other in disbelief.

Tessa nodded over to the sword that lay shattered on the ground and then toward the blade she held. "Guess which is the *real* Sword of a Thousand Souls."

"A blade could mean anything," a man said.

"Not a blade that can break another god's weapon," Hachiman admitted. "That...the one the girl is holding is truly from the Armory."

The crowd of gods and spirits gasped.

"It's not any blade," Tessa said. "This is the Sword of a Thousand Souls. It would devour you rather than let someone unworthy handle the blade. It's letting me use it for a little bit, until I reunite it with its true owner."

As if to answer, mist swirled around Tessa's hands clutching the hilt, forming, for the briefest of seconds, the shape of wolf's face; it snapped at the fake Lord Taira, who squeaked.

Jin leaned in, eyes sharp. "In other words, listen to her."

Tessa dug her sword a little sharper into the side of the fake Lord Taira's neck, between the plates of armor, and he whimpered. "Have mercy!"

"Tell me your name."

He shook his head, eyes wide.

"Tell me your name or you won't be able to tell us anything at all," she hissed.

Again, he shook his head; she pressed in firmly, and Jin dug his staff in on the other side, and he let out a gasp.

"Fujiwara!" the imposter squealed, finally. He closed his eyes in a reluctant surrender. "I'm Fujiwara Hidesato, now let me go!"

Jin gasped. "I learned about you in history class! When you were a mortal, you were the one who assassinated Taira Masakado. You were his ally. His friend. Until you rallied his family to kill him."

"It wasn't my fault!" Fujiwara whimpered. "The government demanded me to! I was honored for saving the prefecture! Taira wanted to overturn the government, it was chaos!"

"I'm not a fan of people who betray their friends, you know." Tessa slid her sword closer to his neck, and he yelped. "The least you could've done was stand up for him."

"I was set up," he blubbered. "If I didn't fight, I would lose everything I had—"

Tessa shook her head. "*Don't* try to blame someone else. *Why* did you pretend to be him, then?"

Fujiwara slumped. "I...When I finally materialized, after all those years, Taira didn't know who he was. This—*this* was my chance to become someone powerful! If I could take his power, take all that he was, then I could finally be everything I wanted to be! You know how that is, too, right? To finally become someone feared, after being so weak my entire life!"

Jin and Tessa stared at him coldly.

"Oh, please, boy!" Fujiwara reached out toward Jin. "Those I work for will reward you greatly. It won't matter if you're a mortal, you can achieve—"

"I'm no traitor," Jin said coldly.

"Little girl! What if I help you get stronger?" Fujiwara whispered. "Imagine—someone like you, with my support! You'll be marvelous, the gods will notice you and accept you in as one of their own—"

"I don't need that. Even if I'm weak, I'm not going to wreck an entire city just for my own gain."

Then Fujiwara's lips curved. "I have something you want."

"We would never—"

"Your little fox friend?" Fujiwara simpered. "What if he's alive, still?"

Tessa's eyes burned. "Show us."

Fujiwara shook his head. "I refuse. Not until you let me free."

A new voice chimed in, "Is that so?"

Jin spun around, but Tessa kept her eyes on Fujiwara, her blade pointed firmly at his neck. She wasn't going to let a distraction allow the traitor to slip away.

"The Seven Lucky Gods!" the crowd behind them gasped.

Light shot out, melting away Fujiwara's black armor. The samurai shouted. "Wait! That's mine—"

Bishamonten growled, "I'll have to have a talk with Kagutsuchi. How *dare* he betray me by giving away his stock of godfire. I'll take the armor for myself, thank you."

Then Tessa slid down her katana. Fujiwara let out a shriek, flailing, but she didn't slice his skin. Instead, she pulled up a red string from around his no-longer-armored neck. With a swift movement, she plucked it off.

She stared down at the gold fox charm cupped in her palms. "Kit? Please be alive."

"Shall I help you return that charm into your friend's proper shape?" Kuju asked.

"Yes, absolutely!" Jin said.

Tessa clutched the charm in her hands, feeling like she was holding her entire heart outside of her body. "Would you be able to?"

Kuju inclined his head. "It is the least I can do for a mortal who has stopped a great evil at—or shall I say, *inside* our doorstep." Then he paused. "I have my suspicions now, but may I ask who your friend is?"

Tessa nodded, looking down at the small, sharp-nosed metal charm of the kitsune. "I think he's the *real* Taira Masakado."

Jin stared. "*Kit?*"

"After I saw that my sword matched the fake Lord Taira's, I got to thinking.... Remember all those facts you mentioned?" Tessa said. "That Kit was from the Heian period, that he used to sword fight...And Kit doesn't know who he is, but this guy with a fake sword is trying to claim his identity, and would do anything to kill Kit. And when I realized something wasn't right about *this* Taira Masakado, I started realizing that our Kit might actually be the real Taira."

Jin stared at her. "You really did listen to me."

Tessa grinned at him.

There was a flash of light, and then a voice said, "How about someone listens to me? Hello, do you two even see me in front of you?"

Tessa looked up, and a tall samurai stared back. He

was outfitted in gold and scarlet armor, but there was an impish look to his eyes that she recognized all too well. "Kit!"

She and Jin threw their arms around the samurai— although, in his real form, they barely reached up to his stomach plated in armor.

Kit looked at the Seven Lucky Gods and then at the crowd of onlookers, and stepped forward, gesturing Tessa and Jin to stay at his side, so that they stood in the center, like the connection between them all. And it was true; he, Tessa, and Jin had brought all of the City back together.

"I am Lord Taira Masakado." His voice was deeper than when he was in his fox form, but it had that steadiness and the rich tone to it that was undeniably him. "My memories are shaky, still, but I know this for certain. Nearly a dozen years ago, I was going to meet my friend—at least, I thought he was a friend." His eyes cut to Fujiwara, who whimpered. Kuju shook his head, and Fujiwara shut up, casting his eyes about imploringly for help.

"I had wanted to ask my *trusted* friend for a favor," Kit said, "but the moment I saw him, I knew something was wrong: He had come up behind me with a poison dart. Before I could defend myself—he shot me, wounding me gravely."

The Seven Lucky Gods were strangely quiet, looking between each other; so was the crowd, waiting in anticipation for the rest of Kit's story.

"Nearly close to being extinguished myself, I trapped Fujiwara in the clay body of a daruma owned by mortals, though, as weak as I'd become, I wasn't able to make it as strong as I could."

"I bound myself, reaching the end of my powers as I was, into the form of a fox charm," Kit said. "Then I secretly attached myself to a newborn girl, nearby; she was the last person anyone might expect to be connected to me. That way, I could watch over the daruma. To make matters difficult for her, no one could see the bracelet, unless they were god-blessed. However, I did not expect that her family was only here on a trip, and I was pulled away from Tokyo, to live overseas."

Tessa breathed out in shock.

"Through our close connection, she found she was god-blessed. But my connection was also a curse. My sword called to her; trying to bring me back to my full strength, as any true partner would, and sent two of its souls out to find her."

The woman in white, with the wolf. Being god-blessed, this chance she had now, it was all because of Kit.

"That newborn—now grown—is Tessa Miyata, the girl who has saved the last magical city."

He nodded at Tessa, and everyone turned to stare

at her. She wanted to duck her head, but instead she met their eyes bravely. To finally know more about her past and about the bracelet—and Kit—was a relief; it hadn't been all in her mind all along. And, she was much, much stronger now.

"And this is Jin Uehara, her friend, who was also key in bringing this truth to light." Kit gestured. "He is noteworthy amongst mortals for his fighting skills, and that was shown along with his many other assets as he protected the sanctity of the Last City."

Jin gave a solemn bow, his ears turning pink.

Kit continued with his story. "It was only after Tessa released me, in that alleyway during her plea for help, that I was able to return to corporeal form, albeit not a strong one. With the powers I had to use to fight off Fujiwara in that assassination attempt, I sacrificed *everything*, including my memories. Those trickled in like water after a drought, and I will continue to work to regain what I have lost."

"But there is one thing I have not forgotten, through this all, and the reason why I was able to keep my powers, though the prayers for me were weak."

Kit—no, Lord Taira looked around, his eyes dark, his hand on his hilt, like he expected to have to swing out his sword. "I am the Eighth God. The Unlucky God."

The crowd gasped. Tessa whispered, in disbelief, "You...*you're* the terrifying god that we're all supposed to be afraid of?"

"Pretend to be a little scared, okay?" Kit murmured out of the side of his mouth. "It'll ruin the effect if you two start laughing."

"No!" a voice cried out. It was Fujiwara, from where he was contained by Hachiman's spear. "I was set up!"

Kit looked over to the Seven Lucky Gods, meeting them eye for eye as the god that he was. "My heaven-sent role, as the Unlucky God, is to keep balance within the City. After all that has happened here, I will fight to keep the connection between us and the mortals strong. None of this shimenawa roping off the City from the rest of Japan, no closing the gates."

"That's right!" The crowd began cheering. "We deserve more ku, too!"

Kuju spluttered. "The Unlucky God is not supposed to be known by their true name or face!"

Kit had told Tessa that. And he'd also mentioned that those in the City had never favored the Unlucky God.

Until now.

Tessa could feel the hopes and wishes, carrying belief in Lord Taira, thick in the air, as the crowd continued shouting, "No more shimenawa!"

"There are grave consequences to cutting the rope," Ebisu said hastily. "This will mean we will have to serve the mortals, many of whom are not worthy—"

But the crowd only grew louder. "Let us walk amongst the mortals and answer their prayers! We'll get more ku!"

"And this will restart the Cycle—"

Tessa wasn't sure what that was, but the gods and spirits were cheering too loudly for her to hear anymore.

The gods looked between each other, and then Ebisu spoke, amplifying his voice to echo out throughout the City. "Before we came out here, we had come to that conclusion as well. We will remove the shimenawa and reconnect with those that we are to serve."

Tessa grumbled under her breath, "They just made that up."

From Kit's other side, Jin made a disgruntled noise. "They're trying to save face. Typical."

Kit winked, but tapped a finger to his lips for them to stay quiet. Then, with a serious look on his face, he asked, "If that is the case, and if the Seven will have new receiving hours"—Ebisu reluctantly nodded, wistfully looking at his home, where his TV was—"then I would like to request the first case."

"And that is?" Kuju inquired, peering over his glasses.

"Fujiwara's fate. I think he deserves a thousand years encased in a charm, so that he'll remember what he did to me," Kit responded.

Fujiwara yelped. "But—"

"He used ku to coerce Tessa's family to take the daruma out for mending, so he could try to break out," Kit said. "Perhaps he'd like to return to that shape."

Ebisu snorted. "I've been looking for a new art fixture

for my study. I'll keep you there, and my staff will ensure you'll be there for the next thousand years, which will give you more time to think about what you've done."

"Please! Honorable Lord Ebisu—"

Ebisu passed his gaze over the other gods—including Kit—who inclined their heads.

With a snap of Ebisu's fingers, Fujiwara disappeared. In his place, a red daruma sat on the ground. The figurine had a rather shocked look on his face. As he'd just been created, his other eye, to signify a wish come to fruition, hadn't been filled in. There was a stubborn, downward tilt to his painted frown, like he was still in the middle of a protest.

The crowd let out a resounding cheer. Hachiman trotted off to Ebisu's shrine, holding the one-eyed daruma carefully in his hands.

Kuju's lip twisted up as he gave an ironic salute. "Maybe we'll bring him back during our upcoming receiving sessions for entertainment."

Tessa gestured at the godfire fading away down the street. "I think he's provided enough entertainment for several lifetimes."

The god gave her a wry smile. "Fair enough."

All around, the crowd was on the verge of starting a party; their excitement only grew louder as Ebisu gestured for the gates to open and fountains of jewel-colored drinks popped out of nowhere with a snap of Kichijoten's fingers.

Then Ebisu, the Leader of the Gods, cut his eyes to Tessa and Jin. "We will meet with you mortals soon, at the torii gate behind Kuju's shrine, after the Seven Lucky Gods have a moment to discuss your fate."

Tessa and Jin glanced at each other. *That* didn't sound promising.

IV

A New Legend

38

Kit, Tessa, and Jin loitered in front of a red-orange torii tucked behind Kuju's shrine. Out in the main street of the City, gods and spirits mingled, celebrating the reopening of the Seven Lucky Gods' gates with lots of sweetened drinks and delicate desserts. Bells rang merrily through the air; even the gods and spirits had wishes of their own.

Kit's shrine, apparently, wasn't part of the Seven's compound; he would be heading off to find his (if his memory was working right) after Tessa and Jin returned home.

If they were allowed home.

A chime tinkled in an unfelt breeze, and a throat cleared from behind them. The Seven Lucky Gods stood there, resplendent in shimmering robes.

Hachiman cleared his throat and pounded his hands

together, sounding like a drum. "The Seven Lucky Gods have voted on the futures of Lord Taira Masakado and the mortals Tessa Miyata and Jin Uehara."

The Seven Lucky Gods looked down at them (well, straight at Kit), and nervousness fizzed through Tessa, like sparks of ku.

"For returning the City, the last magical city of Japan, and the rest of Tokyo into a state of peace, we hereby will negate the destruction you have caused in releasing Fujiwara Hidesato."

Tessa opened her mouth to protest. *Negate?* They were using fancy words to hide how the Seven had done *nothing* but show up at the end, pretending like they'd saved the day.

But Kit whispered, "Let's hear the rest of what they have to say."

Ebisu cleared his throat, and in his jolly voice, he said, "The Eighth God, the Unlucky God, preserved the balance in our land. As such, he has requested that we return Tokyo to what it was before Fujiwara's meddling."

Hachiman gaped. "Honorable gods! Turning time itself? The magic required—"

"Will require everything the Seven Lucky Gods have stored up over the past decade, yes," Kit said smoothly. "And, as the Unlucky God, I made this demand as it is what is owed to the city—and its people—at the very *least*."

Ebisu waved the other six gods to him. "We must deliberate, as is our custom."

Slowly, the Seven turned in toward each other.

"This may be the last time we agree on a matter," Hotei murmured. "I sense dissonance in the future."

"I'll only do this because it's the right thing to do to take care of Tokyo—everyone in the city has prayed for me, you know," Daikokuten sniffed.

Ebisu dropped his jolly tone. "Let's get this over with. We must serve Tokyo and the rest of Japan honorably."

Kit whooped. "Honor in times of need, indeed!"

Jin beamed; Tessa wanted to dance with joy.

The Seven Lucky Gods shifted their circle to have one empty spot. Lord Taira Masakado stepped forward, as the Unlucky God. They bowed their heads, and Tessa's skin prickled.

After a few murmured words from Ebisu, the Seven Gods—and Kit—began to chant, soft and low. A breeze pushed and tugged at their clothes, fierce and coming out of nowhere. Then the giant torii blazed. A shimmery light covered the gate, like a see-through curtain. Through the glow, she could glimpse the rest of Tokyo: busy city streets, with people going about their daily business; the skyscrapers stretching tall, like they were watching over the city; and trains zipping along the tracks.

Beyond the torii, Tokyo was at peace.

Tessa breathed out a huge sigh of relief.

Then Jin leaned toward her and whispered, "I was wrong."

"What?"

"This city, it's yours, too." He looked at her, and then quickly cut his gaze away. "It's in your blood, same as me. That's how you won over the blade and saved us."

"I don't think it's the city," Tessa countered, and Jin opened his mouth to protest. "It's the people."

A shy grin tugged at his lips, like the sun inching out from behind clouds. "I'll take some of the credit for that."

Kit looked over his shoulder, raising an eyebrow. "Excuse me, I deserve that claim to glory."

A chime tinkled, and Tessa tensed. But this time, it was just Hachiman holding a bell. The gods nodded to one another and stepped back. Tessa couldn't miss how all but Kuju ignored Kit, and she took a step forward. Jin put a hand on her arm.

"He's the Unlucky God, remember?" Jin whispered. "He's the one that's supposed to keep them in check, so it's no surprise they're not happy to see him. Plus, you want to take on all seven of them? We need more than hinoki for that."

She gave him a half smile. "Fair enough."

With a swish of their robes, the Seven Lucky Gods turned toward the party. However, Kuju, the God of

Wisdom, stopped in front of Tessa and Jin. "Are you sure you don't want to stay?"

"Stay?" Tessa echoed.

Kuju's eyes crinkled around the corners in a gentle smile. "It's an offer worthy of a god. You can become part of my clan, and serve me, learning from the wisest of the gods. With this comes immortality, riches beyond measure, and glory for every mission that you accomplish in my stead."

Glory. A world that *wanted* her.

Tessa rocked on her heels.

No more of Allison's taunts in her dreams.

No more worrying about her family forgetting about her.

"Kuju forgets to mention that if you join his clan immediately, you'll be stuck with him for eternity," Kit said, leaning in. The samurai crossed his arms. "And, by the time you finish training, everyone you know as a mortal will be long gone."

Cecilia. Peyton. Ojiichan. Obaachan. The people she loved and cared about, infinite times more than any NowLook comment. They were the people who picked her up when she was feeling down, or always had the perfect snack ready for her. They were the reason why she'd fight evil spirits or gods or anything in between that might put them in harm's way.

Jin glanced over at Tessa and then met the god's gaze. "I need to return to my father. I want to try to work on my relationship with him. Some things are repairable, after all."

"I must admit, I will regret not having your strength as part of my clan. And I do believe you have a wisdom I haven't seen in a while. It would be ideal for learning from me; after all, I cannot rule forever," Kuju said.

But Jin shook his head. "I must tell my father about my future. I need to be honest with him."

The god's gaze shifted to Tessa, and she gulped. There was a strange depth to his dark eyes, like she was looking into a bottomless ocean. This was a god who had seen time ebb and flow, who had seen mortals flicker out like lights. What would it be like to have that power? To be able to be everything she'd ever wanted to be?

She looked at Kit for answers, but the samurai shook his head. "If you really want to return to the path of gods, you should go to the Academy—which hasn't opened for years. So this kind of offer might not ever come again."

Tessa swallowed. A lifetime of being an ordinary mortal or—*this* world. A place that wanted her...

Slowly, she shook her head. "I'm sorry. I need to return to my family, too."

The truth of her realization tickled her with surprise: She didn't need endless glory to be happy. She didn't need to be some god or hero to be proud of herself.

Kuju still studied her thoughtfully. "I'm glad there are mortals out there like you."

The god finally turned away with a snap of his robes, leaving Kit, Tessa, and Jin alone in front of the torii once more.

"I thought you were going to take his offer," Kit said.

"I thought so, too." Tessa looked up at him. "But if *you're* the Unlucky God, I can't imagine being around you for so much longer. You might rub off on me."

Kit let out a barking laugh. "Most would still consider that an honor, shrimpy human." Then he paused, thoughtfully, and kneeled in front of Tessa. "This may not make sense to you right now, but I remembered something."

"What, did you remember where you live?" Tessa asked teasingly.

The samurai snorted. "I'll figure it out sometime. But what I wanted to remind you of is that you wouldn't have been able to carry my sword if you weren't worthy of love—whether from your sisters, from your grandparents, or even grouchy old me. I know that for certain. Never forget that you are worthy as you are. All the rain in the world has only made you stronger. Ame futte, ji katamaru. After the rain, the earth hardens. You may have seen lots of rain, but you've become some pretty tough soil, shrimp."

Tessa's eyes burned. How did this fox—no, Unlucky God—know just the right thing to say? "Thanks, I think.

But, you know, you already helped me figure that out, Lord Taira."

He lightly rested his hand on her shoulder. "You can still call me Kit. It's the name you chose for me, after all, and I've gotten pretty fond of it."

A throat cleared. Jin waited by the torii, rolling on the balls of his feet.

"Um, how do we get home?" he asked. Tessa had never seen him look so impatient.

"Just step into this torii. The way into the normal world is more like a bridge, and the winds of my blessing will take you all the way across." Kit winked. "Ready?"

The two of them glanced up at the gigantic torii, swirling with a strange glow, and then at each other. They were truly heading home.

"Go on, you two, before it's too late," Kit said. "Don't make me throw you in."

But right as they stood in front of the shimmering light, something seemed to stop them.

They turned to look over their shoulders at the samurai, who stood proudly in his dark robe, with his sword sheathed at his hip, looking every inch the god that he had always been.

Her eyes burned. If it weren't for Jin, she wouldn't know what it was like to have a real friend. If not for Kit, she wouldn't have been able to fight her way back home.

Tessa spoke up first. "Kit, we'll mi—"

"Don't!" The samurai had his sword out in a flash. "Nope!"

Jin grinned. "We'll miss—"

"Nope, nope, nope!" Lord Taira shook his head. "If you say that, I'm going to curse you into a life of unluckiness."

The two of them roared, "We'll miss you, Kit!"

He mimed impaling himself on the sword. "Yup, you two have gone and done it."

"But, really," Jin said softly, tilting his head up to look at the samurai. "We will miss having you around."

"The City is connected to the rest of Tokyo." Kit tugged a flyaway hair from Tessa's bangs. "I'll be there for you, in spirit. Literally."

Jin snorted, but Tessa shook her head threateningly.

"Don't make me get out my throwing stars," she said. "Don't cause any more trouble, Mr. Super Powerful and Unlucky God."

Kit raised his hands in mock surrender. "No more trouble. I'm here to usher in peace for all of Tokyo. And I'll be providing balance to the Seven Lucky Gods, day by day, spirit by spirit."

Jin frowned. "If we light a prayer, will it help you?"

Kit snorted. "Do you think we need you mortals to remember us?"

"Yes?" Jin said.

He snickered. "It helps our egos. And, okay, prayers

to the best god of Tokyo *do* help." Then he took a look at the two of them, and Tessa swore his eyes looked faintly misty. "But I want you to remember me for more than just 'because you have to.'"

Tessa reached up and lightly punched Kit on the shoulder. "You're unforgettable. In the worst way ever."

"Hey!" Kit growled. "I am unforgettable, lovable, the best—"

Tessa stepped forward, opened her arms out, and hugged him tightly. "You are. You are the best Lord Taira Masakado and the best kitsune I've ever met and amazing and unforgettable and so much more. Stay safe, okay? No more impostors."

Kit stiffened from her words. And then he growled a little too fast as he swiped at his eyes. "Go on, you two, before I turn evil and trap you here."

Jin and Tessa laughed. She didn't know how to explain the way her chest tightened strangely or how Jin's frown had smoothed out and looked somehow softer and sadder and joyful, all at the same time, mirroring her feelings.

Then Jin extended his hand out to her, looking oddly nervous. "Just...just for safety to get through this last magical torii together." His dark hair fell shyly over his eyes.

"Sure, for protection." Tessa couldn't quite tease him.

She did feel safer with Jin at her side. She reached out and slipped her hand into his. It felt strangely comforting. They stepped into the torii and looked over their shoulders, waving and waving until Kit and the last magical city disappeared in a searing, pure white blaze.

39

A FLASH OF LIGHT. THE CREAK OF GEARS TWISTING, A groan of metal. The wind was too strong; Tessa could barely open her eyes, but she and Jin stumbled forward, hand in hand.

Wood planks clanked under their feet, as if they were walking across a long bridge. A sudden gust pushed them off the ground, and they let out cries of surprise that were torn from them by the fast-whirling air. A faint sensation of something soft brushed against her arms, as if Kit was giving her one last hug.

Then Tessa and Jin were falling, tumbling through a sky that shifted from neon orange to pastel oranges and yellows and—

Thump.

She stumbled onto her knees in a faintly lit entranceway.

All around her, the wood walls and the curio cabinet to her right were colored with faded gray shadows and the faint pastel-yellow midmorning light shimmering from the crack through the door. She was home. Back in her grandparents' house.

To her left, Jin was sprawled out on the stone, eyes closed and unmoving. Directly outside the front door, Obaachan and Jin's father's silhouettes were outlined in the frosted glass.

Tessa reached out, shaking Jin's shoulder gently. "Are you okay? C'mon, c'mon…"

Nerves pinged through her body. He suddenly let out a loud gasp, as if he was taking his first breath of air in the longest time.

His eyes flew open, staring around stunned as he slowly gathered his bearings and pushed himself into a seated position. For a flash, Tessa thought she saw a faint outline of something more; like Jin was bigger, like the way she'd seen a glimpse of Kit's true form. Then she blinked; things were normal again. It'd just been from spending too much time in the last magical city.

"What…what just happened?" Jin groaned, rubbing his forehead. "Did that…did I…"

He looked at his empty hands, shaking his head in disbelief.

Tessa's stomach sunk. *What if he doesn't remember?*

From outside, Obaachan grumbled, "The door's stuck. It swells and sticks in the summer heat, just like my joints."

"I'll get it," Jin's father said, and sandals shuffled on stone as Tessa's grandma moved away. Mr. Uehara grunted as he pushed at the frame. "Hm. It's really stuck."

"It's the morning before we went to Tokyo," Tessa whispered, in wonder. "The gods…they truly did bring us back in time."

"We went back in time?" Jin echoed, his forehead furrowed.

She glanced over at the curio cabinet. There was a conspicuous gap.

"Where—where's the daruma?" Tessa hissed under her breath, looking around frantically.

But the doll was nowhere to be seen. The smooth black stone entranceway was clear, except for something that rolled to a stop at Tessa's shoes.

It hadn't been there a second before.

A white clay figurine rested on the ground.

"There. There it goes," Mr. Uehara said. With an annoyed squeak, the door rolled open. Mr. Uehara and Obaachan stood in the frame.

"Tessa-chan!" Obaachan said sharply. "What are you doing sitting on the floor? Jin-kun, daijyoubu nano?"

A million stories sprung to mind. But…but what if Jin didn't tell the truth? Or, worse, what if he truly didn't remember? Her chest clenched. She didn't want to lie or hide herself from another friend, not anymore. And he had to remember what had happened, too. She couldn't be alone, *again*. Tessa had to leap, fly…and hope.

"The daruma was breaking, so Ojiichan, Uehara-kun, and I brought it to Tokyo to get it fixed, but it turned out to have the soul of a malevolent god, so we had to defeat it to return home," Tessa blurted out, all in one breath. Then she swallowed deep, shoving her hands into her pockets and wishing she had her hinoki throwing stars to hold on to, so at least something could feel real.

Then the curtain leading into the kitchen rose, and Ojiichan strolled out—no limp from a sprained ankle to be seen. "You said we went to Tokyo? Funny girl, we're not going until this weekend."

Tessa couldn't help but let out a gasp of relief; she rushed to his side—she ran much faster than before—and hugged Ojiichan tightly around his waist.

Her grandpa laughed, but he squeezed her tightly back. "Ah, my little Tessa-chan." She hadn't remembered how simply *good* his hugs felt, better than all the god-blessed meals in the world.

But Obaachan raised one gray eyebrow. "What daruma are you talking about? We've only had that kitsune."

The daruma—her grandma didn't remember it? And wait—

Tessa looked down at her hand, where she held a

white fox clay figurine with curiously familiar red and gold markings. *Kit.*

Then her eyes darted over to Jin, who was brushing off his knees, his messy hair falling over his eyes. *C'mon, c'mon…don't tell me you "forgot" everything, too. Please, Jin…*

Jin glanced between Obaachan, Ojiichan, and then his father. He opened his mouth, closed it.

Tessa's heart shriveled.

Then he blurted, "Yeah, we met the *real* Taira Masakado. We helped him fight his backstabbing friend, and he helped us return home."

Everyone's jaws dropped open, even Tessa's. Jin smiled politely.

"It's appalling you have such vivid imaginations." Mr. Uehara sniffed. "Come now, Jin. You're going to be late for practice. We *have* to get you to place first, or I won't be able to withstand the shame."

"I can place first," Jin said confidently, his shoulders straightening. He had, after all, fought an evil god and *won.* "But I have something to tell you, after."

"If you get first—"

"*When* I get first, I'd like to talk with you about my future," Jin said, looking straight at his father.

Mr. Uehara spluttered, turning pale.

Jin had done it. He'd finally started trying to communicate with his dad.

He shot a glance at Tessa, and her heart sang. Not only that, but he'd taken *her* side. Even if no one else believed them, they knew.

Mr. Uehara let out a disgruntled *hmph*. "We're going to be late. Let's get to practice."

Jin bowed to Tessa's family and followed his father, and Tessa sighed. She was *definitely* glad to be home, but Jin's dad wasn't going to want him to hang around her anymore. Back to being bored by herself at her grandparents' house, back to—

"Hey—Miyata—" Jin paused in the doorway, his forehead wrinkled as usual. "Um. Tessa-chan…"

"What?" she croaked loudly. Really? He…he wanted to call her Tessa-chan like…a friend?

Jin ducked his head down as if he had been attacked by a plague of shyness.

"What's up, Jin-kun?" she asked, softer. It was hard to tell under the bright light, but the tips of his ears, peeking through that messy hair, looked a little red.

"There's…a summer festival tomorrow night," Jin said. "Do you want to go? I'm going with my school friends. But it would be fun if you come with us, too."

A tiny, hesitant smile tugged hopefully at his lips. Tessa's heart thudded against her chest as she turned to Obaachan and Ojiichan pleadingly.

The gate creaked open, and bubbling laughter tumbled forth, sweet as wisps of cotton candy on a summer day. Tessa spun around to stare at her sisters, as immaculate and perfect as when they'd first sauntered off, this time with a few bags from the local shopping area weighing down their arms.

"You're…" *Safe*, Tessa wanted to say in relief. "You're home already?"

Peyton raised an eyebrow and laughed. "See, Cece. I told you she'd have fun without us."

Their oldest sister sighed. "I know. I can't believe you're growing up so fast, Tessa. Oh, and hi, Jin!"

Jin bobbed his head in a polite greeting, his cheeks turning slightly pink. "Hello, it's nice to see you both."

"I'll probably be taller than you in no time, Cecilia," Tessa responded with a fox-like grin.

"You're forever my *littlest* sis," she laughed in return, and waved one of her shopping bags. "By the way, I bought you a bunch of your favorite green tea Kit Kats."

Tessa grinned. They *had* been thinking of her after all.

But, right now, she had big plans in mind. She spun to look pleadingly at her grandparents. "So, can I go the festival with Jin?"

Her grandpa paused, his wrinkled forehead creasing with surprise. "If you have him with you…"

"Please, pretty please?"

"We're going to a festival in Tokyo tomorrow. Are you sure you don't want to come with us?" Cecilia asked.

Tessa loved her sisters with all her heart; she knew

that. But, it turned out, she could love them with all her heart and still stand on her own. "I don't mind doing my own thing."

Cecilia groaned. "You're growing up way too fast, Tessa! Pretty soon, you'll be using all sorts of slang, and I'll be totally out of the loop."

"Let's eat some Baumkuchen." Peyton sympathetically patted their older sister's arm and led her inside. "You always feel better with cake. And even though you got *Tessa* Kit Kats and didn't get me any, I got some Jagabee for you."

"I suppose you can go to the matsuri." Obaachan pinched Tessa's cheek. "Now we're going to speed off before you can ask for anything else." Her grandma shuffled toward the kitchen after Tessa's sisters, humming under her breath; she hooked her arm around Ojiichan and steered him inside, too.

Tessa smiled widely at Jin. "Let's do it."

Jin grinned. "We can compete and see who will win the most festival games. I've learned a few tricks. I think I might be able to beat you."

"Ha." Tessa crossed her arms. "I may not be one of the Seven Lucky Gods, but I'm pretty sure I'm the Guardian Spirit of Games between the two of us."

Jin raised an eyebrow. "I'm not going to give up easily."

Tessa placed one hand on her hip, right where her

hinoki stars used to be. "You know that I've got perfect aim."

Then Jin's father bellowed from beyond the gate. "Jin! Get over here. It's time for practice!"

Jin let out a rueful laugh. "Tomorrow, okay?"

She grinned. "See you tomorrow."

Before Tessa followed her family inside, she leaned against the doorframe, watching the way the bright sun danced against the jagged skyscrapers far in the distance. The cool air of her grandparents' home swirled around her, that familiar scent of sandalwood and a hint of those requisite grandparent mothballs.

She'd been gone for days. She'd gone to Tokyo and back again.

But they'd returned to the day she'd first met Jin. It should've been impossible, but it had actually happened.

She shook her head with a laugh at the fox that now stood in the daruma's place. Kit had kept his promise to still be around, at least in spirit.

Obaachan poked her head out from behind the curtain.

"Come into the kitchen for a snack, Tessa-chan," her grandma said, beckoning just like a maneki neko. "Cece-chan is going to eat all the cake if you don't join us. She's posting a video of it on some sort of social media account of hers, and she wants you in it."

For some reason, hearing about NowLook didn't hurt as much anymore. She slid her phone out of her pocket and opened up the app.

Allison had posted another video of her making funny faces with Jenna, her new best friend. It didn't sting like she'd expected.

Tessa's fingers tapped out a message: *I'm glad you're happy.*

She didn't hit send. This was a message just for herself, that she breathed out into the world like a prayer that became ku. But, to her surprise, she was genuinely happy for Allison—who had *always* wanted to be popular, especially after moving from place to place.

For the first time, Tessa felt okay about no longer being friends with her, with a lot more understanding than when Tessa had watched Allison sashay over to Jenna's side. Tessa had had to move, from the US to Japan, and she'd finally gotten a sense of how bewildering it could feel to be somewhere new. Maybe—*maybe*—that was what Allison had felt, and why she'd wanted to make herself popular again. After all, maybe some sixth-grade friends weren't meant to last forever; they were only supposed to hang out through a few trays of cafeteria french fries and head off on their own ways. But she had other friends—like Kit and Jin—that she hoped *would* stand the test of time.

Tessa exited NowLook and dragged the app into the virtual trash basket. She was okay without it, and without Allison, too.

She could see her family in the kitchen, Peyton barking out a laugh at one of Cecilia's jokes, Ojiichan and Obaachan joining in even if they didn't quite get the punchline. Her perfect, world-saving-worthy family.

As she untied her shoes, Tessa breathed in the soul-warming scent of her grandparents' house. Somehow, it felt like home. Then she froze.

That scent—it wasn't a mothball or sandalwood. It... it was hinoki.

She was surrounded by protection, whether through the wood walls of the house itself, or her grandparents, or friends like Kit and Jin.

Tessa looked at the figurine of the white fox. She swore it winked.

She grinned and winked right back.

EPILOGUE

IN FRONT OF AN ABANDONED-LOOKING BUILDING, COV-
ered in silken spiderwebs and creeping ivy, a light flickered on, illuminating a sign caked in dust.

"Is it time?" a soft, beautiful voice asked.

A thin cat meowed in response, curving around the
sign.

"Almost, then."

The cat's bushy tail swiped along the sign, sending
dust flying like a flurry of cherry blossom petals. The
carved letters shimmered in the speckled light: *The Academy of Gods.*

In Kisarazu, a small seaside town alongside the Tokyo
Bay, Tessa Miyata laughed with Jin Uehara, her friend,
as they played games at a summer festival. She did not

know, yet, of the invitation that would soon come her way, but a gust swirled the edges of her yukata, causing her to pause and look out at the Tokyo skyline, on the other side of the bay.

The city lights sparkled like a perfect mirror of the starry sky above. This moment, to Tessa, was perfection; it was everything she wanted.

All, for now, was quiet.

AUTHOR'S NOTE

I HAVE ALWAYS BEEN SPLIT BETWEEN TWO PLACES. BEING born in Japan but mostly growing up in the US—except for the almost magical summers at my grandparents' house near Tokyo—it always felt like I had a foot in each country, but I never truly "fit" into either. Tessa's search for a place to belong resonated deeply with me as I wrote her story, and it's a story I wish the younger me had.

Like Tessa, there is so much I want the world to discover about Japanese culture. Everything from the samurai who have become a part of history, to the most harrowing folklore of changeling creatures, to some of my favorite foods; Tessa and Jin experience so much of Tokyo and the Japan I know and love.

I only lightly brush the surface of the rich history of mythology and folklore of the land of my birth. Kitsune—like Kit—are renowned for their trickster ways, Taira Masakado's spirit is said to lord over Tokyo even long after his death. The last magical city is based on the legendary Takamagahara, Japan's Olympus. There is so much to Japan that I can't wait for Tessa to discover. To everyone who is caught between countries and identities, I hope this story will remind you that no matter where you're from, you, too, have a place where you belong.

And let's be honest, I'm hoping for my invite to the last magical city, too.

Julie Abe

ACKNOWLEDGMENTS

HUGE THANK-YOUS TO THE MAGICAL SARAH LANDIS, Alvina Ling, and Ruqayyah Daud for making Tessa's story sparkle.

So many thanks to the extraordinary Little, Brown Books for Young Readers team, LB School, NOVL, and the Hachette family, including Megan Tingley, Jackie Engel, Tom Guerin, Janelle DeLuise, Hannah Koerner, Cassie Malmo, Karina Granda, Jensine Eckwall, Karmen Loh, Jen Graham, Andy Ball, Nyamekye Waliyaya, Emilie Polster, Stefanie Hoffman, Savannah Kennelly, Mara Brashem, Bill Grace, Christie Michel, Amber Mercado, Victoria Stapleton, Marisa Russell, Shawn Foster, Danielle Cantarella, and Hannah Bucchin.

To my family, my dear friends, and the book community—thank you so much for your support, always.

To the wonderful blurbers of *Tessa*—Graci Kim, Kaela Rivera, Samira Ahmed, Sangu Mandanna, Xiran Jay Zhao—sending you a magical city full of thanks!

All the green tea Kit Kats of thanks to my fellow book lovers who have supported my stories, including

Alexa (@alexalovesbooks), Carmen (@kindredbooks), Esther Fung (@estherhfung), Lili (@utopia.state.of.mind), Nic (@magic.within.pages), Pei (@peireads), Sachi (@sachireads), Samantha (@bookreststop), Sunni (@vanreads), Tiffany (@quilltreefox), and Tiffany (@readbytiffany).

Chelsea Ichaso—I couldn't do this without you. All the Reese's Cups and boba tea in the last magical city aren't enough to show how amazing you are.

Three cheers and loads of ramen to my early readers and fellow writers who keep me company while writing, even when miles or oceans apart, including Alyssa Colman, Eunice Kim, Graci Kim, June Tan, Karina Evans, Melissa Seymour, Rachel Greenlaw, Sarah Suk, Swati Teerdhala, and Tara Tsai.

Thank you, Emily, May, and Eugene, with all my love.